Vasily Mahanenko

LAW

OF THE JUNGLE

Book Two

*Books are the lives
we don't have
time to live,

Vasily Mahanenko*

MAGIC DOME BOOKS

MD
BOOKS

Law of the Jungle
Book 2
Copyright © Vasily Mahanenko 2024
Cover Art © Linni 2024
Designer: Vladimir Manyukhin
English translation copyright © Mikhail Yagupov 2024
Published by Magic Dome Books, 2024
All Rights Reserved
ISBN: 978-80-7693-474-0

ALL BOOK SERIES BY VASILY MAHANENKO:

The Way of the Shaman LitRPG Series

Dark Paladin LitRPG Series

Galactogon LitRPG Series

Invasion LitRPG Series

World of the Changed LitRPG Series

The Alchemist LitRPG Series

The Bear Clan LitRPG Series

Starting Point LitRPG Series

The Bard from Barliona LitRPG series
(with Eugenia Dmitrieva)

Condemned
(Lord Valevsky: Last of The Line)
a Progression Fantasy series

Law of the Jungle Wuxia Series

TABLE OF CONTENTS:

Chapter 1 1

Chapter 2 17

Chapter 3 33

Chapter 4 49

Chapter 5 65

Chapter 6 82

Chapter 7 99

Chapter 8 115

Chapter 9 132

Chapter 10 150

Chapter 11 166

Chapter 12 181

Chapter 13 196

Chapter 14 214

CHAPTER 15...228

CHAPTER 16 246

CHAPTER 17...265

CHAPTER 18 283

CHAPTER 19 300

CHAPTER 20 317

CHAPTER 1

TURNING FOURTEEN TYPICALLY MEANS a day filled with laughter, gifts, and fun in the company of friends. It's a time of joy when life feels abundant and welcoming. My reality was a stark contrast to that. Mine was the miserable lot of an apprentice under the tutelage of a Diamond-ranked Taoist Master, and so my fourteenth birthday was anything but typical. There would be no fun for me; only pain. In heaps.

"Strike!"

I was compelled into action by my mentor's command, delivered with the force of a whip, overpowering my resistance. My blade found its mark again, severing the head of a lesser demon. The creature's bulk crashed to the ground, its blood soaking the earth, and I was allowed a moment's respite. My body bore the entire brutal testimony of the battle with the demons — it had been bitten and rent by their claws multiple times, yet somehow I was still managing to keep myself upright. Falling now would only invite my mentor's wrath — and no lesser demon's fury or venom would ever match that.

"You pour your heart into this oaf's training, pushing him to his limits, and yet he nearly falls at the hands of those who are little better than mindless beasts," my mentor's critique landed with the weight of a sledgehammer. "What will you do against higher demons? Give up and let yourself be captured? Are you that eager to become some otherworldly creature's next meal?"

"Mentor, those were higher-ranked lesser demons!" I managed to find a shred of defiance within me at last.

"So what? The world's not a fair place, if you haven't noticed yet! We're never faced with enemies that match our strength perfectly. They're always stronger — always one step ahead of you. That's no excuse to let them best you. What if more of these lesser demons appear now? You're slipping up far too often for someone aspiring to immortality. Gather the corpses of these demons — they need to be burned. I'll see to your wounds afterwards. You haven't earned the right to get an immediate treatment.

So that was the backdrop of my "birthday celebration" — an unwelcome gift of encounters with two groups of lesser demons. While the first group posed less of a challenge, being of a rank comparable to mine, the second one proved to be

2

a formidable force, far outstripping me in both strength and agility. It took every ounce of my effort, pushing far beyond my limits to survive and wipe out the bastards. And yet despite my finest efforts, my mentor's approval remained elusive.

How long had we been navigating these demon-infested lands? Long enough to attract the attention and provoke assaults from many such groups. Although the threats had been relatively minor so far, I was sensing a brewing storm on the horizon. Yet, perhaps, it would be best to give the account of all the events in the order they had transpired.

The demon realm sure was a sight to behold — the difference with our world was striking. Red wasn't just a color here — it seemed to permeate the very essence of everything: grass and the leaves on what few trees grew here were all dipped in shades of red. A week in, the toxic fumes hanging in the air had me coughing up blood. But the most unpleasant discovery was that the lands of the demons didn't have the kind of boundaries ours did. There were no tiers or barriers here — just an endless expanse of territory, which meant that Qi energy levels were insanely more intense than anything in the human realm's Tier Zero, even way out here, far away from the Primordial Soul. Bravery aside, my body started to rebel against these harsh conditions within two weeks, leaving my mentor no other option but to patch me up constantly.

Our first expedition into demon lands

wrapped up after just three weeks, forcing us back to our world for a breather. I definitely needed one. As for my mentor, he seemed to pay no attention whatsoever to the harsh nature of the demon world. The man was indestructible! His idea of recovery was to cut my training from eighteen to a mere sixteen hours, generously allotting two hours for meditation. In the demon world. Where the very air's Qi continued to lash at my already battered body ceaselessly.

The second foray lasted a month, and we even stumbled upon a small walled township, having steered clear of the smaller settlements along the way. Wiping out everything in sight like some rampaging force didn't sit right with us — why would we turn into monsters attacking those who couldn't fight us back? However, higher demons — those at the Silver and Golden ranks of the Candidate stage — were fair game. My mentor looted workshops and stores without a second thought. According to him, the loot was part and parcel of any venture into the demon realm. The more spoils you carted back, the higher your rep back home. He went all out when we hit a castle ruled by a high demon who was the local prefect. First, the defenders fell, then came a little chat with the boss (who, sadly, didn't make it through the conversation), and finally, we hit the jackpot in the treasury. I'd never seen so many spirit stones in my life — there was a whole room chock-full of them. But my mentor passed on the "trinkets," as he called them derisively, his eyes set on herbs, woods, resins, and other resources neatly organized on separate shelves. Nothing there screamed "valuable," yet what we'd managed to haul back was enough to keep us busy crafting pills and artifacts for weeks on end. And no, training was nowhere near being put on pause.

My mentor decided against taking the spirit stones, but he didn't have the right to just leave them there, either. Why would demons need such treasures? The Taoist sent me out of the town and then did something that turned the solid-looking stone castle into ruins. The explosion was so powerful that half the town must have felt it. Looking pleased with himself, Master Guerlon climbed into the passenger seat and ordered us to head towards the wormhole. That marked the end of our second expedition into the demon lands. By the way, this time it had taken three weeks before the toxic air had me coughing up blood, not one. It appeared that my body was gradually getting used to the local atmosphere. Even the Qi energy didn't scratch up my insides as badly as before.

Two months of recovery followed, but this time the mentor spent a couple of days setting up our first cache in Tier Zero. He'd taken so much loot from the demon castle that even his seemingly bottomless spatial pouch was full. We created the cache in a cliff from which demons quarried stone for their walls. Having found a small cave, my mentor spent some time enlarging it, slicing through rock with his techniques, and then started stashing what he deemed excess. The result was a massive pile of goods, including resources from the blue anomaly. He blocked the entrance with stones and sighed heavily, assessing his handiwork.

"To guarantee the cache's security, we'd need a protective formation. Special artifacts to disguise the entrance and obliterate any curious intruders. I have the formation; setting it to recognize you and me isn't hard. But what's the point? There's hardly any energy in Tier Zero, so the defense would last a year at most. Useless. It's more secure this way — burying the stuff under rocks. Make sure to collect everything here before heading to the First Tier."

Then came our third foray. This time my mentor made it clear we'd be going long and hard because my body had now adapted to the hardships of the demon world. I had my doubts, but who was going to listen? Our mission was straightforward: find as many castles, outposts, training camps, and other weapons-filled demon gatherings as possible to draw the inner territories' inhabitants' keen attention, snaring a Master demon in the best-case scenario. When I asked the logical question why we should take such risks, my mentor answered with a bloodthirsty grin. The more high-ranking demons died in their world, the fewer would venture into ours. But the real goal wasn't just about thinning their ranks. Once the demons realized humans were wreaking havoc in their lands, they'd have to summon a wormhole coordinator to close the passage. That would be when we'd catch them. The fewer wormhole coordinators, the more peaceful our world would be.

"Can't the wormhole just be destroyed?" I wondered.

"A rip in the fabric of space between two worlds? It's not that simple, apprentice. Even I would need to exert myself, though I've done it more than once. If we can catch the coordinator before they close the breach, I'll teach you how to seal it. Your ascension level doesn't matter here. What's important is a precise and specific sequence of actions."

The first weeks of our third venture into the demon realm were a blast — several castles lay in ruins behind us. It wasn't long before squads of fighters started showing up, specifically assembled to hunt us down,. My mentor left one or two demons alive after each encounter, engaging them in lengthy, probing conversations. Sadly, none of the captives knew the whereabouts of the Jarming tribe, but we gradually pieced together a map of Tier Zero's environs. Demons might not officially use tiers to divide their lands, using the term "circles" instead that roughly corresponded with our world's terminology. We were roaming Circle Zero, a territory under the control of the Barnutal tribe — not the largest or wealthiest, given the scarcity of its resources. The tribe clearly wasn't thrilled about a rogue Taoist traversing their land, sending wave after wave of groups after us. The eight demons I'd dispatched earlier were from the twenty-seventh squad we had faced that week.

A blaze shot into the sky, annihilating a group of eight lesser demons. At long last, my mentor took pity and healed my wounds — just in time, as my vision was already blurring and I was staggering like a drunk. Casting another one of his dissatisfied glances my way, he conjured a self-propelled cart and took control of the levers. The role of the driver in the demon world had yet to be entrusted to me.

"Meditate!" commanded the Taoist, and off we sped towards our next target. I closed my eyes, immersing myself in a world of pulsating energy. At least I had made some headway in this aspect during our stay in the demon realm. Slipping into a state of spirit vision that allowed me to track energy flows came easily enough. I watched as particles pierced my long-suffering body, though the marks they left were fewer than before. My body was gradually adjusting to this hostile environment. Occasionally, we passed by power centers — plants or small animals on their path to immortality. These beings harbored slightly more energy than the surrounding environment, but my mentor drove past without a second glance. The thought that the Taoist simply couldn't see these plants and small animals never crossed my mind. He had hunted creatures for Vyllea, so he clearly knew where to find anything imbued with energy. And he could certainly detect both Taoists and demons. In short, my mentor saw everything but chose to ignore most of it.

Until suddenly...

"Stop!"

I whispered the phrase so softly it was as if I feared my own audacity. Daring to command an Elder! Such boldness would have earned me a thrashing back in my village. But instead of a reprimand, my mentor abruptly maneuvered the cart, and we skidded across the stones. I jumped off as soon as we halted, without waiting for any questions, and headed back to where a massive light shone — far brighter than the spirit stones my mentor usually gave me, albeit located deep underground. If I hadn't fully opened myself to the energy during meditation, I'd never have detected this bright mishmash of energies from such a distance. Approaching the site proved impossible; a narrow chasm, barely thirty feet long and just over two feet wide, suddenly split the relatively even surface. The bright energy spot I noticed was within this fissure, about ten to fifteen feet down.

"There," I pointed towards the crack, unsure of what to do next, but my mentor managed to surprise me. Without uttering a word, he leaped and descended vertically into the crevice, not even inquiring about what I had found. Moments later, he emerged just as abruptly, landing a few feet away. I closed my eyes to take another look with my spirit vision. Using it alongside normal sight was beyond me, so I had to choose one or the other. The bright glow beneath the earth had vanished — my mentor had either destroyed or taken whatever it was with him. I couldn't say exactly what he did; in the realm of energy, a Master Taoist of the Diamond rank appeared as an utterly black spot of a human shape. Energy threads flowed into this spot and vanished without a trace. I saw none of the artifacts or spirit stones he carried — just the black silhouette. I had to open my eyes, returning to normal vision.

"Oh wow…" I couldn't help but react to what my mentor held. A skeleton. Or, rather, the lower part of a skeleton. The lower right part of a skeleton, to be even more precise. It lacked one leg, along with everything above the waist. The clean cut suggested a brutal end. The fabric had long decayed, remnants of a now-useless boot clinging to the lone foot, but I finally saw the source of the energy that had drawn my attention. It was a small plaque — an exact duplicate of which my mentor had once shown me. A creation of the Clan's head, granting the bearer the right to be called a Seeker. My mentor laid the remains on the ground, keeping only the plaque, which turned out to be the sole item of any value.

"So, this is where you've ended up," the Taoist said gruffly, twirling the plaque. "Heeding the voice of reason was never your forte, was it? You've always fancied yourself a formidable hunter."

"Mentor, who was this?" Keeping my composure was challenging. It seemed the Taoist knew the deceased personally and might share an intriguing story. I adored stories! Especially ones like this.

BOOK TWO

"This is what remains of one of the younger heirs of House Kahn, which governs the Second Tier on behalf of the Phoenix Clan. About sixty years ago, when I was still just a Warrior, I crossed paths with him. Back then, I wasn't yet a Seeker, just a junior instructor at one of the ascension schools... But Dmyt Kahn dreamt of becoming a free Seeker. Too many relatives stood in line for inheritance ahead of him, so he could never aspire to a decent position. That was when he decided to become a Seeker. The clan didn't skimp on his gear — Dmyt Kahn had everything others could only dream of. Artifacts, pills, techniques, you name it. Without rivals in the second tier, he claimed to be the world's best Seeker, but then vanished suddenly — so suddenly that no one knew what happened to him. House Kahn had even offered a reward for any information about one of their younger scions, but nobody ever found out anything. Everyone thought Dmyt Kahn had managed to create an elemental core, becoming a Master Taoist and moving on to the Third Tier, especially since the clan's resources permitted it. Turns out, this madman thought he was stronger than the demons, found a wormhole, and came here. Judging by the clean cut on the bones, some technique has been used here. The seeker fled here from the Second Tier of this world, hoping to escape, but met an inglorious end instead. It's a shame his gear has been taken. As I said, the Kahn clan was generous. There must have been some truly valuable artifacts on him."

"Why didn't they take the plaque?" I wondered.

"Because demons can't touch it. Well, they can, but not all of them. Those who aren't Seekers or haven't been given the plaque by its owner cannot touch it. It's an artifact made by a Nascent God stage Taoist. Do you think the maker wouldn't ensure that even after the Seeker's death, they could still wreak vengeance upon their foes? What puzzles me, student, is how you saw the plaque."

"It was shining like the Earis," I blurted out, surprised by the question. "You told me to meditate, so I was observing the world through Qi energy. Compared to other spots, this one glowed so brightly..."

"Other spots?" The tone in my mentor's voice had notes I had grown to profoundly dislike. He used it every time he devised a new kind of training.

"Plants, small animals, that kind of thing. They had slightly more energy than the surrounding world, so I thought they weren't of interest to you and that you were bypassing them as something trivial. But this glow was so bright, I couldn't help but stop you."

"How do I appear in your world of energy?"

"Like a black spot." I felt my cheeks redden. "I can't see you at all. Not you, nor anything you carry."

"But you still tried to look at me? A couple of days ago, when you suddenly got a nosebleed during a break. Right?"

"Yes, mentor," I admitted, now genuinely flushed with embarrassment. Caught red-handed!

"All right, we'll delve into that later. Along with why you didn't tell me about this world of energy you've uncovered. For most Taoists, apprentice, meditation is about drawing Qi energy into their body, restoring their meridians. What they usually see are just their nodes and meridians — not the surrounding world suffused with energy currents. That insight is reserved for spirit absolutes, which, as we know, you are not. Are there any of those spots you mentioned around here?"

I had to close my eyes and dive back into the energy realm. So everyone else saw nothing but darkness? How strange that was. The same landscape I saw with my eyes open unfolded in front of me — except it was rendered in shades of blue. I could even navigate like this with a bit of adjustment.

"There." I finally spotted a small cluster of energy about two hundred feet away. It was stationary — clearly not an animal. As we approached, we discovered a small clump of dry grass. The mentor leaned down, and the grass leaped into his hand.

"Ten-year-old wormwood of the Apprentice stage. Worth three, perhaps even four spirit coins. Not a bad catch in the midst of a barren desert. Tell me, student, how many such places have we passed?"

"Twenty-eight." My accursed memory didn't

let me err. The Taoist just smirked and shook his head. Taking this as a good sign, I ventured a crucial question.

"Mentor, you found beasts on the path to immortality when you fed Vyllea. You knew in advance when and how many bounty hunters would come for us. Isn't that the ability to see energy?"

"You're right — it is the ability to see energy. But not Qi energy, apprentice. What I see is the energy of life pulsating within living beings. And this energy can be concealed, as you've witnessed. Recall our first attack — the one who'd set the seal in front of the Seekers' tavern in Vorend was hiding under a protective canopy. I didn't see the energy he emitted, and without your tip about the thread, I might not have noticed him. The higher a being gets on the path to ascension, the brighter its life energy burns. Yours, for instance, barely flickers, as if you've just embarked on the path to immortality. Which, frankly, is infinitely disappointing. After two years of training, I expected more progress. Stand still; I need to check something."

The mentor placed his hand on my chest and closed his eyes. After a moment, he opened them and shook his head.

"No nodes yet. I don't even see the beginnings of them. Your body still isn't robust enough to resist Qi energy. You're still weak. How long will it take you to reach the Silver rank at this rate? Ten years?"

B O O K T W O

The question clearly didn't seek an answer — my mentor often talked to himself. What troubled me was something else.

"Mentor, if you can't see the world's energy, why can I? You said it yourself that I wasn't a spirit absolute."

"You're a mental absolute, and I know next to nothing about them. Never did I imagine, heading into Tier Zero, that I'd encounter my first apprentice here — especially one like you. One thing's clear — we need to test your ability thoroughly to understand its limits. You see me, a Taoist at the master stage, as a black spot absorbing all energy. Yet you spotted an artifact made by a Nascent God-level Taoist. This raises many questions, which you'll answer right after we deal with that group of demons approaching."

The mentor gestured towards the horizon, where several specks were moving closer. They were too far for me to consider using my spirit vision on them, but the task was clear — the mentor wanted to see if my vision worked on objects and creatures alone, or also on beings on their path to immortality of a similar rank to mine. The Taoist himself didn't say so, but I remembered the writings of Huang Lung. Knowing an enemy's ascension stage, along with all their nodes and meridians, granted a Taoist a huge advantage in combat. Each technique used specific meridians, and if an opponent lacked certain connections, they couldn't use any of the corresponding techniques.

I closed my eyes and submerged into the world of glowing forms. A dense energy construction enveloped me, and I grinned. The mentor had employed the Spirit Armor technique to protect me from harm. He'd never mentioned always shielding me, and I had no way of seeing it before. This was my first meditation during combat, especially in a fight where the mentor would allow an opponent to get within striking or throwing distance. No distractions now — I was genuinely curious about what my spirit vision could unveil. I felt I had discovered another reason why free-roaming mental absolutes didn't exist in the world. We simply saw too much. People got killed for a fraction of that.

CHAPTER 2

"I NEED ANSWERS, apprentice."

"Yes, mentor," I nodded, once again suppressing the urge to voice all my thoughts about this method of instruction. To provide answers, one should at least hear the questions! Yet there were none, which forced me to independently determine which information was valuable, which was useless, and which didn't need to be mentioned at all. Why couldn't I just ask a question and receive a straightforward answer, I wondered?

"We were attacked by three demons. One was a Golden-ranked Candidate, and the other two were Apprentices, although I couldn't determine their rank. I identified the candidate's rank by the presence of four nodes among which an energy thread occasionally flickered. This demon hadn't yet formed its meridians. Regarding the apprentices, the first had a core and two emanating meridian threads. One comprised three links heading towards the right hand; the other had two meridians and went straight down. The second apprentice differed only in the number of meridians in the first thread, which had just two links."

"The apprentice stage for any being on the path to immortality involves preparing the body to forming an energy core. This is the criterion for advancing to the Warrior stage. To open the core, a being needs to unlock all growth directions of the meridians: two arms, two legs, the abdomen, chest, and head. Then these seven threads will expand throughout the body, forming two hundred and fifty-six meridians, but this process can only be completed at the Warrior stage. The threads are unlocked first. At the Bronze rank, the right arm and abdomen are unlocked. By opening ten meridians in these threads, one gains the ability to unlock the thread of the left arm and right leg. That's the Bronze rank. At thirty meridians, the opportunity evolve into a Silver Apprentice presents itself — the threads of the left leg and chest are formed. To start on the head thread, one needs to have opened fifty meridians. That's the Gold rank — the most challenging at the Apprentice stage. Once at least one meridian appears in the head thread, one can begin forming the energy core."

"Understood. So, these two demons were

Copper-ranked Apprentices. Odd. Haven't the demons realized yet that they're up against a formidable opponent? Why send such weak demons after us?"

"Since when did Copper-ranked Apprentice stage creatures become 'weak opponents' in your books? Need I remind you what a group of mere lower demon Candidates stage had done to you just recently?"

"I misspoke, mentor," I grumbled unhappily. It seemed that particular incident would be remembered at every appropriate and inappropriate occasion henceforth. "These aren't the first Apprentice-stage demons you've dispatched, right? These are the twenty-eighth group, to be specific. Surely, there were formidable foes among them. But none returned. Even to me, a guy from a distant village, it's clear you can't just keep sending ordinary demons at us. They'll be killed outright. You need to find someone more serious. But that's not happening. Why's that?"

"You have a minute to answer this question," the mentor smirked unpleasantly, causing my teeth to grind in frustration. His laughter only fueled my anger — my mentor was clearly pleased by the effect of his words.

"Someday, I'll rid you of the habit of asking questions when the answers are glaringly obvious, and are of the kind that any person — not just a mental absolute — could reach on their own."

"Obvious?" I couldn't hold back. "Obvious how, mentor? This is my first time in the lands of demons! Two years ago, I thought demons were mere myths! How am I supposed to know why no powerful beasts are sent against us? Maybe they're just not in the mood! Or they can't fight because of some demonic holiday! Or maybe they've all run out! We're so mighty and strong that we've killed them all, and…"

I faltered, struck by a sudden realization. Killed… We had indeed slain all the strong demons — and not here, but in our own world, right near the wormhole! They were bringing food from the First Tier for these creatures with the specific purpose of prolonging their stay in our realm. I had personally piled all the demons into a huge heap and gutted them. I knew the exact number of Candidates and Apprentices among the fiends… Prisoners mentioned that the Barnutal tribe was weak and insignificant. Where would they get an army of lesser and higher demons? They gathered whomever they could and immediately sent them after us. Meanwhile, their neighbors from the inner lands probably scoffed at requests for reinforcements. Helping a weak tribe was pointless by any account.

"Emotions are one of a Taoist's main enemies, apprentice," my mentor stated calmly, as if my outburst hadn't occurred. "You must learn to control yourself, no matter how nonsensical or foolish your interlocutor, enemy, or partner seems. Anyone. By displaying emotions, you lose focus. You become vulnerable. This is especially dangerous in the world of demons, where no help is to be expected from any party. We're completely on our own here. Look at what became of the Taoist who fancied himself godlike. His thirst for glory and his desire to be someone important to the masses had brought him here. Where is he now? He had lost focus and allowed himself to be caught and destroyed. If you don't learn to control your emotions, you'll meet a similar fate someday. It may happen in the world of humans or in the world of demons — it doesn't matter. What matters is that your emotions will betray you and cloud your judgment at the very moment when you need to be most concentrated."

"Thank you for the lesson, mentor," I replied after a pause, even bowing, a gesture long unused. Mentor Guerlon didn't care for excessive formality. But now it somehow seemed appropriate. The Taoist was right — I was paying too much attention to my emotions and how I felt about various assignments. Even if I wished to dispute them, it needed to be done with a calm spirit and not in a flash of anger.

"I have no idea how to train what you call 'spirit vision' for use in everyday life. That's a path you'll need to tread on your own. For now, your task is to scan your surroundings every thirty seconds for centers of power — the very plants, small animals, and hidden artifacts you've mentioned. Despite seeming trivial, items from the demon world are highly prized in ours. And... I was planning to tell you this when it was time to return to the Third Tier, but since today is your birthday, you've earned yourself a little gift."

With these words, the mentor once again pulled out the Seeker's plaque we'd found in the demon world.

"This isn't just an item that certifies one's right to be called a seeker. Whoever returns the plaque to the clan is granted the right to receive their own. And their ascension level does not matter. Even a Bronze Candidate Taoist can become a seeker. All you need is enough spiritual stones to activate the portal in Vorend. Yes, the capital of Tier Zero has its portal, too. But the cost of opening it is not as important as the outcome you'll achieve. Becoming a Seeker of the Phoenix Clan grants you complete freedom. In Tier Zero, it's House Wang that calls the shots. They're used to thinking of all people living in their territory as their servants, obliged to satisfy any whim. Suppose Hurikki Wang decided to send you into a black anomaly — you'd have no right to refuse him, because that's the mandate of the house head you belong to. Well, you and your village are exceptions — House Wang didn't bother with border territories and granted them autonomy. But everyone else is far less fortunate. Anyway, those are Tier Zero affairs. When you enter the First Tier, you'll immediately find yourself in an absorption center. That's the place where the houses pick worthy candidates. They sign long-term contracts with them, which only the heirs of great houses of the inner tiers have the right to refuse. All the others are compelled to sign under threat of retribution. It's disadvantageous for the houses to have independent Taoists roaming their lands. I thought House Soth might take an interest in you, and was even ready to give you some contacts that could be useful. But that was before I thought you could only become a Seeker by reaching the golden rank of the Apprentice stage. Everything changed when you saw the plaque. Heaven itself is on your side, apprentice. By becoming a Seeker now, you can ignore the requirement to join any of the houses of the First Tier. You'll gain your freedom."

"And a host of enemies," I retorted.

"There's no such thing as a Seeker without enemies. After all, where else should we acquire our resources from? Fools who fancy themselves immortal serve as a splendid source of income, especially those from affluent houses. So happy birthday, apprentice! Even though a quartet of lesser demons had nearly managed to finish you off. I'll hand over the plaque when we return, but now it seems the time has come to pay a visit to one of the largest cities in the demon world's Tier Zero. If the Barnutal tribe refuses to summon the wormhole coordinator, we'll have to disturb others — those who have more say in the local tribal hierarchy."

It took us nearly a week to reach the city the mentor had mentioned. The amount of energy floating in the air grew daily, making me feel increasingly uncomfortable. My mentor healed me just once an hour, claiming that only through hardships would my body eventually adapt. The days weren't that bad, but after the nights, I resembled a battered leather bag. Everything that could hurt did hurt — and how. Yet the heartless Taoist remained unmoved. He restored me to a tolerable level, placed me in the cart, and made me work, searching for valuable plants or animals. The essences of demon world animals were as valued in our world as the herbs and trees, which the mentor also made me inspect. But I hadn't found anything valuable yet. Interestingly, we hadn't engaged in any battles anymore. Apparently, the demons had finally run out, or the Barnutal tribe decided it was easier to forget about our existence than to sacrifice the remnants of their warriors. Either scenario suited my tormentor, and we proceeded almost non-stop.

That was until the stone walls of a large city rose before us. A banner with an unfamiliar symbol fluttered above the towers — the city definitely wasn't controlled by the Barnutal tribe. We were spotted — movement began on the walls as demons near the gate dropped everything and rushed into the city; the gates started to close, and the carrying sounds of horns called for the city's defense. In less than ten minutes, the demons had barricaded themselves and bristled with crossbows. It seemed every second warrior on the wall was equipped with this weapon. Despite the fact that we were close enough to the walls, the demons didn't yet fire. They were probably hoping we 'd be scared off and retreat back to the red steppe. So naïve. I closed my eyes and viewed the city from an energy construction perspective, describing what I saw.

"The gates are protected by some technique. On the nearest wall to us are Copper Apprentice demons. Three of them. They're wearing some artifacts around their necks, similar in energy to the herbs we found. All the others are mere Candidates. I see nothing else filled with Qi energy. We're too far away from the city."

"Reinforced gates?" The mentor smirked viciously, turning the self-propelled cart towards the city. "Not every tribe can afford them, especially here in Tier Zero. For instance, the House of Wang in Vorend has never managed to set up any worthy defense. If such a wealthy tribe lives here, I don't even know what more we'll have to do to attract the attention of the more serious demons. Be warned, though — I'll hold you strictly accountable for every miss!"

My mentor handed me one of the crossbows taken from the enemy along with a whole bag of bolts. He was irritated by my helplessness and inability to use strike techniques, and so he'd found a perfect role for me — eliminating the enemy with their own weapons. After a month of training, I had become quite proficient at shooting up to a hundred paces, thanks to the crossbow's range, which made me slightly better than completely useless — in fights against Candidate demons, at least. I had taken a couple of shots at the Apprentices only to watch in frustration as my bolts bounced off their protective technique, which my mentor called a Cloak. This technique was the first learned by all those on the path to immortality, both demons and humans. The reason was as clear as day — activating the simplest Cloak required just one meridian in the abdominal thread. This defense was enough to block most physical attacks from ordinary beings and even Copper and Bronze Candidates. As the number of meridians increased, the technique evolved, too, becoming capable of blocking not only physical blows, but also techniques. In short, my crossbow was useless against demons who possessed a Cloak.

But against all others, it was an excellent weapon — as deadly as they got.

I couldn't make out the streams of energy rushing from my mentor's hands, so swiftly was the technique employed. A fire serpent lunged forward, and nothing remained of the reinforced gates, ditto part of the wall — my mentor had put too much force into his attack. The cart charged into the breach, and I began swiveling from side to side, picking off the city defenders stunned by the assault. I felt no pity for the enemy — if they had come into our world, they would have slaughtered everyone, simply because they could. I only shot those who carried weapons. Ordinary demons, scattering in terror in all directions, were no enemies of mine.

A habit formed over the last few days made its presence known. Closing my eyes, I assessed the world from the perspective of the surging Qi within it and habitually began to report to my mentor,

"Two demon Apprentices to the right! An Apprentice demon straight ahead! The house to the left! There are many energy sources there!"

It seemed the mentor had jumped from the cart before it even stopped. Back in the ordinary world, I saw we were near an alchemical workshop — no one else would hang a sign featuring an alchemical cauldron and a heap of pills. I was nudged in the shoulder — a city guard's arrow had hit, but it couldn't penetrate the spirit armor the mentor had draped over me. I doubted anyone in this city could. So I grabbed the crossbow again, aiming at my opponents. But these scumbags had hidden well, and the crowd of demons, panicked and scattering, hindered me enormously. Shoot ordinary passersby? I couldn't bring myself to do that, my disdain for demons notwithstanding. Yes, everyone running here would gladly devour my core once it emerged, but should they be killed for that? It was their nature. As for the ones continuing to shoot at me, I'd happily end their existence at first opportunity!

My mentor appeared shortly, looking smug, with a huge flame igniting behind him and causing even more panic. He flashed a bloodthirsty grin, stretched out his hands, and started hurling fireballs into nearby houses. Watching this was... scary? Perhaps, "disconcerting" would be a better term. I never liked how the mentor dealt with the castles we destroyed. Too relentless for my taste. He took the phrase "fewer demons here means fewer demons in our world" a touch too literally, in my opinion. I doubted the lady lying on the stones, her bright yellow eyes filled with terror and staring into the sky, would have ventured into our world. What saddened me the most was the injustice — the demons were desperately defending, but what could they do against someone several tiers of ascension above them? Nothing! Yet I understood the necessity of such cruelty. Without suffering enough, they wouldn't summon the wormhole coordinator, leaving our world defenseless. Not from the likes of that lady, but rather those who kept shooting at me! How much more could I take?!

We reached the palace at the city center with three stops along the way — for more workshops lay in our path, and my mentor's hoarding tendencies didn't allow him to pass by just like that. The destruction of the palace itself went without saying — the mentor had left me at the entrance and entered alone. Unwilling to chase demons throughout the building, he activated his Master's aura upon entry and crushed everyone with his power. Servants, defenders, and bystanders all perished. Black smoke billowed shortly, signaling the mentor had completed his mission of destruction.

We left the city in silence. The streets we used to enter the center were ablaze, forcing us to take alternative routes. This time, however, the Taoist didn't bother hurling fireballs, only employing techniques a couple of times when lesser demons blocked our path and sparing the defenders who continued to shoot at us with their futile crossbows.

"It was necessary," the Taoist said once the city was far behind. His intonation was just as calm and confident as always, but his voice sounded low and I thought I detected a somber note in it.

"I understand," I replied. "I've seen villages ravaged by demons. Witnessed what they do to people. We must close the wormhole."

"Understanding and accepting are different things," the mentor observed. "I saw your face when you exited the alchemical workshop, apprentice. You understood, but you did not accept."

"It's hard to accept such things, mentor," I confessed honestly. "Demons... It's not their fault they are as they are. They cannot be otherwise. And the fact that our worlds were bridged by the Primordial Soul wasn't their doing, either. I'm not saying we should pamper these beasts. I've seen what they do to people. I repeat myself, but it's worth saying it again. Just... Sometimes I think your bloodlust is excessive. Those demons simply couldn't fight back. You said the Heavens never sent us weak enemies. It seems this city must have greatly offended the Heavens for us to have been sent here."

"So you stopped shooting for that reason?"

My mentor smiled with unexpected warmth. I looked down, unsure what to say, but the Taoist didn't need my response.

"What we've been doing lately will profoundly affect me, and you too, in the future. The Heavens dislike unequal fights, seeing no valor in them. There is no overcoming. By destroying so many demons today, I've delayed my own ascension by at least ten years. Even if I sit by the Primordial Soul and meditate all that time, the Heavens won't allow me to ascend to the Master tier. That's the price, and I've accepted it, deciding on this madness. I needed to test you, apprentice. To see if you're ready to destroy the weak to satisfy your thirst for blood. And whether you have such a thirst. This test will echo in your future. Someday you'll hit an ascension wall that you'll have to break through with great effort. And the reason will be what we — no, what I did today. But we had no choice. The Heavens see all, so we have no other option but to destroy the wormhole coordinator, even if it costs us decades of ascension blockage. We cannot achieve our goal without causing chaos here and without instilling terror in demons. If the demons don't decide to destroy the wormhole after what transpired today, we'll have to destroy another city of theirs. Then another. And another. We'll stay here as long as necessary, even if we pay a monstrous price."

"But how will we know if the coordinator starts closing the wormhole? We're here, and the wormhole is weeks of travel away."

"We'll know, trust me," my mentor said, his smile boding no good. "As I mentioned, closing a wormhole isn't that simple. It requires a precise sequence of actions. And I've left a little surprise at the place where those actions are supposed to begin. To you, a Seeker's plaque might be the most precious item, granting freedom in the future. To me, the Phoenix clan's creation is one of the most effective ways to deal with careless demons."

"Do you have many of these plaques?" I asked, realizing an uncomfortable truth. Seekers could also die. And nothing remained of them but these plaques that other Seekers carried as weapons. As a memory that they, too, would someday become a weapon in the hands of their more successful brethren. Did I really want to be one of them?

"Sadly, yes," the Taoist replied calmly, but I had been with him long enough to sense his mood darken. Probably many of those whose plaques lay in his spatial pouch had been known to him personally. Every man for himself? Was that really the law of the seekers? Sure! It might seem so outwardly, but the more I listened to the mentor, the more I realized that the Seekers, though they may not have showed it, valued each other deeply. Because true Seekers were few. For those ready to go against the will of the entire world were ground into dust almost immediately. Only the strongest remained. As it should be.

We rode aimlessly for several days, disturbing no one, until one beautiful moment, we climbed another hill. Stopping the wagon, the mentor grunted.

"You asked where demons got spirit stones if there were no anomalies in their world. Well, today you have a unique opportunity to see for yourself. There it is, the source of the demons' spirit stones. And, it seems, we're in for an extremely interesting encounter, judging by the fluttering flag. Truly, the Heavens love to surprise us where we least expect it."

I probably should have responded, but all my attention was riveted to the half-destroyed city within which various techniques flickered. Yet, no matter how hard I squinted, I couldn't make out the details. Everything was too far away. One thing was clear — Apprentice demons were at work, and not of the lowest ranks. But it wasn't the city or the techniques that caught my attention. A tent city spread out near our hill, right at the center of which stood a huge tent with a blood-red banner flying over it. Another gust of wind straightened the banner, and I could make out an intricate black symbol. The same was depicted on the chest of Almyrda, the chief of the Urbangos tribe. It appeared I knew who lived in this tent and whose demons were now using techniques in the semi-abandoned city. The mentor was right. The Heavens did sometimes present us with astonishing surprises.

CHAPTER 3

"HAVE YOU CALMED DOWN yet? Or should I explain again how I came here in peace?" Mentor Guerlon hardly glanced at the demon sprawled on the ground. What was the point of observing someone whose limbs were twisted at unnatural angles, with blood streaming from the mouth, their face being one big bruise, and their yellow eyes rolled back, signaling a journey to a better world where strong madmen don't suddenly fall from the sky? Yet, for me and everyone gathered, it was hard not to stare at the defeated demon. It's not every day — heck, not even every decade — that you saw a Golden rank Master turned into mincemeat in seconds.

"What have you done, fake Taoist?!" Unlike most onlookers, Vyllea wasn't stunned into silence. "Make things go back to normal right now!"

"Has the junior forgotten she's no longer my apprentice?"

My mentor's voice didn't waver as Vyllea was slammed into the ground with such force blood splattered in every direction. The mentor might have overdone his show of power, but again, no one dared utter a word. He stood ready to demonstrate, via total annihilation if necessary, that we had come in peace. He leaned over the fallen master and laid a hand on him. Demonic healing techniques differed from the human ones in color. While ours emitted a soft blue glow, demonic techniques blazed bright red. I sighed in disappointment, returning to the normal world. Spirit vision hadn't helped me discern the energy flows. The demon, like my Mentor, appeared to me as a completely black figure. I couldn't peer inside him. My mentor chose not to heal Vyllea, adhering to the principle that a sharp tongue must suffer. If the brat dared to show such insolence, she had to bear the deserved punishment.

Yet, I was no longer sure Vyllea could rightly be called a "brat." Since we last met, she had visibly toughened and nearly caught up to me in height, and I'd grown quite a bit myself. Her short boyish haircut was gone, replaced by a lush mane of auburn hair. Her face had become even cuter — but the most significant change was her body. Even if Vyllea had kept her short hair, no one would mistake her for a boy now. At nearly fourteen, she was beginning to develop the beautiful shape of a grown woman.

"Any more objections to our arrival, or can we talk like civilized beings, junior?" Mentor Guerlon asked the now-standing demon. The horrific wounds had vanished, but it was clear full recovery would take time. Nonetheless, the healing technique bestowed by Lord Shang Li worked miracles. The demon cast a brief glance at Vyllea, sprawled on the ground, before bending in a bow.

"A talk would be nice, Elder. Some tea?"

"I wouldn't say no," Guerlon was the epitome of graciousness. Nodding in my direction, he added, "This is my apprentice. Should anything happen to him, the entire camp will perish — both the ones here, and those storming the city of the ancients. As for this junior, let her remain as she is for another five minutes. If she hasn't grasped that impulsiveness isn't a virtue at her age, it's up to me to instill it in the most comprehensible way. After her punishment, bring her to the tent. Lead the way, junior. Your story intrigues me greatly. Apprentice, you're coming with me."

"Yes, mentor." I bowed, unexpectedly to myself. I had never seen Guerlon like this before. Instead of the irksome Taoist forcing me to seek my own answers, a true Elder emerged, whose will was to be obeyed without question. And should anyone doubt this, they would be punished in the most fearsome manner.

The tale of Nars-Go Li, a Golden-rank Apprentice tier and an inner-circle apprentice of Venerable Shang Li, turned out quite fascinating.

LAW OF THE JUNGLE

The loss of his personal apprentice had severely damaged the Overlord's reputation on two fronts: the apprentice had been so headstrong that he'd ignored his mentor's order, and so weak that he'd managed to die. It had reached a point where several demons even challenged Overlord Shang Li, deeming him unworthy of his position. The Overlord eliminated these challengers, but the damage to his reputation lingered. He had to demote some of his personal students to inner-circle ones, and inner- to outer-circle ones, even parting ways with some of the latter altogether. Nars-Go Li was among those who'd managed to retain their inner-circle status. Since Overlord Shang Li was left with only two personal students and continued to face scrutiny from rivals, he'd sent Nars-Go Li with Vyllea, giving him a clear mission: to advance her to a copper Apprentice by age eighteen. The Urbangos tribe had bought the rights to explore the ruins of an ancient city for six months for this purpose, embarking on an enthusiastic conquest of the location.

At that moment, Vyllea was brought in unconscious. Guerlon placed a hand on the demon's shoulder, and several unpleasant crunches followed — the broken bones set themselves right. Vyllea inhaled deeply as if surfacing from underwater where she'd remained for at least two minutes, then began coughing to clear her lungs of residual blood.

"Has the junior learned her lesson, or does it need repeating?" Mentor Guerlon asked as if

36

nothing significant had happened. Vyllea glared at the Taoist with hatred but remained silent, seemingly gathering her thoughts.

"A question was asked, junior. If you lack the brains to understand that you must answer your elders faster than they even pose the question, I will have no trouble teaching you another lesson."

Vyllea screamed in agony — her legs turned into a pulp of flesh and bones. Guerlon didn't bother with lengthy discussions or attempts to appeal to reason. He acted as the strong should. The law of the jungle, as my mother would say. Might makes right. The rest must obey or die. Or, in this case, suffer.

"Did she make it to Bronze?" Guerlon turned to the hushed Nars-Go Li, seemingly forgetting the howling girl. I might have been mistaken, but what seemed to have impressed the demon the most was the Taoist's tranquility — no emotions, no raised voice. Nothing but a clear sense of superiority.

"Yes, Elder. Six months ago."

"Late. I had hoped for a promotion within three to four months of our parting. Did Overlord Shang Li take long to find her a mentor?"

"Yes, Elder. The loss of his personal student greatly affected the Venerable Overlord Shang Li. He took a while to decide, and my apprentice was unable to train for some time."

"What are her prospects for reaching Silver?"

"Perfect. She'll get there within a month."

"A month," Guerlon nodded respectfully and

looked at me. The Taoist said nothing, but his gaze conveyed much. It seemed I'd disappointed him again — the Silver rank remained elusive to me, while Vyllea would reach it in just seven months. Exhaustive training had toughened my body, but its energy volumes had not increased. Crafting two artifacts, whether a year ago or now, remained an unreachable goal for me.

"Junior, are your healing techniques sufficient to restore the apprentice?" Guerlon glanced at Nars-Go Li, who nodded. "Then heal her. I don't want to waste time on trifles. If she can't temper her spirit, we may need to repeat the lesson."

Vyllea had enough sense to stop whining. She sat down in one of the chairs, hands on knees, gazing into the void, effectively becoming a piece of furniture — quite an attractive one, admittedly. It seems I hadn't interacted with girls for a while, even forgetting what they looked like. However, such behavior didn't satisfy Guerlon. He turned to her and announced,

"The Urbangos tribe used the wormhole to infiltrate the human world. I know the name of the demon coordinator — Lensor from the Jarming tribe. Now, I need information on his whereabouts. And this question is directed at both of you. I presume the inner-circle student of the Overlord Shang Li might also possess such knowledge."

Silence fell in the tent. Vyllea's eyes widened. She began to look at the Taoist in a way she never had before, with fear in her gaze — something unbecoming of someone who deemed herself a mistress entitled to command the lives of servants and slaves.

"The information about wormhole coordinators is a secret for which demons are obliged to die," Nars-Go Li stated. "Such are our laws."

"I don't care about your laws," the Tapost shrugged. "If you're not sure you can withstand our conversation, you might as well end your ascent here and now. I won't bother reviving you. Breaking a Master demon, especially of the Golden rank, is too challenging a task. I don't have time to fuss over you now. But you, girl, won't get off so easily. You can't stop your heart, you have no poison in your system, and you haven't even heard what real pain is. Torturing you won't please me — you were once my temporary apprentice. I know your potential. I see how confidently you progress in your ascension. It would be a pity to cut it short, but I will if I must. And don't tell me you have no idea who Lensor is or where to find him. You're the elder daughter of the chief of the tribe that has paid for the wormhole's opening. You surely know where to find the coordinator. I give you ten minutes to collect your thoughts and prepare to answer my questions."

A daunting silence fell in the tent again. My mentor leaned over to pour himself some tea. After a moment's thought, he filled my cup as well. I had to join the table, although being near him when he looked and behaved like this felt somewhat intimidating. Guerlon had never been this ominous, even when annihilating demons in cities.

"While our esteemed hosts ponder over who will answer my question, it's time for a lesson. So, apprentice, in the world of demons, spirit stones are mined in two places. The first is special mines — a highly secretive and closed location, inaccessible to ordinary demons. All we know is that the stones grow deep underground, and the main problem lies in excavating them. The second source is what you've just seen — the ruins of ancient demons. I suppose if we ask the venerable Master Nars-Go Li, he'd be pleased to tell us the history of these places. Fundamentally, they are a mix of battlefields and our anomalies. Here in Circle Zero, some techniques will work inside the city, but not all of them. Am I right?"

"Yes, Elder. What works here is Spirit Arrow, Cloak, and Steps — only at the initial level, though. This place is perfect for training those aspiring to immortality at the Candidate stage."

"Exactly as I surmised. Cities like this are akin to our anomalies, apprentice, harboring a heart that spawns golems at a much faster rate. There's substantially more Qi here than in our realm. Demons venture into the city, obliterate groups of golems, scour sectors for resources, and retreat. These ruins aren't just a source of spirit stones and materials; they're perfect for teamwork practice."

"We don't refer to the ancient cities as ruins, Elder. They're training grounds that we use for skill refinement."

"So be it — a training ground, then. Now, our time's up. I require an answer, and I'm about to — "

I couldn't catch the rest of Guerlon's words. Suddenly, I felt as though drenched in something unsettling. Emptiness engulfed me, a void formed in my chest, and circles danced before my eyes, swapping with alarming speed. A bitter taste lingered in my mouth; I might have even blacked out briefly. When the eerie sensations ebbed away, I found myself staring at Mentor Guerlon, sitting upright, his face deathly pale as if drained of all blood. I first thought it might be some invisible arcane technique the demons had employed to shock us, but then my mentor's face broke into a knowing smile. He even closed his eyes as he leaned back in his chair.

"No need to probe about Lensor from the Jarming tribe any longer. My gratitude to the Urbangos tribe for their hospitality and the delightful tea. I hope it'll be long before we cross paths in combat again. Whether it's you, my former apprentice, or you, most esteemed inner-circle apprentice of Overlord Shang Li."

Guerlon refilled his cup, savoring a sip. He clearly understood what had just transpired, yet he chose not to divulge this to the demons.

"Does this imply we're free to go, Elder?" Nars-Go Li inquired.

"This camp is yours, junior. We're merely visitors. You're at liberty to do as you see fit.

Though, I'd like to make a request."

"A request?" The demon's tension was palpable.

"The training ground is reserved by the Urbangos tribe. I've observed its worthy members confidently navigating the city, sharpening their prowess. I wish to assess my apprentice, hence I seek Vyllea, the tribe chief's elder daughter, to grant Zander access to the training ground."

What in the world? Just moments before, my mentor had seemed ready to resort to torture for information on the wormhole coordinator. Now, he transformed into a gracious guest, overflowing with compliments and geniality. This abrupt shift left not just me, but everyone else as well, especially Vyllea, dumbfounded.

"Do you merely wish to train, or do you intend to destroy its heart?" Nars-Go Li sought clarification.

"It's not our training ground, junior. If the Urbangos tribe allocates us a district, we — my apprentice, that is — will not step beyond its limits. There's nothing for me there."

"In that case, Elder, I have a counter-request," the demon spoke. "If you permit, I'd like to send my own apprentice along with yours. She needs to practice interacting with someone close to her rank. Sadly, within the Urbangos tribe, there are no demons whose rank is low enough. And inviting someone from a different tribe would be improper. Servants shouldn't see their masters as weak."

B O O K T W O

Vyllea's cheeks flushed — her current level of ascension was clearly troubling her. Had she been born in her world's Second Circle, she would already be at the Apprentice stage — and not at the lowest rank, either. Yet, climbing higher than a Warrior would have been impossible. Demons faced restrictions similar to ours. Vyllea had to claw her way up from the very bottom, breaking through each rank's barriers. While her peers had long stepped into the Apprentice stage, this temporary setback frustrated her a lot as the tribe chief's daughter.

"That's not just a good idea — it's an excellent one!" My mentor acknowledged. "Such a proposal is beyond what I had even dared to ask for. What could be better than a joint deadly training of two Bronze-ranked Candidates?"

"Deadly?" Nars-Go Li frowned.

"Oh, let's say, fraught with danger. Surely junior doesn't think he'll accompany his apprentice onto the training ground? It's improper for mentors to interfere in their apprentices' endeavors. They're given a task, and they must accomplish it. Succeed, and they move closer to ascension. Fail, and everyone questions whether the weak are truly deserving of life. When shall we begin?"

"I suggest the morning. Will the Elder stay in the camp overnight?"

"Why not? As I've said, I currently bear no grudges against demons. We are guests in this world, and will return to ours at the earliest

43

opportunity."

"So there's no such opportunity now?" Nars-Go Li seemed to be catching on.

"There isn't," Master Guerlon's smile was disarmingly sincere. "Unfortunately, the wormhole through which we'd entered this world has been detonated."

"Not closed? Specifically detonated?" the demon clarified.

"I'm still at an age where the ability to choose words with precision isn't clouded by the years, junior," the Taoist's voice carried an underlying chill despite his smile.

"Please forgive my imprudence, Elder. It won't happen again. As an apology, allow me to offer you and your apprentice this tent for tonight. Dinner will be served in two hours."

"I'm not accustomed to inconveniencing hosts, junior. A regular tent will suffice for me. But thank you for the offer of dinner. If it's half as good as this tea, my gratitude will know no bounds. And if you could provide us with an opportunity to bathe... I swear by the Heavens, I'll pay for it with a full spirit coin!"

I couldn't fathom what had gotten into Guerlon all of a sudden. There he was, brimming with joy for no discernible reason at all. Our gateway had snapped shut. That empty feeling clawing at my chest had probably signaled just that. Hold up — my mentor was right. I needed to start thinking more! He mentioned our wormhole wasn't just sealed; it had exploded. Shortly after, his interest in the coordinator evaporated. Earlier, he'd shared that the Seeker's plaque, a creation of the Phoenix Clan's head, wasn't just a badge of honor, but also a formidable weapon against demons of any tier. Piecing it all together, it seemed Lensor of Jarming tribe had attempted to seal the wormhole, brushed against the artifact crafted by a Nascent God stage Taoist, and — poof — vanished into thin air, wormhole and all. Thus, despite feeling like I'd just been sucker-punched by the universe, I witnessed Master Guerlon morph into Mr. Congeniality. He'd kept his vow to the Heavens, erasing the wormhole's coordinator from both our world and the demons'. Locating a replacement wouldn't be easy. A Gold-ranked Master being ready to die to guard this secret suggested that such demons weren't exactly dime a dozen.

Now the real puzzle: how were we supposed to get back home? But I had that figured out too — Zou-Lemawn. The city we'd holed up in for four months was linked to demon territory by a wormhole. If we made it to Zou-Lemawn on this side, we could hop back to our realm. I doubted the demons would fuss over our right to pass through. Who would dare to face off against a Diamond-ranked Taoist, anyway? I sure wouldn't. The kicker? It was a two-month trek to Zou-Lemawn. I'd likely croak from the rampant energy of the demon realm before we ever make it. Qi was completely overwhelming here. My cough was making a comeback to boot. Bad news all around.

But then the morning kicked off splendidly, especially after soaking in a warm bath — a rarity in our endless hustle. Contrary to my grumbling, training felt surprisingly refreshing. With our insane mobility, finding time for a decent workout was a luxury.

Near us, Vyllea and her new mentor's training markedly contrasted ours. While Mentor Guerlon honed our hand-to-hand combat and weapon skills, the demons engaged in something that struck me as quite odd. Vyllea meditated, and Nars-Go Li intermittently struck her shoulders with a stick. That was their entire routine for two hours, as we exhaustively practiced our strikes. I was tempted multiple times to inquire my mentor about the demons' peculiar training, but each time he discerned my intent, he intensified our pace, making questioning him suddenly seem a less appealing prospect.

When we wrapped up, Vyllea received a dose of healing, unlike yours truly. Guerlon opined that if I were too frail to dodge his bone-crushing hits, I didn't merit healing — though he did alleviate the overall strain my body was suffering from the energy abrasions.

The moment for our combined training arrived eventually. Vyllea and her mentor, standing not far off, seemed deeply engrossed in a serious dialogue, probably setting some detailed task for her to accomplish. As for Mentor Guerlon, he merely gave me a succinct rundown, evidently considering it sufficient for my survival on the training ground. He'd even managed to assign me a task!

"Your only companion will be your sword. Golems demand decapitation and dismemberment; they're mechanisms, oblivious to pain. Keep a close watch on Vyllea — your mission is to ensure her safe return."

"Why's that?" I blurted, astonished.

"Because looking after yourself is the easy part. The real challenge multiplies when you're accountable for someone else. Aren't you here for a rigorous training and not a leisurely stroll? Bear in mind: should Vyllea suffer any harm, you'll face repercussions. Now, off you go. It's rude to keep the demons waiting."

Wait? Their conversation seemed at its peak! Still, I often found my mentor's motives enigmatic. One day he was on the brink of executing Vyllea, and the next, he demanded I safeguarded her, notwithstanding her nearing the Silver rank. Could enduring pain be essential for advancement? Why else would Nars-Go Li strike his apprentice with a stick if not out of sheer sadism or as a manifestation of some demon trait I was unaware of?

"Stop dawdling, runt," Vyllea snapped, as "courteous" as ever. At least some things remained unchanged in this world. "Cross me, and it'll be the end of you!"

"Move, demon wannabe," I retorted with a smirk, using a form of address she detested the most. "I wager a spirit stone that you'll..."

An overwhelming force brought me to my knees mid-sentence, Vyllea collapsing beside me. As our entire camp succumbed to this unseen pressure, only our mentors remained standing, Guerlon brandishing his sword and Nars-Go Li bowed in respect. Devoid of the strength to even turn my head, I awaited the outcome, which swiftly arrived — a deep scornful voice broke the silence.

"You have destroyed a city full of my slaves, you worm. You've made me expend resources to teleport here. You've forced me to come to this accursed place, devoid of energy. Your punishment will be death, and I will feed your apprentice to the lower demons. He's good for nothing else. I just want you to know who kills you, runt. So that in your final moments you realize just how pathetic you are. To curse the day you decided to enter my world. You will be killed by Overlord Lurth Mink of the Copper rank! These are my lands! This Circle Zero is mine! This is my world! And now die, human scum!"

CHAPTER 4

"PLEASE FORGIVE ME, Overlord Lurth Mink," Guerlon bowed his head and kneeled before the demon. "I have erred in attacking your city. I acknowledge my fault and am ready to atone. Just tell me how: with spirit stones, artifacts, or service? I don't seek forgiveness but hope for your leniency and... Hey, Overlord, stop crawling away! Or do I need to sever your other leg, too?"

"Do you have any idea of what's happening here?" Vyllea whispered right in my ear. The scene unfolding before us seemed so surreal she forgot to maintain her usual insolent demeanor.

"Nothing unusual — the Taoist deigns to ask for forgiveness, apparently," I responded, equally stunned. Huang Lung's texts mentioned that a Taoist of the Diamond rank could easily handle an opponent of the lowest rank of the next ascension stage, but I hadn't imagined the gap in their power to be this colossal. Deadly lightning roamed the vicinity for mere seconds. The arriving Overlord had acted recklessly — his element was earth, and so he had obliterated half of the Urbangos tribe camp with sharp stones and compressed soil. And it wasn't just the camp — many demons got caught in the crossfire and became pulverized as well. We would have suffered, too, had Guerlon not shielded Vyllea and me with spirit armor. Sharp earthen spikes tossed us into the air a few times, but they couldn't breach the Taoist's protection. Hence, Master Guerlon decided not to prolong the battle — the actions of Overlord Lurth Mink were too wild. The demon collapsed, and to prevent further reckless actions, the Taoist amputated a leg and an arm. That was enough.

Yet, what followed next... I couldn't fathom Guerlon's actions, even after pondering over it at length. Instead of finishing off his dangerous foe, he kneeled and begged for mercy, all the while thoroughly looting the Overlord — taking his spatial pouch, rings, several amulets, and leaving him only a local artifact that allowed ignoring the energy hunger. Everything else was taken from the demon Overlord.

"But how?" Vyllea continued to whisper. "He's an Overlord! I know him — he was among those who challenged Overlord Shang Li, thinking him too weak. Has your mentor become an overlord? Answer me, human! How did a mere master defeat an overlord? It's impossible!"

B O O K   T W O

I wasn't planning on answering listening to the mentor intently instead.

"Overlord, it seems that I've inadvertently inflicted wounds upon you. Would you permit me to heal them? Hey, I've asked you a question, Elder! Don't make me repeat it!"

The venom Guerlon infused into the word "Elder" was palpable, as if he had condensed all the contempt of this world into it. Yet, credit where due, the Overlord ceased crawling away. Glancing around for aid and finding none, Lurth Mink conceded,

"Yes, Junior. You have my permission. Heal me."

In a flash, Guerlon became lightning, and when he materialized again, the severed hand and leg of the demon were in his grasp.

"This will hurt, Overlord. Oh, but it will. You'll just have to endure, I'm afraid."

The shriek that followed suited a stuck pig a lot more than it did a demon Overlord. The scream ceased abruptly as Lurth Mink fainted. Yet the objective was achieved — the leg and the arm were back in place.

"What an intriguing technique," the Taoist mused as he turned to me: "Apprentice, come over here."

I got up and approached Guerlon on stiff legs, fearing the Taoist now even more than Overlord Lurth Mink.

"Look at the Overlord with your spirit sight," my mentor ordered me as I drew closer. "What do you see?"

"A black figure, mentor," I replied, following his order.

"Place your hand on his body and use the sight again."

Touching the overlord was daunting, but not following the mentor's command was even more so. I knelt, laid a hand on the unconscious demon, closed my eyes, and immersed myself in the world of energy. For a while, nothing happened, but then the darkness lifted from the overlord's body, revealing something unimaginable. All seven meridian threads glowed with overflowing energy. Yet nothing seemed to be moving through a couple of them. The energy core and the spirit core were constantly connected — there were flashes moving between them, which I couldn't track. The center, originating all meridians, seemed disproportionately small against this backdrop, as if taken from another body to be transplanted into this one. Continuing my examination, I noticed that the threads of the leg and arm, which the mentor had severed and then reattached, appeared lifeless. The Taoist had failed to reconnect the meridians with the center. Moreover, the thinness of the energy channels struck me as uncanny. I had seen demons with far sturdier meridians. Here, the channels seemed like mere threads.

"What do you say?" Mentor Guerlon asked as I returned.

"It's beautiful," I confessed honestly. "Never

seen anything like it. It's both beautiful and terrifying at once. If the overlord doesn't heal the damaged meridians in his leg and arm, he might lose the threads. Taoist, can an immortal regress to a lower rank?"

"No. An Overlord remains an Overlord, even if all their limbs are severed. They simply won't be able to use corresponding techniques. But that wasn't my question."

"You didn't actually ask anything," I muttered, yet proceeded, "The Overlord's meridians are alarmingly thin. There is hardly any energy coursing through them. Several demons at the 'apprentice' stage that we've encountered in this world had much sturdier threads. Here, everything seems fragile, as if it might snap at any moment."

"You didn't notice the spirit core, then?"

"Sorry, mentor, never heard of it. If the energy core is identified by the power it emits, and the elemental core by the color of its energy, then I know nothing of a spirit core. Does it really exist?"

"Not in any pure form, but we'll discuss this later when you reach the Third Tier. Nonetheless, you haven't answered my question."

"Mentor, you've posed no question," I retorted, my fear of the stern Taoist evaporating. "You have tasked me to report what I saw. Task completed."

"No," he simply replied. "You've only told me what any student from any school of ascension could have. Everyone knows an Overlord has all meridians formed, possesses cores, and that limb injuries harm the threads. But I'm curious about something else, apprentice. You were on the right track but somehow didn't pursue the topic."

The right track? Was he hinting at the thinness of the meridians?

"Is Overlord Lurth Mink an irregular Overlord?" I started reasoning aloud, pretending not to notice Vyllea and her mentor, who had come closer. "The excessively thin meridians suggest he... didn't cultivate them? Didn't develop? But how is that..."

The realization hit me quite suddenly, as was usually the case.

"Overlord Lurth Mink hails from the fourth circle of the demon world! His meridians developed almost in infancy, but he'd never bothered to strengthen them, focusing instead on his elemental core, which is significantly larger than his energy core. His center and meridians are so weak they can't sustain technique usage for long. Yes, that had struck me as odd — some threads seemed as if they had run out of energy, becoming nullified. Yet his elemental core was vast... The overlord used only one element throughout the battle! Earth spikes, stones, and dust — those aren't techniques, but pure element manipulation. But is such active elemental use even allowed in Circle Zero?"

A satisfied smile crossed the Taoist's face.

"No, apprentice, one shouldn't do that in Circle Zero. In fact, it's strictly forbidden. You'll understand why when you reach the Master stage. Am I right, junior Nars-Go Li?"

"Yes, Elder. Using elements in Circle Zero is very dangerous," the demon's voice conveyed unabashed respect. My mentor looked at me again, prompting for more. But I was nearly done.

"Overlord Lurth Mink couldn't use techniques for long. Why? Because he wasn't a true Overlord. He lacked battle experience in Tier Zero, had never faced such formidable foes, and came here without any of his apprentices, as if he never had any. He's of the Copper rank, and I'd say he'd attained it relatively recently."

"What..." It was precisely that moment that Overlord Lurth Mink chose to regain consciousness. My mentor knelt once again in what I realized to be a very fine mockery of the demon.

"I beg your forgiveness, Overlord Lurth Mink! Your body has been healed, but you'll have to mend the meridians yourself. In seeking your pardon, I offer you these spirit stones. I hope for your mercy."

Two sizable chests appeared next to the Taoist. Sealed. The overlord started to rise but froze when the Taoist's steel voice commanded,

"You weren't given permission to stand, Elder! To the ground!"

The overlord's eyes widened, a mix of surprise, fear, and bewilderment evident. Not just I, but everyone around struggled to comprehend the Taoist's actions. Continuing his play, Guerlon announced,

"Do you forgive my audacity, Overlord Lurth Mink? Are the spirit stones sufficient? Do you relinquish all claims against me for the destroyed city and the accidentally slain demons? My soul grieves for the misdeeds committed, and I submit myself to the fair judgment of the Elder." Once again, the term "Elder" was imbued with a tone that seemed to cross well into mockery.

"Yes," the overlord managed to blurt out, thoroughly confused. "I have no claims against you. I forgive your attack on my city and my demons."

"Thank you, Elder! Your forgiveness means a great deal to me! As for these spirit stones, I will hold onto them for now. I see you've misplaced your spatial pouch and would not be able to carry such a burden. By the Heavens, I promise to return every last spirit stone at the first opportunity. Now, overlord, you may rise and depart at your leisure, pondering the purpose of existence as you do so. Cross paths with me in Circle Zero again, and I'll end your existence permanently. Seeker's word! And now, be gone!"

A fiery serpent erupted from Master Guerlon's hand, scorching the earth a step away from the fallen overlord. That was enough to make him jump up as if stung, even attempting to flee, but a technique hurled at his back knocked him down again.

"Is the Elder so deaf as not to heed my words? I said, proceed with dignity and grandeur!

Overlords do not run! They grace their lands with their majestic presence, bestowing joy with their mere existence!"

Taoist Guerlon had to approach the fallen adversary to heal him — the blow had pierced the demon through. Forgetting to erect a shield was another major oversight on the part of the Overlord. The second attempt achieved exactly what the Taoist had demanded — the demon started to move towards the horizon slowly and with great trepidation, making no efforts to hasten, only casting terrified glances back at my mentor, anticipating another strike. None came.

"Overlord Lurth Mink will seek vengeance," Nars-Go Li remarked calmly as the departing demon's figure dwindled to a speck.

"That's a problem for the Urbangos tribe and Overlord Shang Li to deal with," my mentor responded, his smile turning predatory. "I shouldn't concern myself with the honor of the tribe and the Overlord, but I'll make sure to mention how an overlord of the Copper rank attacked an inner-circle apprentice of Overlord Shang Li and the eldest daughter of the Urbangos tribe's chief. Instead of retaliating against such audacity, they simply looked away, pretending nothing had happened. If Overlord Lurth Mink and all his apprentices continue to live, it speaks only to the weakness of Overlord Shang Li and the Urbangos tribe. It suggests they are unworthy of their current standing. But, as I said, it's none of my concern."

"So, you've let him go just to harm my tribe?" Vyllea flared up, but quickly caught herself, adding, "Elder!"

"The reason I did this shouldn't concern you, junior. Your duty is to defend the honor of the tribe. If you're incapable of that, get used to being smeared. The weak have no place in your world. Right now, you are weak. Your tribe is weak. Overlord Shang Li..." The Taoist's gaze shifted to Nars-Go Li. "It's up to him whether he's weak or strong enough to protect his inner-circle apprentices. I suspect Overlord Lurth Mink will return to Circle Zero in no more than a week, gathering whomever he can. Disciples, mercenaries, friends, if he has any, and so on. His honor is wounded; he'll crave vengeance and the eradication of all who've witnessed his disgrace. How untimely for the Urbangos tribe to have claimed the right to this training ground. It will soon become perilously hot here for demons of lower ascension stages. But we digress. Apprentice, aren't you supposed to be carrying out my task?"

"I beg your pardon for my sluggishness, master," I managed to keep my smirk at bay. It seemed I finally grasped why the Taoist had staged the entire spectacle of begging for forgiveness. Yet, I harbored significant doubts about the effectiveness of such a method. The Heavens must witness sincere motives, not just outward actions. Or was the exterior enough in some cases? I definitely needed to read up on what the Heavens were and how they influenced the lives of Taoists. Demons, for instance, never appealed to them. The Taoist received official forgiveness for killing defenseless demons. But was that enough to avoid barriers in ascension? I didn't have the slightest idea.

"So? I hear words, but see no action!"

"I cannot fulfill your task alone, mentor. A clear order was given — to ensure that demon Vyllea faces no threats as vigilantly as possible. How can I obey if Vyllea refuses to go to the proving ground? Who am I to protect there? Myself? From some golems?"

"Protect me?!" The girl flared up at such audacity once again. "What have you deluded yourself into thinking, runt? I'm almost at the Silver rank, and you're still stuck at Bronze! It will be me who has to protect you!"

"So? I hear words, but see no action," I echoed, almost biting my tongue. I sounded just like my mentor!

"Let's go! Mentor, we're off to the proving ground! I'll show this human that demons are superior!"

Anger fueled Vyllea, rendering her... breathtaking. That blush on her cheeks, her heaving chest, sharp movements, and an astonishing figure. No, I definitely needed more practice interacting with girls if I was feeling attracted to a demon. The scent hadn't changed! Vyllea still reeked of death, just like...

The scent! What a fool I'd been! That was

what the Taoist had been probing me about! Overlord Lurth Mink emitted the same sickly sweet odor as all the others! Despite proclaiming himself an Overlord of the Copper rank, he wasn't one at all! Just a Master of the Golden rank, most likely! That was why my mentor had dispatched him with such ease. And that was also why he had inquired about the spirit core. It was a leading question to make the obvious dawn on me.

"Are you coming, runt? Or did you chicken out when it got real?" Vyllea taunted me. She was clutching her jian in her hand, and, unexpectedly, I found myself eager to test how much her blade mastery had improved. I used to win ten out of ten bouts against her, but the girl was tenacious and never gave up. I'd have to ask for a sparring match after we'd clear the training ground.

The ancient demon city had a clear boundary that the local heart didn't cross. Golem beasts prowled the city's perimeter, the local ones resembling huge cats akin to panthers — just slightly smaller. The guardians lunged at anyone crossing the line, but seemed oblivious to those a step away. Golems couldn't venture outside the city.

"Watch, runt, and see how real demons act! This is what will happen to you when I gain more power!"

With those words, Vyllea crossed the line and charged at the golems. She moved quickly, and her sword flew in a way that spoke of significantly increased skill. Yes, I definitely wanted to spar with her. I hesitated before following her without any spirit armor on me, taking a moment to view the world through spirit sight. The golems were not so simple, as it turned out! Two tried to snatch Vyllea, while another two lay in wait on the roof of a nearby two-story building, ready to pounce from above. Vyllea was pressing the golems and cackling maliciously, pleased with the effect. She had no idea they were letting her win. And she had no time to clutter her mind with such nonsense. She was showing off her valor and strength to me because I needed to be impressed and acknowledge that she was far stronger than me. Another Elda-grade nuisance on my hands...

I leaped, slicing my golem in half and, knowing time was tight, hurled my sword with all my might towards the ones lurking on the roof, poised to pounce on Vyllea. As expected, the golems ducked, letting it fly overhead before straightening up — and one promptly toppled back onto the roof. It was hard to leap at people while decapitated, even if you were a dangerous mechanism.

"Above you!" I yelled, rushing to Vyllea's aid. The creatures she had easily corralled suddenly realized their ambush had failed and stopped holding back. They lunged at the girl so swiftly she missed a block and fell. As the mechanisms converged to finish her, I was already there.

"So this is how real demons act? Falling under golems?" I couldn't resist taunting her as I fended off the beasts. From what I had glimpsed through spirit vision, these golems ranked as Silver Candidates, making them formidable foes for Vyllea and me.

"Kill that bastard! Move over!" Vyllea sprang to her feet, standing beside me. A chill ran down my spine — there was a scratch on her cheek. Nearly bloodless, but that wouldn't stop my mentor. I'd failed his task, unable to protect this headstrong demon. Where were those golems? I needed to vent my anger before I lashed out at the stupid brat!

* * *

"Elder, I have a request."

"I need the complete collection on demon artifact crafting up to the Second Circle," Master Guerlon replied, keeping a watchful eye on his disciple's actions, ready to intervene at any moment. Despite the proving ground's apparent simplicity, mechanical creations were not to be underestimated. After all, this was Zander's first real battle with golems.

"Elder?" Nars-Go Li was taken aback.

"That's the price of my assistance, junior."

"But how did you..." The demon began, baffled.

"You need to rush to Overlord Shang Li and inform him of what has just transpired. Vyllea will die in the inner circles. This means you'll need to ensure her safety first, which will create an inevitable delay before you can race to your teacher. Over this time, the one who calls himself Overlord Lurth Mink could cause a lot of irreversible damage. For example, he could annihilate the Urbangos tribe from the Second Circle without much trouble. The news of her mother's death would erect such a barrier to Vyllea's ascension that she won't be able to overcome it until she is eighteen at least. You would fail your teacher's command and never become one of his personal students. Have I made myself clear, or do you need more details?"

"No, Mentor, you've been most succinct," the demon pressed his lips together.

"Then you've heard my requirements — I need textbooks on artifact crafting. Both the textbooks themselves and any supplementary guides. They should await us in Zou-Lemawn in a year and a half. I believe that time will suffice to advance Vyllea to the Golden Candidate stage, possibly even to Apprentice, though I'm less certain about the latter. I've never worked so closely with demons before. What musical instrument does she play?"

"The pipa, Elder. Though I wouldn't exactly say she 'plays' it — we've only just started our lessons."

"Chess?"

"Demons prefer Go, Elder. She's quite good at it."

"I need a board and stones. I don't have any."

"Yes, Elder. Also, Vyllea is learning alchemy."

"I'll need resources for pills; I have my own

alchemy furnace. Anything else?"

"Just personal belongings, but not many. All materials related to demon artifact crafting up to the Second Circle will be waiting for you in Zou-Lemawn in a year and a half, Elder."

"Agreed. You'll pick up your apprentice there, too. One more thing. Tell Overlord Shang Li that seeker Guerlon would be greatly appreciative if he could be informed about the workings of demon artifacts that block energy hunger. I'm intrigued by things I don't understand. The principle behind this artifact eludes me, hence my interest."

"I'll convey your message to the Overlord," Nars-Go Li nodded, struggling to stay put as he watched his apprentice topple under the assault of three golems. Only the heavy sigh and mutterings of the eccentric Taoist stopped the demon.

"I'll have to discipline both of them. Their teamwork is abysmal. Did I undercharge for my services, I wonder?"

CHAPTER 5

"JUST ONE WRONG MOVE, and you'll regret it. Look away and forget you even have hands. And I dare you to smile, human. By the honor of the tribe, I'll end your miserable existence there and then!"

Vyllea's menacing whisper in my lap boded ill. After exiting the proving ground, our mentors sprung the news: for the next year and a half, the girl would be Master Guerlon's apprentice, while her former master, Nars-Go Li, needed to head off on some important business. This was perhaps the only time I fully sided with Vyllea — our outrage knew no bounds. But of course, no one cared to listen. My mentor gathered the girl's possessions, a map of the demon world's Circle Zero, clarified a few details with Nars-Go Li, then conjured his two-seater self-moving cart, took the controls, and stared into the distance. He didn't even speak. It was clear what we were supposed to do.

The only available seat was singular, and Vyllea and I were no longer twelve-year-olds. But, as I noted, this detail didn't bother my mentor — or, rather, our mentor — in the slightest. I cursed having agreed to this lunacy of venturing into the demon world as I took one look at the girl. Vyllea's gaze was nothing short of incendiary!

Master Guerlon coughed, as if by accident. With a heavy sigh, I settled into the seat, trying to sink as deep into it as possible, brought my legs together, and turned away, unwilling to face the girl. The only way to fit on the passenger seat was for Vyllea to sit sideways on my lap and, as Master Guerlon favored fast rides, wrap her arms around me to avoid getting shaken off the ride. To make us both comfortable, I also needed to embrace the girl, pressing her close. This arrangement formed a rather stable structure capable of withstanding the rough terrain. Two years prior, such a mode of travel hadn't particularly bothered us, but, as I had already observed, we had grown somewhat since then. Vyllea took her place on me after the Taoist's second cough. Her body was as rigid as steel, and so tense it seemed that if I made even the slightest wrong move, she would leap from the moving cart and flee as fast as her feet could carry her. Our mentor pulled the levers and we tore off, leaving dust clouds in our wake. The girl swayed, forcing me to pull her closer to prevent an accidental ejection, which required her to hug my neck. It was at this moment that she uttered her formidable threat.

But smiling was the last thing on my mind. The Taoist's decision had unsettled me considerably. I couldn't fathom why we needed Vyllea. She was useless — nothing but trouble all along! Not only did her idiocy make me run laps around the training grounds three times as punishment for failing in my task, but she herself kept venturing where the most dangerous creatures lurked, clearly seeking death in her attempts to prove superiority. I found myself repeatedly dragging her out of complete disaster scenarios. She blatantly ignored me, persisting in her own ways. The relief I felt as we were leaving the training grounds was indescribable! Master Guerlon was right after all. It was one thing to be responsible for oneself, and quite another to ensure a brainless team member survived as well. My time on the training grounds had fully convinced me of Vyllea's utter lack of brains. I even began to understand why her mentor would hit her with a stick during meditation — nothing else seemed to reach this mule-headed creature!

Fortunately, we began our journey towards the end of the day — Master Guerlon drove the cart for only a couple of hours. He remained indifferent to mentions of energy clusters en route. Spoils of hunt held no interest for him, apparently — he aimed to distance us from the proving ground as far as possible. I understood his rationale — there were certain risks that the disgraced demon Lurth

Mink, who was posing as an Overlord, might return with reinforcements.

When we halted, Vyllea leaped to the ground like a cat. She seemed fairly fresh, despite having sat tense for the entire two hours. In contrast, I resembled a dried-up cucumber — only a wrinkled husk of me remained. My legs were pricking as if several hundred heated needles had been thrust into them at once. The mentor stowed away the carriage, and I collapsed onto the ground, barely holding back a groan — standing on those legs was out of the question.

"You will meditate all night," came the command, after which the mentor only took out one tent from his spatial pouch. His own. "Do not light a fire, do not wander far for personal needs, and do not talk to each other. Split the water between the two of you."

A small flask appeared on the ground, after which the mentor disappeared into his tent. It felt as though he was entirely unconcerned that we had stopped in the middle of an open field. No trees, no elevations, no lakes. Nothing. Just reddish grass, small stones, and some animals that scurried at the very edge of my spiritual vision. Despite my inability to stand, checking the surroundings was the first thing I did.

"And how long do you plan to lie there, runt?" Vyllea's disgruntled voice rang out. I had to roll over and look up at her.

"Don't tell me you're so hopeless your legs have gone numb!"

BOOK TWO

"We are but mere mortals — what chance do we stand against great demons of nearly Silver rank!" I replied. The needles gradually receded, allowing me to sit up. Standing was still out of the question.

"I'm serious, Zander," Vyllea suddenly seemed like a different person. She even called me by my name, which had never seemed to happen before. "Why didn't you strengthen your muscles during the trip?"

"To strengthen muscles, one must know how to do it. I don't."

"Oh, come on! That's the foundation of ascension! Look, all you need to do is..."

Vyllea didn't get to finish — we got engulfed by the monstrous aura of our furious mentor. He even emerged from his tent.

"You were explicitly told what to do. Why do I see two foolish chattering teenagers instead of two apprentices meditating? A hundred push-ups, squats, crunches, and five minutes of plank. Since you have enough energy to talk, let's have a little evening warm-up. Begin!"

The hundred repetitions weren't the worst punishment, but they sent a clear message — next time, the count would double. Then quadruple. Eight hundred was my limit; I understood it was wiser not to infuriate the Taoist beyond that, He'd flatten me into the earth, then gather me up only to do it again, and still ensure I served my punishment. Talking was off-limits. Meditation was the order of the night.

Yet Vyllea's words lingered with me. Body strengthening was foundational — something her mentor must have emphasized. Mine, however, acted as if I should stumble upon every insight by myself. Even Huang Lung, who'd penned the explanatory grimoire, skipped over the Candidate stage as trivial, assuming any Taoist would evolve past it naturally. He focused on forming nodes, meridians, and fortifying them into thick ropes. but glossed over body preparation. Disappointing, really — the founder of the Silver Heron School should've considered his works might reach a layperson far from any thoughts of ascension.

What exactly was Vyllea trying to convey? The essence of ascension? "Why didn't you strengthen your muscles?" Was that what she said? Muscle strengthening... nothing came to mind. Let us assume that during our two-hour ride she wasn't tense, but engaged in strengthening. Once the journey ended, she became all supple and soft, just a moment before she leapt to the ground. Observing Vyllea through spirit sight revealed nothing beyond what was expected of a Bronze-ranked Candidate. Yet, her mentor believed she'd reach Silver in a month. Oddly, I understood the distinctions among Taoist ranks at the Apprentice stage, but remained clueless about the Candidate gradations. I knew the Golden rank entailed forming at least two nodes, with some demons showcasing four. But the specifics of the Silver rank remained a mystery. The golems we had defeated were classified by the energy in their spirit stones, an unmistakable measure. But our energy wasn't like the golems'. It was the energy of the body, so...

Body energy... body strengthening. What if those two concepts were meant to interact somehow? But how? I told myself I needed to quit jumping from thought to thought and leverage my advantage. I was a mental absolute, for Heaven's sake! And my mentor, may his years be long, was teaching me precisely how a mental absolute ought to be taught — to figure things out on my own! No! That wasn't why he was making me think! He'd leave me in two years! If he spoon-fed me everything, how would I survive with him gone? Expect him to come running from the Third Tier to wipe my nose? He was preparing me for independence, no less! And my failure to realize this was entirely my own fault.

What did our training sessions entail? The mentor honed my mastery of hand-to-hand combat, jian, spear, crossbow — no training directly aimed at body strengthening. Nothing that would turn me into the burly type whose broad shoulders didn't fit through doorways. But that was irrelevant. The goal of the Candidate stage was to prepare the body for the formation of additional organs — nodes, cores, meridians, and, eventually, three types of cores. But we didn't focus on strengthening the body. We refined our skills instead. Why was that?

Could the reason be that physical strength development wasn't the foundation? Everyone said we needed to "prepare the body," not "buff up the body." Now, back to Vyllea's words — "body strengthening." Something that would allow me to comfortably support her weight for hours without worrying about circulation disruption. How could one achieve body strengthening? Only through its development. But I had just concluded that mere physical training wouldn't help. It seemed a dead end...

Could it have been that I was approaching this from the wrong angle? Carrying weights developed muscle mass, addressing the external aspect of my body. What I needed was to cultivate the internal. The internal volume... of muscles? No — this was about body energy! My mentor often lamented that I could only produce two artifacts at a time. And yet, he continuously had me create more. By that point, all our crockery had gained the property of repelling dirt. I was seriously considering applying this to clothes, but I was afraid I might not have enough juice in me. At any rate, the point was that repeated creation of artifacts hadn't increased my body energy levels. Why was that? Because I wasn't retaining energy within my body — I was expelling it outwards, into the item I was creating. I was giving it a part of myself. This made me more resilient, but it wasn't what was needed. I needed to circulate energy within my body without letting it escape. I had to make it work — to pump it up without letting it spill over my body's boundaries! I had done this in the anomaly! I had been pumping body energy! I had created warmth and kept it near my skin. It had been challenging, but now, as logic suggested, I needed to complicate it even further. I had to circulate heat throughout my entire body, constantly feeding it new warmth, not letting it stop for a second! I had to have so much energy in my body as I could possibly hold! Why hadn't I reached such a simple conclusion on my own, when the Taoist had left so many hints? Why had it taken a conversation with Vyllea? Maybe she was right, and I really was a bit on the slow side?

Warmth cmcrgcd in my chcst and instinctively moved towards my hands, ready to emerge outside, but I managed to halt it. It became uncomfortable — my body wasn't ready for such treatment. The warmth concentrated in my fist, which immediately started to ache with pain. Not knowing how to control body energy yet, I simply imagined it returning from my hand back to my chest. It seemed to work — the pain in my fist ceased.

But my shoulders began to ache instead — the heat didn't go back into my chest but stopped in them, refusing to descend any lower. Unlike with my fist, the pain here was bearable, prompting me to add more energy. Doing so for the second time proved difficult, but since all my life force remained inside my body, I didn't faint. The heat made another rapid dash towards my fist but then returned to my shoulders, obeying my will. That was when the discomfort became quite palpable. My shoulders swelled with heat, feeling like they were about to burst, and forcing me to risk using a tried and tested method — directing the heat towards my skin as if to shield myself from the detrimental effects of Qi energy. However, there wasn't as much energy here as in the anomaly, and the pain nearly suffocated me — it felt as though I was dunked in a vat of boiling water. I had to quickly revert everything to how it was before — the body's energy once again flew towards my chest area, pausing in my shoulders for some reason. A wave of pain that overwhelmed me was so intense that I couldn't hold back a groan. The thought arose that I needed to urgently rid myself of the body's energy, or I would be in trouble, but I immediately dismissed it.

I wasn't a masochist reveling in self-torture — I simply knew what would follow the abrupt removal of warmth: much of my life energy would leave me. If it didn't kill me instantly, recovery would take at least a week. I had generated too much heat in one go. It wasn't just dangerous; it was potentially lethal. Thus, sitting and enduring was the only option! My shoulders burned as if set aflame.

Then, a life-saving idea emerged: redirect the energy elsewhere. Perhaps not to the fists, but maybe to the legs? As if obeying a command, the heat began to flow through my body downwards. For a moment, I felt nothing, but then I was hit with such a charge that I couldn't help but yelp. The energy swiftly returned to my shoulders — moving it to my legs had been foolish. I hadn't felt such pain in a long time. Again, a moment of calm while the energy transitioned from one place to another; then all the world's weight seemed to crash down upon my shoulders.

"Don't touch him!" My mentor's formidable roar cut through the murky veil of my meditation.

"But he's going to die!" Judging by Vyllea's voice, she was on my side, surprisingly enough. "He needs to get struck!"

"He needs nothing! Your former mentor needs to have his arms pulled off his body for what he's done to you! A Seeker must handle their body energy on their own! I warn you once. Strike Zander on the shoulder, and you'll die. I swear it by the Heavens! Zander must deal with what he's done to his body on his own!"

The pain in my shoulders was becoming unbearable again. I had no strength left to hold back, so I growled like a wild beast. Maybe even cried like a baby. The thought of expelling the energy outward and quietly dying came to me more and more frequently. Perhaps the Taoist would take pity and heal me? Yes, that was what I'd do. Anything was better than this. At least in my last moments, I'd live without pain. After all, as long as the energy transitioned from one organ to another, it didn't inflict harm.

The revelation that enveloped my body was so intense and swift that for a few moments, I forgot about the inhuman pain tearing me apart. Why had my mentor told me about the development of a seeker at the Apprentice stage, but never about the Candidate stage? Perhaps because these matters were interconnected? Something he'd told me a while ago came to mind: *"First, the threads of the right hand and stomach open. Then the left hand and right leg. Followed by the left leg and chest. And, finally, the head."*

When the body's energy flowed from one area to another, it caused no harm. Obeying my mental command, the warmth surged toward my right hand, which immediately started to fill with heat. Before the sensation became unbearable, I directed my body's energy toward my stomach. It felt as though I had taken a dozen blows at once, but then the sensation eased — the energy swiftly moved on to my left hand. Almost instantaneously, it left there and leaped to my right leg, then to my left leg and finally to my chest. Remarkably, this time the energy entered without any issue, bypassing the shoulders altogether. However, I had no intention to let it linger in one place for too long — the pressure around my chest began tightening like steel bands, prompting me to push the heat further through my head. While my brain still functioned, I closed the loop by sending the body's energy back to my right hand.

The pain receded. Nothing burned anymore and there was no pressure. The sole issue was that I couldn't afford even a moment's distraction — shifting the energy from one organ to another demanded my full concentration. I understood that should I pause even for a moment, my body wouldn't withstand it, and not even my mentor would be able to assist me. I would perish. Thus, all that remained for me was to keep circulating the warmth following the path of the meridian threads' formation. Soon, this began to yield results — the turbulent energy within me started to decrease. With each circuit, a portion of the warmth remained in my muscles and internal organs, dissipating within them harmlessly.

When the last remnants of energy were absorbed into my body, and the frenzied circulation of warmth ceased, I opened my eyes. The luminary of the demon world hung high in the sky, indicating that I had sat immobile throughout the entire night and the better part of the day. The first thing I noticed was the absence of needles throughout my body. Despite having to sit still for so long, my body felt thoroughly rested. Rising to my feet, I saw Master Guerlon assessing Vyllea's jian skills nearby. The girl had improved significantly. Yet, as soon as I stood up, my mentor effortlessly disarmed her and halted the fight. He concealed the weapon, approached me leisurely, placed a hand on my shoulder, closed his eyes, but there was no healing. It seemed as though he was examining me. Eventually, he removed his hand and declared,

"It's taken you too long, apprentice. The task was to meditate through the night — without encroaching upon the following day."

"My fault, mentor — I'd lost all track of time," I replied, surprised to find that no anger stirred within me. Now that I had realized the motivations behind my mentor's actions, his words were perceived entirely differently. Everything he did and said was aimed at ensuring my survival in the future. How could one be angry at that?

"This is no excuse — you will be punished regardless. Let's move out!"

Given Vyllea's stiff movements, it was evident that Guerlon had been training her rigorously since the small hours of the morning. She looked exhausted to the core, and for once skipped the customary unpleasantries as she settled onto my lap. Even more surprisingly, she laid her head on my chest and fell into a deep sleep almost immediately, undisturbed by the bumps along our path. As time passed, my legs began to numb, prompting me to recall the body strengthening techniques I'd recently grasped. Unsure of the exact method, I opted for a familiar approach — generating small amounts of warmth and circulating it throughout my body. This temporary measure provided relief for about ten minutes before I re-emerged into the larger world, waited for the numbness to return, and then submerged back into the realm of surging body energy. This cycle continued for an extended period, as Master Guerlon showed no intention of stopping.

Eventually, the landscape transformed before us. Initially, sparse trees dotted the horizon, gradually becoming denser until we found ourselves enveloped by an immense forest. Our Dark Forest back in Vorend resembled a well-maintained park in comparison. Utilizing my spiritual vision on the forest unveiled a rich concentration of energy clusters — a sight that made me swallow hard. As if responding to my realization, Guerlon halted our journey. With adept movements, he leaped from the carriage, stowing it away in his spatial pouch, which caused both Vyllea and I to tumble onto the grass, though we quickly scrambled to our feet. Vyllea, who had woken up during the ride, but remained silent, now looked around with wide eyes.

"Is this the Forest of Dandoor?" she exclaimed in astonishment.

"Correct, apprentice," Guerlon confirmed, setting up a table laden with various foods. "Eat up and listen. We are indeed in the Forest of Dandoor — the southern boundary of Circle Zero in the demon world. As I've come to understand, this expanse of trees is deemed a rather unwelcome place by the locals. About seventy miles from here lies a battlefield, and the creatures that inhabit it sometimes make their way to the forest, managing to survive here. We are currently at this location."

Master Guerlon laid out a large sheet on the table and pointed at it. My father had taught me how to use maps, so I appreciated the level of detail. It detailed the lands of demons in the southern part of Circle Zero with precision. The map instantly became etched into my memory. The Forest of Dandoor covered a vast area, and its isolation was marked by the absence of any nearby major cities. The battlefield he had mentioned was also indicated, lying almost at the ocean's edge.

"Your task," Master Guerlon pointed elsewhere on the map, "is to reach this point within three days."

"But that's the Forest of Dandoor!" Vyllea was aghast. "It's notoriously avoided for a good reason — it's dangerous!"

"Dangerous indeed," the Taoist agreed with ease. "Deadly, I'd say. But how do you plan to pursue immortality if you shy away from danger? Victories on training grounds will not teach you the most important skill, apprentice — and that is survival. The ability to assess your strength accurately. This forest will have no wise mentors to heal your wounds and no aides to bring you a flask of cool water or wipe your sweat as you rest after killing another golem. Here, everything will try to kill you. The beasts, the mists, the plants, the aura. You cannot learn to survive while always relying on those stronger than you. Here, take this."

Master Guerlon tossed two half-empty backpacks to the ground.

"You're going armed with swords. Food and water should last you three days. Fail to make it on time, and you'll have to travel to Vorend on your own. I refuse to wait for incompetents who cannot make a twenty-mile trek through a forest in three days. Turn back, and you'll fall into the clutches of Overlord Lurth Mink, in which case death will seem like a luxury. So, apprentices, the countdown is on!"

Master Guerlon materialized the self-moving carriage and sped off in the opposite direction, quickly disappearing among the trees.

"I always knew humans were mad. But this mad..." Vyllea looked at me. Fear was evident in her gaze. "How have you not died with a mentor like that?"

"It's precisely because I have such a mentor that I haven't died," I hoisted my backpack over my shoulder. "If I was coddled every time I got a boo-boo, I'd have been dead a year ago. Faced with choosing between a terrifying forest and my mentor's wrath, I'd choose the former. At least there's a chance to survive. Coming? Or do you need a moment to gather your thoughts?"

"Let's go. Wait, hold on. Zander, I know we're enemies and that our alliance is only temporary, but... How did you manage to harness your body's energy?"

CHAPTER 6

SUNSET WAS ONLY A FEW HOURS away, so we decided to wait for morning. Moving through an unfamiliar forest at night — especially one that even demons feared to enter — was ill-advised and fraught with health hazards, to put it mildly. While Vyllea busied herself with her own tasks, I approached several clusters of energy, becoming the owner of simple plants that had embarked on the path of ascension in the process. Vyllea's reaction upon my return was priceless — her eyes widened in astonishment. It turns out that foraging was a highly respected profession, and demons who ventured out often return empty-handed. It required a special intuition for herbs and strength to fend off dangerous predators that fed on these plants. Yet here I was, a simple Bronze-rank human Candidate who had never been in this forest before, and within about ten minutes, I had gathered a forager's monthly quota!

"So you've never wondered about the power spots I mentioned to the mentor during our journey?" I marveled.

"How was I supposed to know? Maybe it was a quirk of your communication or some such! Zander, you still haven't answered me! How did you master body energy?"

"Let's trade information — tell me everything you know about it. How do you master it?"

"That's just it   I don't master it!" Vyllea surprised me. "I can generate it and concentrate it in one place, but when its power becomes unbearable, the mentor relieves me of the generated strength. That's why I can't train on my own, and when I asked Mentor Guerlon for help, he got very angry."

"Are you talking about the stick?" I guessed.

"It's the most effective way to release accumulated body energy. After the strike, it disperses throughout the body, allowing it to strengthen. This is the path to the Silver rank. Therefore, you can't train body energy alone — you might die in such a scenario. But you... You've done it on your own! How is it even possible?"

I wanted to say it was none of her business, but then I remembered how Vyllea had defended me. She demanded that the mentor allow her to hit me on the shoulders to save my life. Yes, we were formally enemies, but Heaven wouldn't forgive me if I didn't repay kindness with kindness.

"Alright, sit down. This will be a long talk. It's not enough to know what to do. You need to understand why it works and how to avoid mistakes. They almost finished me off, and there's no mentor here who can heal you."

I had to explain everything. Starting from the generation of body energy, methods of controlling it, and redirection, to the process of forming the meridian through which this energy must flow. I detailed every nuance I encountered myself, from the heat and excruciating pain to the perils of losing concentration. I even mentioned that a minimum amount of body energy was necessary for a test — this would still be harmful if control was lost, but not fatal. Vyllea listened attentively, without interrupting me once, and then sat down, closing her eyes. Soon she started growling in pain, screamed a couple of times, and staggered, forcing me to find a stick to hit her on the shoulders — but it wasn't needed, as it turned out. She found balance and quieted down, and only the large drops of sweat streaming down her face spoke of the monstrous tension she was experiencing.

As I couldn't offer any help to Vyllea, I decided to explore the surroundings. Why else would the mentor give us only half-full backpacks? Given the abundance of power centers here, it made sense to collect everything I could find. As I started exploring, I immediately stumbled upon a tree that had adapted to the ambient energy and embarked on the path of ascension for the first time. I puzzled over how to take it with me but, failing to come up with a solution, left it to grow further. Only about two feet of the trunk at the base would be useful, but accessing the wood required cutting down the tree and sawing off the unnecessary parts. I lacked the tools, and even if I had them, a whole chunk of the trunk wouldn't fit in my backpack. However, I gathered enough herbs for ten foragers! The Forest of Dandoor proved to be quite generous with plants, even if they didn't hold any exorbitant value. They were worth merely two or three spirit coins each, and that was if I managed to bring them back to our world. Compared to the thousand-year lotus hidden in our first cache, these were beyond trifles. Yet they still had their use — besides food and a water flask, the mentor had included artifact crafting tools in my backpack. The plants I'd found were just enough to turn my cloak into an artifact. I was tired of washing it every day! While I couldn't enhance its durability yet — meaning it would tear from any snag — it wouldn't get dirty. Good enough for a long trek through demon lands.

Vyllea meditated until the next morning. I had returned, loitered about, and even had breakfast by the time she finally opened her eyes.

"It works!" Vyllea whispered in astonishment. "This method really works! But why didn't my mentor tell me about it?"

"Because if you make a mistake, you die. Draw too much energy, you die. Lose control, you die. Release the energy from your body... You get it."

"Die," Vyllea echoed, as if tasting the word. "Do you often find yourself on the brink of death like this?"

"Depends on the circumstances," I could only shrug in response. "The mentor believes you can't head towards immortality without facing hardships. The more there are, the easier the process seems. I agree with him, in a way. Shall we go? Or do you need more time?"

While Vyllea was having breakfast and tidying herself up, I took off my belt and laid it out on the ground. It seemed to me that starting with the smallest of things was the way to go. Transforming the required flowers into fine dust, I began to apply the pattern carefully. Fear clutched at my back and didn't let go until the final stroke — I was doing something without the mentor's oversight for the first time. Vyllea returned and sat next to me, watching my actions attentively. Noticing my concentration, she showed an unprecedented tact for her — she didn't curse, sneer, or mock. She just observed my actions silently. Ensuring the symbol turned out exactly as I had envisioned, I activated a wave of warmth and, after channeling it through my chest, released it into the seal. The belt flared brightly, but immediately went out, turning into a simple artifact. Tuning into my feelings, I even frowned: my body felt weakened, but not as much as before. It felt as though I had spent not half, but at most a third of my available body energy reserve.

"And what's this?" Vyllea finally poked her curious nose into my creation.

"An artifact," I replied. I scooped up some soil and smeared it on the belt for the sake of demonstration, rubbing it in deeper. However, a flick of my creation caused all the dirt to fly off. Only the old dirt, ingrained before the belt had become an artifact, remained. And it appeared to me that it would stay there until the belt's complete destruction.

"I've just gotten tired of constantly washing it. Now I have a dirt-repellent belt."

"Can you only do this with belts?" Vyllea was intrigued.

"Mantles, trousers, leg wraps, boots," I listed the constructions that were mentioned in Huang Lung's book. First-year students of the Silver Heron School fortified their clothing themselves rather than buying it from others. It saved both effort and money.

"How about a dress?" Vyllea asked hopefully. I rummaged through my memory and nodded. Such a foundation was also present in the charts. "What do you need for that?"

"I've gathered enough herbs, so all I need is time. I can manage one item a day without harming my health. Need to meditate more to increase this number."

"Can you only do cleanliness? What about durability?"

"Qi energy manipulation is required for that, so until I reach the Golden rank, it's not even something I should consider."

"You meant to say, until the Apprentice stage?"

"No, Vyllea," I even smiled, "I meant the Golden rank of the Candidate stage. Though I won't have meridians yet, I'll be able to manipulate the energy of spirit stones without putting my life at risk. Listen, we can chat all we want, but it doesn't get us any closer to our goal. If the mentor were here, he'd say he sees two chatty teenagers but not any work aimed at the completion of his task. Personally, I have no desire to trek to Zou-Lemawn on foot."

"You do realize he was just scaring us, right?" Vyllea snorted. "He wouldn't dare leave the two of us on our own. Especially not in this forest. I bet anything that he's watching us even now. Mentors do nothing but shout and scold their apprentices, yet they're really very kind to them deep down. Yours is no exception. And you know why I think so? Because he didn't leave us a map. Pointing out a spot and saying he'll be waiting there for us — that's not just foolishness. It's madness."

"Actually, we do have a map." I recalled the very map of the demon world's Circle Zero that the mentor had shown us in my mind. "Considering I'm a hunter's son and can not only read maps, but also trek through unfamiliar forests with ease, I see no problem covering thirty miles in three days to reach the designated point. The mentor knows this, hence the task. You can stay here if you want, but I'm definitely going."

"Zander, that's ridiculous! No one treats their apprentices like that! A mentor is supposed to guide, hint, and help us. Do everything to facilitate things. What does yours do? He just dumps us in the middle of a forest!"

"Not 'yours,' but 'ours,'" I corrected her. "Your demon gave up on you so easily — as if you were a burden to him. Were you also expecting special treatment and demanding his undivided attention?

"What do you know, you little runt!" Vyllea flared up. "My mentor had brought me to the Silver rank! And yours didn't even explain what that is!"

"Remind me, wasn't it you who nearly knelt before me last night, begging me to tell you about the circulation of body energy? Don't your delicate shoulders want to thank me for sparing them from being beaten with a stick?"

"I'll kill you, you little bastard!" Vyllea even drew her jian, looking ready to attack. Every single last vestige of her previous prudence and reason was gone.

"Are you going to hit me in the back?" I smirked, not even thinking of drawing my own jian. Unlike this madwoman, it would take me but a moment. I just needed to clench my hand, and the sword would jump into it.

"I'm off. Are you coming with me, or will you wait for Overlord Lurth Mink? I reckon he'd have no trouble following the tracks of our wagon."

My first impression of the Forest of Dandoor was one of utter mundanity — nothing but a tangle by near-impassable thickets. I had to pull out my jian and hack my way through dangling branches — there seemed no other path forward. Usually, the deeper parts of a forest offered more room: towering trees prevented the undergrowth from becoming too dense. In the demon world, however, trees acted as if they had every right to grow with unbridled voracity. They sprouted from everywhere, seemingly needing no light for their sustenance. There were no customary layers here — grass, shrubs, and tall trees. Everything was jumbled together, creating a monstrously inconvenient terrain for traveling over.

The map in my memory became useless after just a couple of hours. First, I had no idea which direction the sun rose in this world. Second, the dense canopy of towering trees obscured everything — even the sky. Therefore, I couldn't reliably determine the direction of the sun to get my bearings. Moreover, the standard hunting methods for finding direction were futile. In the demon world, there were neither anthills, nor moss on the trees — nothing that could help determine where north was. Vyllea just shrugged at my queries, claiming such useless information had never been necessary for her. In the end, I simply had to forge ahead, breaking a path through the underbrush and branches.

"Alright, break time!" I declared, chopping down another branch. We'd been in the forest for six hours and hadn't encountered a single beast with either my normal vision or its spirit counterpart. I checked our surroundings every minute, fearing an Apprentice level beast might sneak up on us unnoticed, but it never happened.

"Zander, he's not here!" Vyllea kept looking back, hoping to spot Mentor Guerlon. "Not a single branch has stirred! Even an Overlord couldn't move through this forest so silently!"

"Didn't I say as much?" I smirked. "You might as well get used to the idea that we're on our own."

"You don't understand! This is the Forest of Dandoor! Even warriors are reluctant to deal with it! There are battlefield creatures roaming in its depths!"

"That's why we're skirting its edge and not even thinking about venturing deeper. By the way, can you explain how a battlefield is supposed to be located here? As far as I know, it's a wormhole that had collapsed and merged our worlds. But there's not even a hint of such a battlefield anywhere in my world. The mentor and I have traveled through many lands of Tier Zero. There are definitely no battlefields there."

"How should I know?" Vyllea was clearly nervous. The girl couldn't stay still, constantly looking around as if she expected Mentor Guerlon to appear. Yet he was nowhere to be seen. "Zander, are you sure we're going in the right direction?"

"No," I honestly replied. "We'll have to wait until morning to check with the position of your sun. By the way, what do you call it?"

"Hurban. Since you have such a remarkable memory that you remember everything, can you repeat what the mentor had specifically said about our expedition?"

"Our task is to reach a specific point within three days."

"So, not a word about having to trudge through the forest, then?"

"No," I frowned, replaying the conversation in my head. Indeed, the mentor hadn't mentioned we had to move towards our destination in a straight line.

"Then explain, oh great hunter of the human world, why did you drag us into this impenetrable thicket? Why couldn't we skirt the forest's perimeter?"

"Because that would take three times as long as going straight through." I pulled up the map from memory once more.

"Like we're making any serious headway here! Ninety miles in three days is child's play for those of us on the path to immortality! But no, you've decided to go straight through! Naturally, the mentor isn't here: he couldn't even fathom someone being such an idiot to charge through a dangerous forest! What was the point of him showing you the map?"

I think I blushed. The shame felt like a sucking void in my chest. We'd lost an entire day because of my stupidity! The mentor always said to use our heads whenever he gave us a task. Why did I think going straight was the right call? Why didn't I consider there were different ways to accomplish the same task?

"We're going back," I sprang to my feet. "We need to make it back by the end of the day. Tomorrow, we're in for a serious run."

Vyllea just shook her head but didn't voice her thoughts. Though she could have — and had every right to. I had indeed acted like a complete fool. Heading back proved easy enough: a path had already been cleared. The thought even crossed my mind that we might manage not just to return but also to cover a solid six miles or so today, but the heavens decided to play a cruel joke on us.

I stopped so abruptly that Vyllea bumped into me. Yet she didn't complain: a fearsome roar silenced her. In my haste to return, I'd completely forgotten to check the forest through spirit vision, and the result of my carelessness was a few dozen yards ahead. A battle was underway.

"Freeze and don't move," I whispered, trying not to even breathe unnecessarily. The roar repeated, one of the trees wobbled menacingly but didn't fall, prevented by the dense crowns of its neighbors. The red leaves obscured the view, so I closed my eyes and instantly plunged into the world of Qi energy. Chills ran down my spine when I realized what I saw: there were Apprentice-stage beasts fighting ahead. One of them was of the Silver rank — I could clearly see six formed meridian threads; the other four had reached the Bronze rank, each with just four threads. Judging by the way their meridians flared up, the beasts were actively using techniques against each other. More precisely, the four Bronze creatures were trying to overpower their Silver foe, and they were hardly successful. I noticed the bodies of two Copper-rank beasts on the ground, along with a trio of common Candidates. They were almost completely drained of energy. I would certainly not confuse the nodes of their energy structures with anything else.

As I returned my attention to the material world, I realized that Vyllea was clutching my hand tightly. The girl was scared but had no intention of leaving me behind. Without a word, we took a small step back. Then another. And... I didn't even know how I managed to react. It felt like a spear had pierced my back. Without fully understanding my actions, I pushed Vyllea to one side and moved in the other direction, just as a black, hairy mass with a bunch of thin legs crashed down where we had just stood. My jian appeared in my hand before I could fall. And there was nowhere to fall to — the side was blocked by dense branches of a shrub. The recoil sprang me forward, and using this acceleration, I lunged at the bizarre creature, plunging my sword into what I assumed was its head. Only my jian bounced off its body as if it were made of some kind of steel! The creature recovered from the fall and began to rise, but then Vyllea appeared beside it. The girl acted with terrifying efficiency: she didn't slash but simply stabbed the creature somewhere in its torso. The blade went in completely, after which the monster twitched and went still.

"You can't just pierce them randomly; you

need to know the spot," Vyllea commented, looking up. Finally, I could make out the beast we had killed. It was a huge spider, the size of a calf, pitch black. Four tar-like eyes bulged out as if it couldn't quite believe it was dead. Long, hairy legs ended in nimble fingers, suitable for clinging to branches or sturdy webs, and its entire body was covered in small hairs, surprisingly pleasant to touch. The carcass was quite heavy, and had it landed on us from above as it intended, we would have been in serious trouble. I wasn't sure body fortification would have helped, especially since we hadn't activated it.

"Follow me," Vyllea commanded, darting under the nearest branching tree. She continued to peer into the reddish leaves from underneath a branch. I had to press closely to Vyllea, but she didn't even hiss. I closed my eyes, surveying our surroundings with my spirit vision. The fight between the creatures ahead still hadn't ended, with more parties joining. There were about ten attackers, but killing the Silver-ranked Apprentice wasn't easy. It was destroying spiders, which were likely the attackers, with terrifying ease. The creature that had attacked us turned out to be a Silver-ranked Candidate, maybe even a Bronze one — I could be mistaken here. One thing I knew for sure was that it hadn't reached the Golden rank, as it had formed no nodes yet. Several more spiders passed over us, two of which had reached the Apprentice stage. The enemies were deadly, and I completely agreed with Vyllea that we should wait out the fight under a sturdy branch. This way, no one would crash down on us from above.

Gradually, the spiders started to thin out, as did the energy of the beast fighting them — its meridians flared up very rarely now. Seizing the moment, a couple of remaining Bronze-ranked Apprentice stage spiders descended on the beast swiftly, and the bodies of the monsters intertwined. A pain-filled roar echoed — the creature fighting the spiders was wounded. Yet it had no intention of surrendering, and one of the spiders was sent flying into a barrier invisible to spirit vision, its body merely slumping to the ground afterward. The Candidate-stage spiders scattered quickly, as if waiting just for this moment, allowing the beast to deal with the last enemy.

An oppressive silence hung in the forest so dense that it made one uneasy. It seemed even the wind had died down. The victor remained motionless — its energy structure was still intact, but remained stationary. Just like its enemies. We sat for about ten minutes, but nothing changed: the beast didn't move, and the spiders didn't rush to finish off their foe. There wasn't a single living being within my sight that carried even a trace of energy.

"Shall we check?" I suggested, emerging from under the branch.

"Are you out of your mind?!" Vyllea hissed, pulling me back by the sleeve.

"We don't have a choice." I carefully pulled my

sleeve back. She clutched it with a death grip. "Or do you plan to spend the rest of your life under a tree? The beast isn't moving. It's probably wounded, maybe even fatally. Its meridians are depleted, so it can't use any techniques. We'll skirt the edge and dash out of the forest. While the spiders haven't returned, we need to act. I doubt they'll leave the beast alone, considering how many it has slaughtered. They might even kill us incidentally. As far as I can tell, there's no one nearby. This is our chance."

Vyllea couldn't argue against such logic. She herself understood that sitting under a tree was the least prudent of plans, yet she hadn't come up with anything better. We moved forward slowly, clenching our swords, ready to jump back at the slightest noise. I had to keep a constant watch on the world through my spirit vision every moment to ensure the beast remained motionless. The scene gradually changed: torn-apart spiders appeared in sight, and many of the trees were broken or uprooted. Soon we came upon a small clearing that hadn't been there before. There were lots of spiders lying around. If one were so inclined, they could probably be counted, but the exit on the opposite side of the clearing was too enticing. I moved forward, but Vyllea's hand clutched my sleeve again, stopping me. I followed her gaze and finally saw the heroic beast that had caused such great upheaval. A striped tiger lay on the ground, virtually buried under spider carcasses. The tiger was severely wounded, with a pool of blood forming under its body, but miraculously, it was still breathing. I had seen enough wounded animals to know this one was a goner. The tiger was dying, but dying gloriously. It had killed all its enemies and emerged victorious from the battle, even if it was its last.

"Let's go," I whispered, not wishing to disturb the heroic animal's peace. "We need to leave."

"No." The girl's eyes were wide open, and I distinctly disliked their expression. Madness gleamed within them. "That's a freaking tiger from the Forest of Dandoor! Zander, I must devour it!"

CHAPTER 7

I WAS DUMBFOUNDED. "You're out of your mind!"

"I need to! It's a tiger!" Vyllea's statement sounded as though it explained everything. Perhaps it did, but it meant absolutely nothing to me.

"So what? Have you never had tiger before? Want to diversify your diet with stripes? Then chew on wasps! By the handful! Want me to catch some?"

"Idiot! It's a tiger! If I consume its essence while it's still alive, I can gain a part of its strength! I can advance my mastery of the Tiger Style!"

"What Tiger Style? Have you completely lost your mind?"

"Look who's talking! Mentor Guerlon probably doesn't even know what martial arts styles are! He teaches however he pleases. I, on the other hand, am an adept of the Tiger School and have followed this path since childhood. Now I have a unique opportunity to grow stronger! Zander, step back and don't interfere!"

"The tiger deserves a peaceful death. Eat it afterwards."

"You don't know what you're talking about, you nincompoop! Afterwards, I'll gain nothing but its energy! Strength can only be obtained from a living beast! Though why am I even explaining! You're human — you wouldn't understand! That's it, I'm going! Try to stop me, and I'll kill you! When Vyllea sees a tiger, Vyllea will consume the tiger!"

The girl didn't just look insane — she was acting insanely.

"If it moves, you'll die!" I warned.

"Then I'll die full and satisfied! Away, human! Don't stand between me and my strength!"

Vyllea had lost all reason, so I had no choice but to step back. The carnivorous demon made her way to the tiger, which didn't even twitch as she approached. The beast was already at death's door. It had to take just one small step, but it clung to life tenaciously. I really wished I could never have seen what came next — or at least could forget as soon as possible — but I feared this moment would haunt me until my death. Vyllea couldn't penetrate the beast's thick hide. However, she could thrust her hand into the beast's wound and push it in up to her shoulder, growling like the tiger itself. Vyllea's eyes widened, and with a swift motion, she yanked her hand out. In her palm, she held a shimmering bloody clump with meridian threads trailing from it. The demoness swallowed the clump with a guttural growl, and then began to pull the meridian threads from the tiger and stuff them into her mouth. Vyllea's body shook, she growled like a beast, her eyes rolled back, but she continued to tear out the energy channels from the animal.

The tiger died, and the frenzy ceased. Vyllea discarded the now-useless meridians, which evaporated mid-air, releasing their remaining energy into the environment. She turned her blood-stained face toward me, sending shivers down my spine. There was nothing human in the gaze of those golden eyes. A bloodthirsty demon was deciding whether to kill me immediately, or to leave my yet-useless carcass for later. Deciding I wasn't worth the effort, the demon growled gutturally and fell asleep sitting right next to the tiger's corpse. Vyllea's body twitched periodically, so I observed her with my spirit vision. Something unimaginable was happening inside her — energy surged throughout the body of the demoness without causing her any harm. Whirlwinds of Qi periodically concentrated in her limbs, causing them to twitch, but this happened so quickly I even doubted my own eyes. A look of boundless happiness was frozen on Vyllea's face. I had seen such an expression a couple of times in the village — some particularly gifted individuals would often get soused on sour homebrew, and then sit by the fence with their faces looking exactly like that.

Vyllea clearly wasn't going to get up anytime soon. Apparently, she wouldn't return to her normal state until the energetic madness inside her ceased. And I had no idea when that would happen — it could be five minutes or three days. I got the impression that Vyllea had bitten off more than she could chew, and was now suffering for her greed. Perhaps, even touching her wasn't wise — to avoid causing harm. And, honestly, I didn't want to touch her. Any charm her appearance had held was now gone. Not long ago, I could look at her as a beautiful peer, enjoyed hugging her and holding her close to me, but after what had just happened, I was reminded of who I was dealing with. A demon. And not any simple demon, at that.

I didn't wish to remain idle, so I decided to walk around the clearing. As the mentor liked to say, the prey wouldn't collect itself. Spirit vision revealed twelve energy-filled essences. Lacking a knife, I had to hack at the bodies with my sword. However, not all the bodies could be processed. The creatures that had reached the Bronze rank of the Apprentice stage were too tough for my jian. I had to act as Vyllea had recently done — insert my hand into wounds left by the tiger to extract the essences in a rather grisly and unpleasant way.

Unable to harvest anything more of value from the spiders, I found that my spiritvision still detected something energy-filled within the carcasses. However, when I extracted this "something," the energy evaporated, leaving me with a useless piece of flesh — dirty, oozing with some liquid, and extremely unpleasant. It was likely something valuable and useful to alchemists, but I lacked the proper tools to extract it correctly, a container to store it, or the knowledge on how to collect it properly. I decided to walk over to all the carcasses, piercing their power centers with my jian, and releasing the energy back to the world. Since I couldn't use it myself, I wasn't going to leave it for the spiders that would undoubtedly return. I didn't even glance towards the poor tiger, although it also contained many useful things. Unlike Vyllea, I couldn't bring myself to pierce the heroic beast's carcass.

The demoness showed no signs of coming to her senses. She just sat there with a mad grin on her face, her limbs twitching periodically. I didn't like the silence or the unpleasant feeling developing between my shoulder blades. It wasn't painful yet, but it felt as if a heated needle was being held close to my skin, searching for the right spot to pierce. This boded ill. I had no choice but to pick Vyllea up: I couldn't leave my fellow apprentice behind. However, this immediately posed a problem: she started thrashing about so violently that I could barely hold her. Spirit vision revealed that the already chaotic whirls of energy in Vyllea's body had gone completely berserk. When I laid her back down on the tiger, the flows immediately stabilized. They were still raging but didn't linger or obstruct each other. So, what was happening? Did she start shaking because I picked her up, or because I separated her from the tiger? After some experimentation, it became clear: Vyllea's condition worsened when she wasn't touching the tiger. Furthermore, the more of her body surface remained in contact with the deceased beast, the more stable the raging energy in her body became. As I evaluated the beast's carcass, I realized I couldn't carry it along with Vyllea. It was too heavy. I needed to think.

A reasonable thought occurred to me: I needed to increase the area of Vyllea's contact with the tiger's body. But how could I do that if I had already laid her on top of the carcass? It wasn't like I could insert her inside, right? That didn't seem like a train of thought I wanted to pursue at all.

Alright, suppose it was indeed a bad idea, but potentially effective. How could I cut open the tiger's belly? My jian might not be able to pierce such skin. Or could it? After all, it was a First Tier artifact adapted for a Tier Zero body. I had to try...

Vyllea began to twitch hysterically the moment I lifted her off the tiger, but I had no choice — I needed to flip the beast's carcass onto its back. Once I made sure it wouldn't roll over, I nudged Vyllea close to the tiger's side, and she calmed down. Once she'd wake up, I'd give her a piece of my mind about her unhinged ways. And I'd also complain to the mentor. She'd be left without any essences to chew on for the rest of the expedition!

I hovered over the tiger's carcass, and then thrust my jian into its belly with all the pent-up anger I had. Anger at myself for venturing into the forest so foolishly, and at Vyllea for gorging on something she had no right to. It worked — the blade pierced the belly, albeit only as deep as a hand's breadth, but that was enough for my purpose. For the next twenty minutes I played butcher, enlarging the incision and extracting energy-filled innards. The ribcage proved the most challenging: no matter how much I struck, I couldn't leave even a nick on the ribs. My jian might be a first-tier artifact, but in weak hands, it didn't reveal even half its power. Nonetheless, I managed to deal with the bones too. How? I used my head.

The tiger was a Silver-ranked Apprentice-stage beast. My sword was a First-Tier artifact — an item comparable to the beast. However, in the hands of a Candidate Taoist, the jian seemed like a useless piece of iron. How did one get rid of the useless sword? By no longer holding it! Unlike most weapons, mine could jump into my hands. After thrusting the blade as deep into the carcass as I could, I stepped aside and clenched my fist, summoning the jian back. It worked! A loud crunch sounded, and the sword leapt back into my hand, breaking through a couple of bones in the process. The weapon acted as a First-Tier artifact should. After that, dismembering the tiger was a breeze — the key was to insert the blade correctly.

Finally, the result was achieved: I had gutted the tiger nearly to its spine. The beast was so enormous that not only could Vyllea fit inside, but there was also plenty of room left for me. Placing the girl inside and joining the edges, leaving only her face exposed to the air, I looked at my creation with spirit vision and smiled: my guess was correct. The raging streams of energy inside my companion had slowed down significantly and, as it seemed to me, began to be absorbed into her body. About ten minutes later, this became so evident that anyone in my place could relax and even smile at how clever they were.

But I was far from smiling. Because someone invisible, who had been holding a heated needle near my body, finally decided on the spot and plunged it into my very chest, as it seemed. The sensation between my shoulder blades was no mere prickling — it felt as though a fire had been lit there. There was an immense urge to drop everything and run without looking back so as to flee from this accursed forest as quickly as possible. Not just danger, but death was approaching us, threatening to arrive any minute.

I glanced at Vyllea, her face still stretched wide in a maniacal grin. Her breathing had evened out, she was visibly better. It seemed that in thirty more minutes she would regain consciousness, but we didn't have that time. Death would reach the clearing much sooner. My body had even taken a few steps away from the clearing before I managed to regain control over it. Mentor Guerlon had said that one of the main laws of the Seekers was "Every man for himself." Only the loners survived. However, I couldn't even contemplate leaving Vyllea here alone. Apparently, I was the wrong kind of Seeker. What could I do? Even if Vyllea wouldn't die from being pulled out of the tiger, we couldn't escape the approaching death. I would have to carry my companion's body, significantly impacting our speed. Alone, I might have risked it, but with her, it was impossible. Leaving was not an option. Carrying her wasn't feasible. Defend? Foolish to even try. The burning between my shoulder blades indicated that the creature approaching would hardly notice my resistance. A Bronze-ranked Candidate would be a mere snack for it. There was only one option left — one I deeply disliked. But I saw no other way out.

I gathered our weapons, tilted the tiger onto its side, nearly causing Vyllea to roll out, then climbed inside myself, pressing the girl against the spine. The smell inside the carcass was indescribable. Hastily connecting the edges, I left a small hole for air. My back burned one last time, and unexpectedly, the burning ceased, replaced by a heavy aura.

Death had arrived at the clearing.

Visibility from our hiding spot was nil, so I had to turn on my spirit vision. A monster with seven meridian threads loomed nearby. A Gold-ranked Apprentice stage creature had come upon us. The beast approached the spider carcasses, after which an unpleasant sound followed — the bodies of the slain spiders were torn apart. However, they held nothing valuable; I had taken care of that in advance. All twelve essences were in my backpack, and from the outside, one might assume it was the essence of the defeated tiger that shone so brightly. Eventually, the beast realized it would find no prey among the spiders and moved towards us. A massive hairy paw slammed into the ground right in front of our "window." As I had predicted, the spiders hadn't fled in fear of a dangerous and strong opponent; they had hastened to bring reinforcements. Unexpectedly, the tiger's carcass was lifted, and I had to exert considerable effort to prevent the belly's edges from splitting open. I clenched them with my hands and feet, ready to bite down if necessary, just to avoid falling out, but suddenly we began to spin with incredible speed. Resisting the emerging force was beyond my strength, and Vyllea and I were pressed into the belly, but we didn't fall out — the tiger's carcass was being wrapped in strong webbing. Several threads were woven right in front of my "window," allowing me to assess their width: the web was as thick as my little finger. The shaking ended, replaced by a sensation of flight and speed. I could only see the blurring tree canopies through the remaining open slit. Spirit vision revealed more. We were high above the ground — evident by the clumps of energy below. Alongside our abductor, smaller spider carcasses flitted by, ranging from Golden-ranked Candidates to Bronze-ranked Apprentices, and the longer we moved, the more of these creatures appeared. The tree canopies changed:

webbing began to appear on them. Soon, the leaves vanished. Only bare branches remained. But even they disappeared: we had arrived at a massive tree, which was radiating energy. I had to stop observing through spirit vision to avoid being blinded by the brightness of our destination. I felt uncomfortable at once: the energy floating in the air was so abundant it began to abrade at my body, which I thought had already been completely acclimatized. This was a problem. There was no mentor nearby to heal me. I couldn't even imagine where he might be. Probably sitting near the edge of the forest, waiting for us to run back. It would occur to few that we were inside a tiger, dragged to its lair located on an ascended tree by huge spiders. It sounded utterly insane just when you put it into words.

The tiger's carcass shuddered, releasing an acrid stench. I held my breath, realizing the spiders had injected their prey with a flesh-decomposing venom, intending to return once the tiger's body softened into an appetizing meal. The oppressive aura faded as the spiders departed, deeming their vigil beside the marinating meal unnecessary.

"Zander?" Vyllea's voice broke the silence. "Where are we? What's happening?"

"Quiet," I hissed under my breath. There was no way to silence her physically without risking exposure, so I hoped for her cooperation. Thankfully, she remained calm. Our cocoon was wrapped by the spider colony's mightiest, rendering escape through brute force futile. Yet, my artifact blade and knowledge of handling Apprentice-stage objects gave me a sliver of hope. Positioning the blade through an opening, I leaned heavily on the handle to prevent it from snapping back, then extended my hand towards my throat, summoning the jian.

The blade moved reluctantly. The pressure squeezed Vyllea against me, eliciting a surprised grunt, but I managed to keep the hilt steady, slicing through the dense webbing. Soon, an exit was carved wide enough for escape, which I took immediately, gasping for fresh air. The outside stench couldn't compare to the decay inside the tiger. Vyllea followed, confusion written all over her face, necessitating a quick summary.

"We're in the spiders' den. After consuming the tiger's essence, you blacked out. I thought you were a goner. I had to hide us inside the tiger, but then the spiders hauled us here. In short, that's what you missed. There's also this energy-infused tree, and if we don't leave soon, its abrasive energy will pulverize me."

"I'll get pulverized, too," Vyllea noted, feeling her surroundings. "I don't remember anything. We were walking, saw the tiger, and then nothing... Hey, hold on! Zander, I've reached the silver rank!"

"Could you be any louder? Just in case the spiders haven't heard us. Have you lost your mind? Are you in that much of a hurry to die?"

Vyllea fell silent, but her face made it clear she would remember my words, should a future for us still exist. Finally able to survey our surroundings, I realized we were in a small space — more accurately, a small hollow. Light seeped through several holes in the bark. Besides our cocoon with the tiger, there were about a dozen other bodies wrapped in webbing here. Most appeared to be animals, but a couple caught my attention immediately. It was unlikely that animals would carry spears resembling classical jis. I was tempted to inspect the deceased demons with spiritual vision, yet I knew it would be futile — the tree's light would overwhelm everything. Still, some form of check was necessary. Why? To ensure the spears weren't bound artifacts. Handling one might cost me my hand, if not my entire arm.

Deciding to examine the bodies first, I began slicing through the webbing with a practiced method. Vyllea helped by pulling pieces aside, and soon an excessively bloated corpse was revealed before us. The venom had done its work, preparing the demon for consumption.

"Don't touch," I warned her as she reached for one of the jis. "It's an artifact. Deadly. The corpse has a spatial pouch, typically awarded to Masters. Rarely Warriors. Apprentices can't handle the binding. Moreover, look at the clothing — it's clearly anything but ordinary."

"Indeed," Vyllea agreed, tracing a symbol on the mummy's chest. "The Nurghandal tribe. Our neighbors in the Second Circle. Is this a Warrior? What's he doing here? Who could destroy someone as powerful as a Warrior? These spiders are Apprentices at the most!"

"Then not all spiders are low-level ones," I muttered, regretfully eyeing the ji. Such a weapon would be much more convenient for fending off spiders than our swords, but I had no desire to grasp an unfamiliar artifact. The mentor had drilled such recklessness out of me. Yet it felt like a crime to leave such spoils behind. Even facing death, it seemed better to perish knowing you were hauling a trove of interesting artifacts along.

"What are you doing?" Vyllea gasped as I nudged the spatial pouch with my sword. Direct touch was dangerous, but why not use the tools at hand? No lightning strikes or deadly techniques ensued. It seemed direct contact was needed for those. After setting down my backpack and creating a nest in the collected herbs, I carefully placed the spatial pouch inside. Everything seemed fine, even when I hoisted the backpack again. The same went for the amulets. Rings, one looking like a flame clump, were left untouched. I simply severed the hand wearing them and stashed it with the rest. No time for detailed scrutiny. Nothing else on the demon was of immediate interest. Sure, the clothing and weapon could buy several of my villages, but I couldn't stuff them into my backpack. However, I managed to identify another demon — also a Warrior from the Nurghandal tribe. Indeed, we faced a formidable enemy here, one capable of downing formidable fighters. Their gear indicated a well-prepared expedition into the Forest of Dandoor.

"Ready?"

"Ready to do what?"

"To get out of here. I don't plan on waiting for a powerful enough spider to show up. Better to die trying to escape than turn into... that."

I gestured towards the prepped demons.

"Besides, this energy... I can literally feel my insides turning to mush. Another hour, and Zander's done. So, you do what you want, but I'm leaving."

With the backpack secured, I climbed towards the light-seeping hole. Navigating corridors frequented by spiders was hardly wise. The wood resisted at first, but my artifact again came in handy, this time as a lever, jostling the bark. It snapped, and I nearly fell through the newly formed exit. My enthusiasm vanished as I peered out. The tree we were on wasn't just huge — it towered over the entire forest! No leaves, just a web transforming this giant into a monstrous cocoon. From my vantage point, the ground was obscured, but it didn't stop me from appreciating the Forest of Dandoor from a bird's-eye view. And as a final touch, huge black spiders scurried everywhere. Escape through this route was impossible.

"Zander!" Vyllea's unexpected cry pulled me back. Turning, I saw we had company. Two spiders, lacking any aura, likely just regular Candidates. The decision came instantaneously — as mad as all those taken before, but I saw no other way to survive.

"Kill the bastards!" I shouted, leaping onto the nearest spider. "This is our path to freedom!"

CHAPTER 8

"I WON'T DO IT!" Vyllea nearly shouted.

"I won't force you," I replied calmly. "Just hand the essence back."

"Zander, this is madness! It won't work!"

"It might not," I agreed lightly. "Maybe the first spider we encounter will finish us off. But there's at least some chance that this masquerade might indeed help us. Vyllea, make up your mind quickly. I can't hold out much longer."

I wiped my lips, showing her the blood on my sleeve. My lungs were gradually failing. Not only was the Qi scratching them, but the invisible venom spread in the demon world's air was not being conducive to well-being, either.

"This is insanity," Vyllea whispered, looking at the corpse of the dissected spider. "Plain old madness."

She understood, though — this madness was our only chance of survival. Breaking through hordes of spiders as two Apprentice-stage teenagers was impossible, even if one of us had reached the Silver rank. But if we climbed inside the body of a spider and took two essences I had gathered in the clearing, we might appear to the other spiders as two of their higher-ranking kin. I had no idea how these creatures recognized each other, but it could work. Without the essences, ordinary Candidate-stage creatures would surely pique their interest; with them, however, there was a chance.

As the idea's author, I was to risk first. Climbing into the spider's carcass and wrapping myself in webbing, I even managed to be thankful that this creature wasn't as heavy as I had feared. Bending awkwardly, I moved forward. To avoid getting separated, Vyllea and I stretched some webbing between us. I held one end, and she held the other. The thread tightened, then gave way — Vyllea was following me. Suddenly, several spiders ran past us — I couldn't even tell where they came from. They paid us no mind, absorbed in their tasks. It worked! My crazy plan worked! At least, at the outset.

Finding a path for descent wasn't hard: I simply followed the spiders and ended up on a huge spiral staircase. The tree was hollow and dead inside — a feature the octopod creatures had exploited. Pulling Vyllea closer so our makeshift disguises pressed against each other, I descended.

But it got worse with every turn — the amount of energy floating in the air increased. Barely conscious, I found a side branch and dived onto it, emerging on a large limb. The relief was immediate and significant. There was some powerful energy source inside the tree, spawning all the chaos surrounding us.

Ensuring no spiders were nearby, I pulled Vyllea even closer.

"We need to descend via the web! Inside the tree, we'll be burnt to a crisp."

"Agreed! I nearly died in there. Does this mean there's a source here that spawned a spider capable of killing Warriors? Can you imagine the strength it must have? How did it even get here?"

"Let's think about that once we descend," I suggested. "Come on, we need to reach the edge of this branch. Then we'll figure out what to do next."

The spiders had transformed the giant tree into a bizarre structure: thick strands of web stretched out towards neighboring trees from nearly every branch, some hundreds of feet away. These strands weren't sticky like those of the smaller spiders. For the larger creatures, the web served as a means of transportation, not as a tool for catching prey. Choosing what seemed like a particularly strong strand, I hung from it upside down, grateful that we had thought to wrap the corpses in webbing. Even in such a state, they didn't fall. Waiting for Vyllea to join me, I began to slide down, using my hands to help. The spiders we met on the way didn't seem interested in our strange mode of transportation. Perhaps they were intrigued, but too afraid to question their bronze-ranked apprentice brethren if they were alright in the head.

On the upper tier of the forest, the spiders had crafted convenient pathways for themselves. Several layers of webbing allowed even us to move at a decent speed, so within about ten minutes, Vyllea and I had distanced ourselves significantly from the ominous tree. Salvation seemed close, but my body betrayed me. I was seized by a coughing fit and collapsed onto the webbing. My organs finally gave out. Not only had the tree nearly killed me, but carrying essences of such a high rank had taken its toll, too.

"How are you?" Vyllea settled beside me. Concern was evident in her voice.

"I'm afraid I'm done for," I managed, barely suppressing the cough. My chest was torn with pain, my heart beat erratically, and my vision was filled with dancing circles. "Keep moving. Try to survive."

"I won't leave you here alone!" The girl protested. "You didn't abandon me, so I won't abandon you, either! You have to survive, human! Who will I kill in the future if you die now? I'll drag you to the mentor myself if I have to! Do you understand? Don't you dare die on me here!"

I twitched as Vyllea indeed started dragging me away from the colossal tree. I lacked the strength to protest, managing only a bitter smile, though Vyllea couldn't see it; the spider corpses obstructed her view. She continued to pull me, despite her own deteriorating condition. Darkness began to encroach upon my vision when suddenly I heard Mentor Guerlon's gruff voice,

"If you're hoping to die and thus avoid punishment for your stupidity, I'm afraid I must disappoint you, apprentice. I won't allow you to die. However, I can guarantee you'll regret not dying today a hundred times over."

A jolt of lightning coursed through my body, followed by an incredible sense of relief as the pain receded. The sound of tearing webbing followed, and the spider carcass was flung into the unknown. Struggling to raise my head, I saw Mentor Guerlon tearing through the thick webs and removing the disguise from Vyllea. Placing a hand on her shoulder, the Taoist closed his eyes and activated a red healing technique. Vyllea arched as if in a spasm of pain but soon relaxed.

"To think of the apprentices the Heavens have blessed me with. One cannot use his head properly, and the other shoves everything she can find into her mouth. But even that wasn't enough for you — you decided to climb inside a poor tiger's rear end. Literally! Enough, I won't hear any excuses. Stay here and don't stick your noses out! The local beasts won't see you. If I return and don't find you here, I swear by the Heavens, I won't even go looking for you! No, actually, I will find you — just to personally finish you off for your staggering incompetence!"

With those words, the mentor took out an

object resembling a flag and tossed it in front of him. The flag hung in the air, split into six parts, each embedding itself into the nearest branches to us. In a moment, an energy field formed between the flags. Assuring everything worked as intended, the Taoist explained,

"This is a protective formation capable of shielding you from any beings up to the Bronze-ranked Master stage. Even if a Gold-ranked Master attacks, you'll still have a minute. I'll feel the attack and have time to return."

"You're going to the tree?" I asked.

"To the tree?" The Taoist chuckled. "No, apprentice, I'm heading to the source that has reached the Master stage. I want to understand how it ended up in Circle Zero and why it still emits such powerful energy. Judging by the tree, it's at least a couple of hundred years old. Yet the source remains strong. I need to get to the bottom of this. Wait here."

Having said those words, Mentor Guerlon vanished, charging towards the giant tree visible even from our location.

"I told you he wouldn't abandon us," the girl said, suddenly breaking into tears. "I knew it! I knew it! Mentors never abandon their apprentices! Even one like him! He was just watching over us and refraining from interfering! I knew it!"

Perhaps I should have shown resilience and ignored the emotional outburst, or maybe even reminded myself of Vyllea consuming the tiger's essence, but I acted differently. Rolling over, I moved closer to her and hugged her, pressing her to myself. It felt like the right thing to do. She didn't pull away. Instead, she buried her face in my chest and sobbed, seemingly even harder. Surprising myself with such audacity, I began to stroke her hair, noting with surprise that it remained clean despite everything we had just been through. Then again, my hair, nurtured by miraculous ointment, was also clean. Artifacts, and our hair had become just that, didn't absorb dirt.

"We need to meditate," I said once the crying had subsided. "The mentor will return and proceed with our punishment, so we should use this free time wisely. Sit down."

I distanced myself and sat down opposite the girl. She hiccupped a few times but mirrored my actions. For a while, we sat knee to knee, looking into each other's eyes. I had never looked into a demon's eyes for so long. It was fascinating to watch how her vertical pupil thinned to a fine line and then dilated fully. This dance was so captivating that I didn't notice when Vyllea's palms ended up in mine. She seemed just as unaware of her actions, not taking her gaze off me, making no attempt to pull her hands away.

"Don't take too much body energy," I rasped out and was the first to close my eyes, severing the connection. A strange feeling washed over me again. On one hand, I saw the bloodstains on her lips, a reminder of her treatment of the tiger. On the other hand, I saw the lips themselves. Soft, sensuous, and inviting... I had to retreat into the world of energy.

A warm clot formed in my chest and immediately started on its familiar path. However, being in such close contact with Vyllea, I could see not just my body, but also the body energy she created and its movement, albeit with a reddish hue. It mirrored my warmth, and at some point, our energies synchronized, reaching the same body parts simultaneously. That's when I noticed something odd in both of us. When the energy reached our hands or feet, it hesitated, as if considering whether to rush not along the standard route but into the new body so closely touching mine. I watched this indifferently for a long time; who knew the oddities these energies carried, after all? But the longer the energy remained in the same place, the more pain it caused. We had to either separate or...

I don't know what prompted me to choose the "or" option. Perhaps what the mentor called a lack of brains. When another clot of energy paused at our left hands, I drew warmth from Vyllea, offering her mine in return. I had no idea if such an action was permissible, but an inner conviction told me that if the girl didn't resist, there would be no issues. Both energies trembled, and then unexpectedly flowed from one body to the other, rushing along their usual routes. I almost lost focus upon seeing the reddish clot within me and my blue within Vyllea. The demon's red warmth completed a full circuit and even a bit more — it reached not the left but the right hand. Waiting on the opposite side was the blue energy of humans, and as soon as our flows reached the designated spots, they didn't stall, but rushed forward, returning to their native elements.

It was... unusual. Vyllea's energy didn't cause any rejection or anything similar in me, and that went both ways. I saw an additional stream of body energy forming in the girl's chest. I probably should have objected and said it was dangerous, but instead, I created a similar volume whirl and sent it circling. An unusual sensation emerged: the energy exchange was now happening not only in our hands but also in our legs. The warmth no longer paused, seemingly glad we had managed to break through the dam. Vyllea increased the volume. I did the same. Then again. And again. We only stopped when our energies merged and mixed completely, racing through our bodies at insane speeds. It seemed enough for both me and the girl. All that was left was to sit motionlessly and continue circulating warmth to each other, not losing focus.

Gradually, the whirl of warmth began to subside, settling on the insides. We didn't add any new portions: initially, we needed to understand what had happened and how to live with it. When the last crumbs of mixed body energy dissolved, I opened my eyes. It was dark. A monstrous emptiness churned in my stomach, as if I hadn't eaten in a week. Suddenly, a bright light flashed to the side. The mentor had lit a lantern.

"So, I can't leave you alone even for a minute now?" The calm voice of the Taoist hit harder than a whip. He looked at Vyllea: "You're a demon! You're supposed to consume creatures like him. He's your food. Your power. Your path to ascension. You were supposed to finish Zander off, not drag him out with your last strength, wasting your own life energy."

Mentor Guerlon turned sharply to me and continued in the same calm tone.

"And you? You should be killing the likes of her! You should be repelled by her very stench. You should protect your world. You should have left her to be devoured by the beasts. But as I see it, the laws of the universe are not written for you. You decided to do things your own way."

It seemed as though the very space around us quieted down, fearing to anger the furious Taoist.

"What you've done is called an energetic conjunction. It's a potentially deadly practice that one approaches only after years of preparation. It requires immense trust in your partner to dare such a thing. Had either of you lost concentration, not a single healer, from this world or ours, could have saved you. One connection is dangerous, two is lethal, and only a few dare to attempt three. You, however, circulated energy through four channels as if it were as natural to you as breathing air. And you didn't just circulate any energy — you mixed it, achieving the maximum level of unity. Had I not been nearby, you would have simply burned up! This is not how I planned our training. Not at all.

But the Heavens never give set us on any easy paths. Only through hardships can we evolve."

The mentor fell silent, lost in thought. I looked at Vyllea, and her eyes suddenly widened.

"Zander, your pupils... They're... Yellow!"

"With the level of unity you've achieved here, Zander has turned into a demon for the next day. At least, outwardly," the Taoist explained, still deep in thought. "The effect will wear off, and he will become human again. Well, if the Heavens have decided to put me through this test, so be it."

The mentor stood up, and the flag flew from his hands again, enclosing us in a protective formation.

"This conversation won't be easy, and I don't want anyone to disturb us. The spiders are gone, but other beasts might take advantage. Vyllea, I took you on as a temporary apprentice for one specific purpose — for you to become a counterweight for Zander. I know how you love power. How you despise the weak. How you love to dominate and win. I was more than satisfied with that. Having such a worthy sparring partner, Zander would have breezed through his Candidate stage without even noticing. You were supposed to grow to hate each other to the extent that you'd sacrifice everything for victory. You were meant to work tirelessly, train until you lost consciousness, and consume energy, transforming into beings worthy of immortality. Having a sworn enemy, both of you would have continued your ascension after returning home. Meeting periodically in wormholes and fighting each other, each of you would have become a serious force to be reckoned with. But now...

The mentor paused as if hesitant to voice the next thought.

"When a human and a demon enter a state of conjunction, it's not just an energy exchange that occurs. There's an adaptation of bodies to the specifics of each other's worlds. Zander has become a demon. His eyes have changed, he's acquired a specific scent detectable only by Taoists, losing the human odor that so irritates demons. Didn't you notice this?"

"Indeed," Vyllea said, stunned. "He doesn't smell anymore."

"Even the air has ceased to affect Zander while he's in this state. But everything comes at a cost, including conjunction, especially one as complete as yours. Once tried, you can never give it up. It's not even a drug — it's something much greater. But that's not the main problem. Now your development is predetermined. The Tiger Style, as I understand it?"

Vyllea nodded, still in shock.

"I deliberately did not teach Zander any styles, so that he'd have a choice. He was to base his combat style on what suited his spirit. His and his alone. But now there's no choice, and the foundational style is determined. Tomorrow, we begin training in the Tiger Style, both in hand-to-hand combat and in weapon work. This aspect cannot be changed. Apparently, Heaven itself decided to make you strike fighters."

"Is it just the martial arts style that's predetermined? Or is there something else? If I've become a demon for a day, do I now have to consume essences?" I clarified, a point that disturbed me greatly. The mentor took a long time to respond. He even closed his eyes, as if searching for the right words. Finally, the Taoist spoke,

"There are many paths to immortality, and each seeker chooses the road to follow at any given time. Most people choose the path of harmony — ascension through unity with Qi energy. That's the path I'm on, and that's the path you're following now. But that doesn't mean other paths are somehow flowed. Vyllea, for example, pursues two paths at once. The path of demons — ascension through the absorption of others' meridians, and the path of the beast — through understanding the essence of the beast and absorbing its power. By consuming the tiger, she has comprehended its techniques and advanced in understanding the style. She's become stronger. This power could have burned her, but Heaven did not bring you together for nothing — you did the only right thing to save her. You increased the area of contact with the source of borrowed power and held it long enough for the body to absorb all the energy."

"So, there are only three paths to ascension? Harmony, demons, and beasts?"

"There's another. The Path of Blood. Should you embark on it, you'll become enemies of all living beings. I would personally come to end your existence. This path is chosen by those who hit the limits of their ascension. Those who cannot overcome the barrier. Those who refuse to submit to the will of the Heavens and accept the birth barrier. Yes, this barrier can also be broken, but it's something people refrain from discussing. Those who walk this path are called cultists. They are sought out to be killed in both our world and this one. The Path of Blood is one of sacrifice. A path of madness, pain, and the suffering of numerous victims. The more a victim suffers before death, the more energy they provide to their tormentor. These are extremely dangerous adversaries."

"The cultists wiped out several tribes of the Second Circle," Vyllea said with undisguised hatred. "They... They even killed children."

"Because their energy is purer. Their emotions are brighter. The power they generate is greater. But let's return to ascension. The Path of Harmony is an upward path. Those who walk it strive to overcome the hurdles of ascension, sometimes ignoring the development of their power. To enhance it tangibly without spending countless years, one needs the essences of beasts. My mentor consumed them. I consumed them. Sooner or later, every Taoist consumes them. This cup will not pass you by, pupil. You too will eventually have to consume them to strengthen yourself."

"I will not do that," I said, realizing it was a promise for the rest of my life.

"That is entirely your choice. Each Taoist decides for themselves where to stop in their ascension. However, I must tell you straight: if you build a colossus on clay feet, it will collapse. You'll turn into the likes of Lord Lurth Mink."

"Thank you, mentor, for the lesson, but the Path of Beasts is not for me," I confidently declared. "I like harmony. I will stop there."

"As I've said, it's entirely your choice. Now, as for what comes next. As I mentioned, initially Vyllea was needed in our group only as a catalyst for your ascension. But now everything has changed. So much so that I don't even know how both our worlds will react. Heaven did not provide another way. It's not my place to argue with its decisions."

A golden sheet of paper appeared in the hand of Mentor Guerlon.

"Demon Vyllea from the Urbangos tribe, this is a two-year apprenticeship contract. I, Seeker Guerlon, a human Master Taoist of the Diamond rank, offer you to become my official apprentice. You are the eldest daughter of the tribe's chief. You have the right to decide for yourself who will be your mentor. If you sign this contract, I promise that for the next two years, you will curse the day you decided to enter the world of humans and met me. You will curse the day you signed this contract. But if you sign it, you will enter the world of humans as a Diamond rank Candidate. This I can also promise you."

"Into the world of humans?" Vyllea wasn't the

only one astonished. I expected nothing of the sort, either.

"I thought I was speaking a language everyone could understand. By choosing to merge your energies, you've bound yourselves to each other. From now on, your ascension is impossible without such meditation. I promised my pupil that I would return him to the human world at sixteen. I will do so, whatever it costs me. And you, my potential apprentice, will have to follow him. Without Zander, your ascension is impossible. Just as his is impossible without you. In our world, you will become a human and will be able to live there as long as the two of you remain in conjunction. But the opposite is true as well: Zander in your world will become a demon. From now on, you are residents of two worlds, and you will have to accept this. The Heavens have decided, and it's not for us to argue."

"Just sign this? What happens next?" Vyllea twisted the sheet in her hands, as if seeing paper for the first time.

"The magic of document exchange in this world is the same as in ours. A copy of the contract will go to your mother, Lord Shang Li, your former mentor, and a bunch of Taoists in our world, too. Whether it's for the good or bad is for you to decide. I've described what you can expect to get. The choice is yours, whether to agree or not."

"So, without Zander, I won't be able ascend to the Apprentice stage?"

"Without him, you won't even achieve the

Golden rank of the Candidate stage. Nor will he get his Silver without you. Conjunction grants great power, but also demands significant sacrifices."

"But will I really regret it?" Vyllea seemed to have made her decision. She stopped twirling the paper.

"I can promise you that," the Taoist assured. "You will regret it all your life."

"I don't care! If it makes me stronger, I agree!" The girl took out her jian, ran the blade across her palm, then pressed her bloodied hand to the golden sheet. "Demons don't recognize ink. We only sign contracts like this."

The document flashed and disappeared, after which Mentor Guerlon nodded.

"Welcome to this world, Candidate demon of the Silver rank. This probably concludes our conversation. You should reflect on what has just happened. Stand up, apprentices. I want to show you why demons avoid the Forest of Dandoor."

CHAPTER 9

A GOLDEN SHEET MATERIALIZED in front of Mentor Guerlon before we reached our destination. He scrutinized it, a smirk unfolding. "Overlord Shang Li sends his blessings for your training, Vyllea," he announced. "Your mother, too, rejoices at the thought of a formidable Taoist shaping her offspring. Master Nars-Go Li, on the other hand, voices dissent over having had his apprentice taken away from him in such an abrupt manner. He renounces all prior agreements and declares me and my apprentices his personal foes. He's even promised rewards to anyone who can eliminate me or any of those under my tutelage. Strange, and there I was thinking the demon was quite sensible. Sadly, Zander, it seems you won't be getting those artifact crafting textbooks from the demon world. No matter, we'll claim our spoils from those mad enough to hunt us."

"Mentor, speaking of spoils, Vyllea and I have managed to find these." I dropped my backpack and opened it to show our findings. All of the stuff was beyond my current grasp. I was unlikely to be able to pry bound artifacts open before reaching the Second Tier. Yet if Guerlon could inspect the spatial pouches, he might uncover something of value.

Guerlon chuckled pensively as he took the artifacts. After removing the rings and discarding the hands, he stood silently for a moment with his eyes closed. "Useless trinkets. Those two were Warriors — mediocre ones at best. I assume they'd barely reached the Bronze rank. That they endured spatial pouches' binding doesn't impress me. The amulets are rubbish, and even the spatial pouches, clearly crafted by a complete incompetent, barely hold a hundred pounds. Is that supposed to be useful? I doubt there's anything valuable inside."

"So these can't be sold?" I inquired.

"On the contrary, selling is the only thing you're good for. By the time you reach the Warrior stage, all this will be useless to you. Once we make it to a major city, we'll hand the emblems over to the local authorities. The tribe whose warriors we've found will have some closure knowing the bodies of their kinsfolk have been laid to rest."

Just my luck. I wanted to boast about our loot, but Guerlon dismissed all of it as worthless. Had we dragged along the spear, it might as well have been thrown into the woods as a useless stick. Guerlon seemed different after Vyllea and I woke up. Perhaps he, too, needed time to digest what had transpired earlier.

The web ended abruptly. Guerlon activated some artifacts, and several bright stars soared up, illuminating the area reasonably well. The gigantic tree that once towered over the forest was gone. There was no web or tree anymore — absolutely nothing remained. Just a vast scorched clearing where even the ashes had ceased smoldering.

"How long did we meditate?" Vyllea marveled.

"Four days. The first conjunction is always the longest. Zander, your thoughts on what you see?"

"Could you light up the center? There are too many shadows."

Upon my request, Guerlon illuminated the area further, eliciting a surprised exclamation from Vyllea. "Is that a tortoise?"

There was a shell of a colossal tortoise on the ground where a tree had once stood. Its body was long gone, surrendered to the merciless flow of time. Here and there, the shell bore cracks and holes, yet it remained a recognizable relic, spanning the size of several village houses.

"Not just any tortoise," I confirmed. "This is a beast of the Master stage. Its energy structure is concealed. The tortoise had crawled here... from the battlefield? Is it really that close? It lacked the strength to return and perished here. Yet, in its lifetime, it had consumed so much energy that even the tree that had grown around its shell couldn't fully absorb it."

"That's impossible," Vyllea declared. "Any energy source in Circle Zero will dissipate over time. Everyone knows that."

"Except for this tortoise." I closed my eyes, deeply immersing into my spirit vision and significantly expanding its range. Surprisingly, this proved remarkably easy, and the scope it covered was astonishing — three times as much as before, at the very least.

"Mentor, could you shed some light towards the far edge of the clearing?"

Once again, Master Guerlon complied without question.

"Some sort of energy channel stretches from the tortoise in that direction, now fading. The creature that had come here must have brought something with it. Something connected to a vast source. Look at the trees over there — some differ from their neighbors markedly. Those trees have embarked on the path of ascension. Their wood must be quite valuable. Whatever the tortoise had brought here resides in the Mentor's spatial pouch now, I presume. He wouldn't leave such a treasure unclaimed. Essentially, that's all. The spiders had adapted to the energy and evolved into the monsters we saw. The tree had grown to an incredible size, but perished. Either the spiders had consumed it, or it was overwhelmed by too much energy. Mentor, I've been meaning to ask — where does the battlefield come from? It doesn't exist in our world, does it?"

"Why wouldn't it? It does. That's precisely why the inhabitants of your village never venture to the ocean. Because the creatures that occasionally emerge from the battlefield would devour them."

"The wormhole connects parts of the sea?" I marveled.

"If you overlay the maps of both worlds, it will turn out we've strayed far from the shore in our world. Yet, the battlefield is still a long way off. It intrigues me how it's structured. From the demon world's perspective, it's definitely land — too many indicators point to it. From ours, it's deep sea. And yet, the wormhole is minuscule — essentially just a hole in the ground leading to another world. But how is it structured? Why doesn't water seep through here? I've never encountered such a phenomenon before; it might be worth investigating at some opportunity. That's why we are Seekers in the first place."

"And it's impossible to close it?"

"Closing the wormhole isn't impossible at all," Mentor Guerlon explained, pausing thoughtfully. "Firstly, we must eliminate all the creatures on this side, then on ours. After that, we can proceed to transition. However, a task such as this one, we'd need to invite a Water Overlord; no one else could survive at such depths. Yet I doubt any Water Overlord would turn their gaze to this wormhole. It's too inconsequential and promises no loot. How could they know that occasionally creatures like Overlord-level tortoises crawl out from our world? Not only is it a formidable force in itself, but it had also dragged along the Heart of the Ocean."

"The Heart of the Ocean?" Vyllea gasped in disbelief. "But that's just a myth!"

"I could showcase this 'myth' to you, but I fear you'd be reduced to a handful of black dust as a result," Guerlon continued, his voice carrying a mix of seriousness and a hint of regret. "Even at my rank, it would pose a significant threat to me. Indeed, it is the Heart of the Ocean — a rare, almost unique source of Overlord level energy. Pity that its element doesn't align with mine, really; otherwise, I'd already have transported you to the human world and bid farewell before delving into meditation. Where the tortoise got it and why it stubbornly crawled deep into demon lands is a vast mystery."

"Mentor, you mentioned only a Water Overlord could traverse this battlefield's wormhole. Do such high-level Taoists have pets? Such as an enormous tortoise, perhaps?" I inquired, connecting the dots in my head.

"Which would equate to bringing a considerable force into the demon lands — one capable of turning half of Circle Zero into dust," Master Guerlon interpreted my thought correctly. "You're right, apprentice Zander. The cracks and fissures on the shell aren't the work of spiders. Such creatures could not harm a beast of the Overlord level. These are the marks of techniques used by those who had stopped the tortoise here, managing to protect the southern parts of demon lands. Moreover, they'd even sealed the heart within its body, covering it with several energy domes. Hence, I was able to take it. Stay here; I need to examine the shell more closely. Who — No! I certainly cannot leave the two of you alone now! You'll be coming with me. The energy level near the shell isn't anywhere as immense anymore. Endure it. I've had it up to here with the surprises the pair of you manage to create every time you're left to your own devices. I won't allow such an oversight again."

Mentor Guerlon grabbed me by the waist, snagged Vyllea with his other hand, and propelled us forward, taking an inhuman leap. Breath caught in my throat as we were landing — I had never fallen from such a height before. Vyllea snorted beside me — she was impressed by our mode of transport as well. The impact with the ground was monstrous — no matter how prepared I was, or how much I'd fortified my body, it nearly broke me in half. Something definitely fractured — the crunch was just too loud. Yet, there was no pain — healing had arrived beforehand. As we landed, I noticed Vyllea's stunned gaze next to me. It seemed that I'd found something my sister-in-training couldn't tolerate — namely, heights and falling. Though I had to admit I didn't enjoy any of it much, either.

The healing had only lasted a few moments, and as its effect faded, my body instantly alerted me to the proximity of a dangerous object. The shell radiated such an immense amount of energy that staying close to it was extremely uncomfortable. Vyllea sat down nearby and closed her eyes, starting to meditate. The next stage of ascension involved creating two nodes within oneself, requiring that one did this in such energetically charged locations. But I wasn't Vyllea; it was too early for me to meditate and suffer. Mentor Guerlon walked towards the shell, which indeed was as large as a couple of houses, with confidence, while I instinctively backed away. My foot stumbled upon something that should have been incinerated by the mentor's fire that had raged here four days ago. Bending down, I spotted a shank bone spared by the flames. It clearly wasn't human and likely belonged to some large animal that spiders had dragged into their den. Informed by bitter experience, I refrained from rashly grabbing it, opting for a spirit vision inspection beforehand. Just as I suspected: the bone was suffused with Qi. I hadn't noticed it against the backdrop of the shell as I glanced over the scorched clearing, but now I could state with confidence that the bone belonged to that same Silver Apprentice tiger we had been using as a hiding place. I had seen enough of its energy streams while the spiders hauled us to their lair. Despite the bone giving off a tangible amount of Qi, I picked it up anyway. I'd hand it over to the mentor to stash away and return to me when it would no longer cause me any discomfort. Vyllea had gained an essence from this beast, granting her the Silver rank, while I settled for this item. Did the Heavens arrange our encounter for nothing?

"No punishment, Apprentice Zander," Mentor Guerlon spoke, tearing his gaze from the direction the dead tortoise had crawled from. After a heavy sigh, he shook his head.

"Did you discover anything, mentor?"

"The shell bears the mark of Overlord Nurghal Lee, who had vanished two hundred years ago. This information is invaluable."

"Are there so few Overlords among humans that the mentor knows of those who disappeared so long ago?" Vyllea quipped in her usual manner.

"Overlord Nurghal Lee was a Seeker — one of the greatest geniuses of his era, and an honorary mentor of the Summoning School. His treatises on taming beasts remain relevant to this day. Rather, they are increasingly found to contain hidden wisdom, revealing the secrets of the great Overlord. Throughout the history of Seekers, Nurghal Lee was perhaps the only Taoist possessing all the resources, opportunities, and grounds to become a Nascent God."

"No seeker has ever become a Nascent God?" I marveled.

"The path we tread is far from simple, Zander. Now it's clear where the Heart of the Ocean has come from. The Overlord's element was water."

"So the Overlord's plaque is buried somewhere nearby?" I too glanced towards the battlefield. "Or were they not made back then?"

"They were made," the Taoist slowly confirmed.

"Mentor, I don't understand what we're talking about," Vyllea barged into the conversation without any hesitation. Apparently, she was never taught about courtesy as a child.

"Currently, my spiritual vision extends up to a thousand feet," I mused, ignoring the impudent girl. "The radius increased after exchanging body energy. Theoretically, if we spend some time in conjunction, the distance might increase."

"I've heard of some managing to see up to a mile," the mentor nodded. "But I don't think that's our case. The maximum you can achieve at the candidate stage is fifteen hundred feet. I don't know where the battle took place. If we encounter a beast of the Overlord stage, we might perish."

"Won't the Heavens turn away from us if we just ignore everything we've learned now and leave the forest?" I asked, suddenly realizing I was speaking these words not because I wanted to irk my mentor, but because I believed in them! I, a dweller of a remote village, who two years ago had no idea what the Heavens were, thought it wrong to anger them with improper actions.

"Will you finally explain what you've planned?" Vyllea burst out. "And another thing! Now that I'm one of you, I want to understand what the Heavens are and who the seekers are!"

"One of us?" Mentor Guerlon even frowned. "No, apprentice Vyllea, you are not one of us. You are a demon."

"So what? Zander is also a demon now, albeit temporarily. Is he not one of you, either?"

"He..." Guerlon was taken aback. Externally, he remained impassive, but the pauses in his speech suggested he didn't know how to respond.

"So, until proven otherwise, I am one of you!" Vyllea declared. "You even have a golden paper that confirms it! So it doesn't matter whether I'm a demon or a human being. In your world, I'll have to be turned into a human anyway."

"Fine," our mentor conceded, not expecting such assertiveness from his other apprentice. "Let's go. We need to choose a location for training and discussion. Apprentice Vyllea is right: until proven otherwise, she is one of us. The Heavens never give us easy trials, so we will find a way to overcome this one, too."

We plunged into the forest, circling the shell in a wide arc. The mentor didn't mince steps and carved a wide path with techniques, grinding trees and shrubs to splinters. We headed towards where the turtle had crawled from two hundred years ago, and I constantly checked the space with my spirit vision. No beasts were in sight, but there were so many stationary power clusters it seemed as though someone had sown entire meadows with plants embarking on the path to immortality. When I bent down, perhaps for the hundredth time, to pluck another flower growing right underfoot, the mentor stopped.

"Many of them?"

"A ton. The ground is literally covered with herbs here!"

"How do you even find them?!" Vyllea burst out. She grabbed a whole bunch of grass, but by an incredible coincidence did so exactly where there were no plants containing any Qi. It was even surprising how she found such a place!

"In that case, we stop here. There's a small river a hundred meters from here. Apprentices, grab the buckets and fetch some water. I want to take a bath."

Four buckets, five gallons each, appeared on the ground. Realizing that we couldn't make our way through the forest with the buckets, the mentor cleared the path with several techniques. When we returned with the first four bucketfuls of water, we found a covered tent with a large wooden bathtub inside.

"Pour the water and go fetch some more," the mentor commanded, not even looking at what we had brought. That was a sight to behold — the water in the stream turned out to be very dirty. It contained branches, leaves, sand. No matter how hard we tried, we couldn't scoop up any clean water. The darkness significantly hindered us — the light of our mentor's magic firefly, placed over the camp, barely reached the stream. Vyllea and I exchanged looks and followed the order. The bathtub suddenly filled with foam, began to fizz, and when the foam subsided, we were surprised to find the water perfectly clean and warm. All the debris lay in a small pile next to the tub.

"Take the dirt away with you," Mentor Guerlon ordered, without even entering the tent. I looked at the tub with interest — I had never seen the mentor bring it out during our two years of travels. It was definitely an artifact, and judging by how actively it pulled energy from the surrounding world, it wasn't powered by spirit stones. Amusingly, the energy strands plunged right into the artifact, bypassing Vyllea and me. It turned out this tent was perhaps the safest place for us in the entire Circle Zero of the demon world. Qi couldn't scratch us here.

"What are you standing there for?" Vyllea hissed. "Let's go! I need a bath, too!"

Mentor Guerlon didn't monopolize the experience and allowed us all to enjoy the hot bath, although we had to add a few buckets of water each time. The artifact worked perfectly: the water was always clean, clear, and at the right temperature. After washing our clothes, I emerged from the tent a completely different person. Well, still a demon for the time being — a mirror next to the bath allowed me to assess my yellow eyes. They looked terrifying.

The morning started quite unusually — not with training, not with breakfast, but with Vyllea brazenly barging into my tent. Annoyed that I was still lazing around, she kicked me in the shins.

"Zander, get up! You've got to help me!"

"When you need help, you ask, not demand," I grumbled and pulled the blanket up to my nose. After the hot bath I hadn't taken in what appeared to be two years, and a very filling dinner that the mentor had prepared for us, I most assuredly didn't want to get up. Moreover, today was officially a day off. Our mentor did occasionally arrange such holidays. He said we needed to recover after the first exchange of body energy.

"Get up!" Vyllea kicked me again. "You promised to help me!"

"I did?!" I even opened my eyes, shocked by her audacity.

"You did! You promised to make my dress non-staining! You said you had some symbol for it. And all the resources right here. Look! I've just washed it."

Vyllea threw a bundle, which she had been hiding behind her back, onto the blanket.

"When will you do it?"

"When you ask nicely," I retorted angrily. Sleep had completely and irreversibly fled.

"Fine, then get to it!" Vyllea darted out of the tent so fast I didn't even have a chance to respond. Sitting up, I twirled the neatly packaged dress in my hands and tossed it through the slightly open tent flap.

"Zander!" Her indignant voice rang out. "Do you know how long I spent washing that?! Have you lost your mind?!"

An enraged Vyllea reappeared in my tent.

"Do that again, and I'll kill you!"

"If you need something, you ask nicely," I replied in a calm voice. "Your tongue won't fall off if you try to be polite occasionally. I'm not a slave or a servant. I'm your fellow apprentice, and I won't allow you to treat me like this. If you need help, you come and negotiate, not present me with a fait accompli. If you have nothing to offer in exchange, you ask. I'm not here to be ordered around."

"I'm stronger than you, so you should obey me!" Vyllea attacked. "Once you achieve the Silver rank, then I might, just might, treat you as an equal. And while you remain weaker than me, don't expect respectful treatment."

"Then get out of my tent, Elder," I emphasized the last word in the same tone that Mentor Guerlon used with Overlord Lurth Mink. "Keep washing your dresses and rejoice in your Silver rank."

"Refuse, and I'll force you!"

"You really think you can? Aren't you afraid to lose to a Bronze rank?"

"It seems I made a mistake giving you a day off today," Mentor Guerlon's voice came from near the tent. "Well, it's never too late to admit one's mistakes. You have two minutes to get ready for training. Whoever is late will work until the end of the day."

"It's all because of you!" Vyllea snapped at me and, turning sharply, nearly whipped me with her thickly braided hair. I managed to dodge at the last moment and, not willing to let her have the last word, pushed her out of the tent. She protested outside, as I slammed the tent flap shut. She couldn't really make much of a fuss, especially with Mentor Guerlon standing nearby. Something along the lines of "I'll kill that little pest!" was heard before Vyllea ran off to change. The time Master Guerlon had given us to get ready was quickly expiring.

I noticed something odd as soon as I stepped out of my tent. Mentor Guerlon had laid out three mats on the ground and was sitting on one, waiting for us. When we took our places, the Taoist pulled a lamp with incense sticks from his spatial pouch and lit one. The air filled with a pleasant sweet smoke that started to make my head spin.

"Before we start training, we need to clarify some basic things. Understand who the Seekers are and how the Heavens control the affairs of the human world. Although, as far as I'm concerned, they oversee not just our world, but the world of the demons as well. The more time I spend here, the more I'm drawn to that conclusion. Close your eyes and relax. What I want to convey to you is better seen once than heard a hundred times."

The intoxicating effect of the incense achieved its purpose, and as soon as I closed my eyes, my consciousness drifted, conjuring strange moving images in my head, narrated in Mentor Guerlon's voice. I already knew who the Seekers were — those who were dissatisfied with the overly ritualistic, sometimes pompous lifestyle of the Taoist schools of ascension. Those who went against traditions to establish their own rules. However, the separation of the Seekers from the rest of society had happened quite smoothly.

When problems arose, ordinary people spent too much time on mandatory rituals, while Seekers solved the problem. Wormholes, demons, new and unexplored events — the Seekers didn't need to bend in a hundred bows to their elders. They just moved forward and tackled the task. They often died in the process, but they proceeded nevertheless. Because such was the Seeker's path. As a result, clan heads, schools, and even the emperor himself acknowledged the renegades, creating a separate group for them. Seekers were beneficial and useful, and if they crossed a certain line, they could be eliminated without harming the lineage, since they were initially outside the law and answered only to the Heavens.

The images abruptly shifted to the symbol for "Heavens" — the character Tian. The beginning and end of all that exists. The creator of life and the taker of it. There were many opinions regarding what Heavens truly stood for. Some believed them to be a special realm, accessible only to those who had reached the state of deity. Others thought of the Heavens as an immaterial being with an infinite number of eyes, watching over every living thing. Still, others doubted the very existence of Heavens, considering the very concept a fabrication, a fairy tale, and a foolish superstition. Mentor Guerlon had his own conception of the Heavens. It was the judge, deciding whether a seeker on the path to immortality was worthy to continue or if a barrier needed to be erected in their path. The Heavens introduced various challenges into every seeker's journey, then assessed how these challenges were overcome. Betrayal, cowardice, weakness, and even excessive accumulation — all could erect an insurmountable wall in front of a seeker because it displeased the Heavens. Because there was no overcoming in it. No effort to the limit. No aspiration for elevation. In Mentor Guerlon's view, the Heavens weren't a place, a being, a predestined fate, or any specific object. The Heavens encompassed the entire world and everything that happened within it. Everything that allowed a pursuer of immortality to walk along the path of ascension.

The visions ended, and I opened my eyes.

"Sit facing each other, but don't let your knees touch. First, join hands. Before we begin training, we need to determine your current limit of energy exchange. We need to understand how many channels you can create without a healer's involvement. Begin!"

CHAPTER 10

"SHUT UP, ZANDER! Just shut up!"

"I was silent, o sister in ascension," I responded with such tranquility that even Mentor Guerlon might have envied me.

"But you think loudly! You're throwing me off!"

"Vyllea, the entire Forest of Dandoor would be delighted to interfere in your playing just to avoid hearing those enchanting sounds your pipa makes. Maybe it's time to admit to yourself that music isn't your thing? It happens sometimes. Rarely, of course, but it does. Try practicing on the drums."

"One more word from you, and you can forget about conjunction today!" Vyllea snapped, hitting where it hurt the most. Her struggle with music was the major cause of her irritation. I had no such problems; understanding the notes, strings, and the sounds they produced, I dived into the world of music, offering the forest a captivating melody every time. I didn't even need musical scores — I created harmony as I saw fit. When a musical instrument fell into my hands, it came to life: part of me took control, making my fingers race across the pipa's four strings at an astonishing speed. After hearing my music, Mentor Guerlon flatly refused to give me regular scores. The Heavens would be angered if I were forbidden to create and confined within any bounds. Now, every day ended with me playing my latest harmony for the Taoist and Vyllea. In the six months we'd been in the Forest of Dandoor, I managed never to repeat a piece. Music truly was an infinite ocean for creativity and self-expression.

As for conjunction, the mentor was right — solitary meditation had become useless to us. Sure, it could bear fruits, but only in three to four years, while I was almost at the Silver rank now. In fact, I would have reached it long ago, but I stopped myself each time my body was ready to cross the threshold. To comfortably stand at the Golden rank, I needed a lot of body energy. Every conjunction made me stronger, and by now, I could extend my spirit vision to nearly two thirds of a mile! All in just six months! But I understood this wasn't the limit. More was possible. Seeing no boundaries to body enhancement, I strove to gain as much as I could from the Bronze rank. Mentor approved of this artificial barrier in ascension, especially since I flatly refused to emulate Vyllea, who consumed the essences of tigers on a weekly basis. The mentor caught Silver- and even Golden-ranked Apprentice beasts, broke their paws and spines, and twisted their jaws so they couldn't even growl at the carnivorous demoness, then made an incision in the beast's chest and called Vyllea, managing to heal the animal so it would live as long as possible. After such meals, Vyllea always crawled inside the tiger, where she'd sleep for several days, distributing the borrowed strength. The spectacle was ghastly, but I began to get used to it. After two months, I didn't even pay it any mind. So what if one beast was eating another? Hardly a novelty.

But I was on the subject of meditation. It turned out that by absorbing the energy of beasts, Vyllea could do without conjunction for a couple of days, whereas I had developed an unpleasant dependency. I even had to discuss this with Mentor Guerlon, but he assured me that my dependency was related to my body's demands — it wanted to ascend to match Vyllea's. Once we achieved the same rank, we could do without energy exchange for a week, maybe two. But at that time, I was twisted, turned, and thrown towards the capricious girl, as she was towards me. Her body longed to give me everything it could to aid in my ascension. It turned out that we trusted each other so much at some deep level that we'd managed to engage in energy exchange across all seven directions: both hands, legs, chest, abdomen, and head. To ensure such synchronization, I would lie on my back, and Vyllea would lay on top of me, face to face, ensuring contact at all points. During such sessions, her lips would freeze just a millimeter from mine, sometimes even touching, but there was no feeling of romance in either of us. What we were doing was a necessity.

"How about a game of Go?" I suggested, trying to save my ears from the gut-wrenching sounds Vyllea called music. "It's also a mental exercise, after all."

"I don't think it makes much sense," Mentor Guerlon's voice came. "The Forest of Dandoor has given us all it could; it's time to move on. Apprentice Zander, today you need to achieve the Silver rank. We cannot delay any longer."

"Yes, Mentor," I agreed.

"As if ascension worked on command," the irritated girl snorted.

"One never knows in this world," I flashed her a grin as I spread a blanket on the ground. Over the last six months I had turned all our clothes into stain-resistant artifacts, but I still didn't want to lie directly on the bare earth. It was amusing to watch Vyllea come to "ask" something of me. It was hard for her, but she managed to overcome herself and say the magic word "please." Whether it was the first, second, or twentieth time, it was always with done with such tension as if she was fighting an impossibly hard battle against herself. But the funniest moment was when she came to ask for her underwear. I had never seen a demoness so embarrassed and blushing. It seemed she was ready to die of shame but still handed me six perfectly clean sets. I had to turn them into artifacts all at once, given the amount of body energy allowed, and never mention the bows and ruffles. I believe if I had mentioned them in so much as a whisper, Vyllea would slit my throat in my sleep. She would totally do something like that.

"Welcome to this challenging world of ours, Candidate Taoist of the Silver rank," Mentor Guerlon announced as I opened my eyes. Vyllea had already woken up, but made no move to get up. As we were finishing the energy circulation, I realized I had broken through to the next stage, unlocking new abilities. I began to see not just the surging energy between our bodies, but also the initial attempts of Vyllea's body to adapt to the surrounding world. Unfortunately, the levels of Qi energy in the Forest of Dandoor were insufficient, yet I observed it beginning to concentrate where the first nodes should form. Deciding no harm in checking something, I started working. I mentally began pulling energy threads from the external world and wrapping them around the forming nodes. It felt like I had invisible hands grabbing a heated poker. Through these hands, the circulating body energy still passed, dissipating the unbearable heat throughout my body. Most astonishingly, two tiny peas formed in Vyllea's body. They weren't yet nodes, nor even node embryos. It was merely the body's consent to form new organs — entities that would later develop to allow an immortal aspirant to use techniques. They immediately started working — the energy spread through the Forest of Dandoor entered the girl's body without leaving a mark and ended its journey inside these tiny peas. All Vyllea needed to do now was to meditate near a powerful source of Qi, absorbing it and gradually enlarging these entities into nodes.

"What have you done to me?" Vyllea's whispered voice was so close, her breath scorched my lips, and her lips brushed against mine.

"I have prepared your body for the transition to the Golden rank," I honestly replied.

"How?" The question came from the mentor. Previously, I would have had to extensively describe the body energy exchange process; now, it seemed I had to detail the node formation process, which I did, explaining everything that just happened.

"You see the energy threads and can work with them, twisting them into nodes," the Taoist slowly repeated, then meaningfully added,

"Hm-m..."

While the mentor pondered, I turned my attention to Vyllea.

"Don't you think you've lingered on top of me a bit too long? Get off already!"

The girl only then realized she was still lying on me. She jumped up as if stung. She would have run to her tent, but our mentor's voice stopped her.

"Apprentice Vyllea, come over here."

The mentor placed his hand on her shoulder and closed his eyes. I already knew what he was doing — he was conducting a diagnosis. It was one of the healing techniques that allowed for the assessment of a patient's condition. Unfortunately, I couldn't see it with either normal or spirit vision. Healing techniques eluded me like slippery weasels spotting danger.

"Describe your feelings. What did you feel when Zander was forming the foundation for the nodes?"

"I won't talk about such things in front of him!" Vyllea grumbled, looked in my direction, and blushed. As I said, this happened so rarely with her that now, it seemed, even the Heavens were taken aback. The mentor looked intently at the girl, then turned toward me. Waving his hand, the Taoist materialized a voluminous bag next to my feet.

"Apprentice Zander, by the end of the day, this bag needs to be filled with herbs. Get to it!"

Everything looked so odd that all I could do was sigh and start on the task. The mentor had long since driven off all dangerous creatures from the vicinity, so gathering herbs posed no danger. Thanks to my spirit vision, finding places of power was quite simple, and I had long since picked all the herbs in the area. So now I had to venture further away from the camp, and I only managed to complete the task by the evening. When I returned, the camp had already been struck.

BOOK TWO

Vyllea was sitting silently, trying not to look in my direction, but that hardly bothered me now.

"Mentor, I have discovered something else that seems strange. Could you take out the herbs we found in the world of demons and lay them on the ground?"

Without waiting for an answer, I turned my back on the Taoist. A few moments later, places of power appeared behind me.

"From left to right — clove, geranium, ginseng, clove, celandine, geranium..."

I listed the herbs that were behind me without making a single error. A new ability had revealed itself to me during the search. Having achieved the Silver rank, I had significantly improved my spirit vision. Now, if I encountered a plant I had previously met on my path, I saw not the place of power, but the image of the plant and the amount of energy hidden within it.

Suddenly, a powerful stream of energy scorched my back. The mentor had extracted a plant that emitted such monstrous power that my insides immediately got covered in abrasions. The flower disappeared, and I felt the mentor's hand on my shoulder. He was using healing.

"It was a violet," I managed to say, my voice steadying. "But it clearly wasn't from Tier Zero. Not even Tier One. An unbelievable amount of energy. It nearly incinerated me."

"It's a flower from the Second Tier," Mentor Guerlon confirmed. "The main point is clear; we'll delve into the details of your ability later, when we have time. Let's move out!"

As evening approached and darkness was soon to envelop us — something Mentor Guerlon seemed to momentarily forget, and we dared not remind him — he conjured up a self-propelled cart, and we set forth again. Vyllea held a bright lantern, the mentor cleared the path with his techniques, and I, immersed in the realm of spiritual energy, vigilantly ensured we missed nothing of interest. A daunting task, for now, everything intrigued me immensely. Having learned to identify flowers that brought color to my previously monochrome world of energy, I yearned to examine each energy cluster up close, to understand exactly what I was dealing with. However, such luxury was beyond my reach. My task was specific — to find the site of Overlord Nurghal Lee's demise.

But this place was nowhere to be found. On the second day of travel, the forest began to transform: spaces opened between the trees, the trees themselves became smaller, and the plants and clusters of power virtually vanished, as if devoured by someone. Our speed increased significantly — the mentor even ceased needlessly expending energy on techniques. The cart jolted over the uneven ground, but it confidently made its way forward until, at some point, I said,

"About half a mile ahead, a strange zone begins. There's no energy there at all. However, there's something else. I don't know how to describe it. It looks like clumps of dense light-yellow mush, scattered in various places. Only these clumps are of different sizes. Some are tiny, barely noticeable, while others are as large as a house."

The mentor nodded. Indeed, the forest abruptly ended in about half a mile. It felt as though a giant had cleared a massive swath with a scythe, so straight and sharp was the boundary of the Forest of Dandoor. A fresh scent filled the air — we were greeted by a vast expanse of water. From somewhere in a past life, a fear washed over me. Where there were boundless water expanses, terrifying and dangerous creatures would be sure to dwell. Yet Mentor Guerlon seemed unbothered, and our cart advanced once more, halting about a hundred feet from an astonishing locale.

It was definitely a battlefield. A territory where two worlds had mixed, creating something that was neither, and this mysterious third thing was so terrifying that I had no desire to venture any further. As the mentor explained, battlefields were unique in every location. This one manifested as a perfectly smooth stone that stretched to the water's edge, forming a kind of platform. Yet it wasn't the stone base that was remarkable about this area. Once, monsters had roamed here. Dangerous, frightening, and deadly beasts. But now, something unimaginable had happened to them: they had turned into statues, frozen in strange, unnatural, and sometimes amusing poses. Most were sea creatures — it was unlikely that terrestrial monsters would have fins and gills, but there were also some land animals — tigers, spiders, and even a couple of wolves as tall as me. The battlefield appeared before us as a bizarre, huge collection of animals. Yet their appearance evoked a certain horror. It was as if the creatures had been caught in some invisible bubble, got stuck in it, and were forever immobilized. The parts that didn't make it into the bubble were destroyed. Closest to us was a wolf. The half of the beast that made it into the bubble was intact and seemed alive. The other half was simply missing, as if cleaved by an extremely sharp axe. The cut looked like a picture: nothing moved, there was no blood. A perfect guide for studying the anatomy of a creature on the path of ascension as indicated by the light-emitting meridians. And there were many such "halved" creatures on this battlefield. Rarely did anyone manage to get into the bubble completely. And, strangely, my spirit vision did not detect any energy, despite the visible meridians. The clumps of light-yellow mush scattered across the battlefield were exactly those invisible spheres that had trapped all the animals within. Most of them were empty, as if waiting for the next living being to crawl inside.

"Now it's clear to me why this battlefield has not been destroyed," Mentor Guerlon said, and I thought I detected... fear? Surely the Taoist wouldn't fear some empty space? "It's impossible to fight temporal anomalies. Pity. I really wanted to see the wormhole. We're leaving this instant."

"Mentor, why did you decide to retreat?" I

failed to understand.

"Because it's essential to accurately assess one's strengths," the Taoist explained in a patient voice. "Battlefields with temporal anomalies are classified under the black category — mortally dangerous to any being, regardless of its ascension stage. Look at the wolf. The part that's remained intact is actually alive. Time has stopped for it forever. Its head doesn't know that half of its body no longer exists. That's what happens to objects when they fall into an anomaly."

The mentor bent down and picked up a stone from the ground. With a swing, he hurled it at the wolf's half. The stone hit the carcass, nudging it slightly forward, and then the entire structure froze. A new stone followed, striking precisely the previous one, and thus nudging the wolf a bit further. A third stone came, then a fifth, then a tenth. The mentor created an entire sequence of stones hanging in the air, pushing the wolf out of the anomaly. Finally, the front part of the snout was freed. The nose twitched, as if trying to sniff out what was happening, but at that moment, it unexpectedly fell off and rolled across the smooth base, leaving behind a trail of blood.

"Objects that enter an anomaly transition to another dimension. It's a place where time does not exist. But the trap doesn't spring immediately — it allows the object to get thoroughly stuck. If you step on a temporal anomaly, you can say goodbye to your leg. Any movement in our world will sever the connection between objects of

LAW OF THE JUNGLE

different dimensions. It will be like with the nose of this wolf. But a leg is not the worst. An anomaly might catch the head, or the torso. And then any movement outside the temporal bubble means death. The only way out is to create an internal force that pushes the object out, but this object must be absolutely stationary when it breaks free from the bubble. Otherwise, it will simply be torn apart. That's why such battlefields are never destroyed. They are useless. There are no spoils or resources here. It's just a point that connects two worlds."

"So temporal bubbles are dangerous because they are invisible?" I clarified. "And if we don't step into them, there won't be any problems on this battlefield?"

"Are you saying that the light-yellow mush you talked about isn't beasts, but temporal anomalies?" the mentor frowned.

"Exactly! I don't see any beasts with my spirit vision. It's as if they didn't exist. But I can clearly tell where each bubble begins. Even to this extent."

I picked up a small stone from the ground, approached the sphere where the wolf's half still hung, and pressed the stone into the bubble. A large part of the stone was enclosed in the temporal bubble, but some of it remained outside. After waiting a few moments, I lightly flicked the stone, and it split into two parts. One remained hanging in the air, transitioning to another dimension, while the other fell onto the smooth platform.

"If that's the only danger, then I see no problem with entering the battlefield. Mentor, do you know of many battlefields in the inner tiers where there are temporal anomalies?"

"Two of them," the Taoist answered after a moment's thought. "They're located on the border with the demon territory. Perhaps you're right, apprentice. The reason no one bothers to seal them isn't that they're dangerous, but because it's unprofitable. Mental absolutes are rare, but they do exist, and at a very high level at that. Creating a map of the location and guiding an Overlord to the wormhole is not a problem. It just makes no sense... Can you build a safe route to the center of the battlefield? As I've said, I want to see the wormhole. To understand how our worlds are separated and why this place isn't flooded."

I looked over the battlefield again with my spirit vision. There were many light-yellow blotches, but it was entirely possible to walk between them without much trouble.

"Yes, but you'll have to follow in my footsteps exactly. How to do this..."

"Wear these." The mentor pulled out a pair of strange boots from his spatial pouch. They had a very thick sole, and when I took a few steps, getting used to the unusual footwear, I saw that I left green tracks behind. There was paint inside the sole, and as I stepped, I left a kind of stamp behind me marking the exact spot where one needs to step. What an interesting invention! And it didn't consume so much as a speck of energy!

My mentor really had a trove of amusing things. I'd give anything to rummage through his spatial pouch. I was sure there'd be a lot of valuable stuff to be found there.

I led the way, leaving a green trail behind me. We couldn't go straight due to the enormous carcasses of monsters that had crawled out from the depths of the ocean. Some looked so horrendous that a mere glance at them sent shivers down my spine. The creatures within the temporal bubbles were alive and dangerous, despite time being halted for them. Bones littered the stone plaza, but due to the battlefield's peculiar nature, they had been drained of energy over the years.

Circling another deep-sea monster that had managed to get caught in four anomalies with different body parts, I stopped abruptly. Ahead were two temporal bubbles, and I was uncertain how to react to their contents.

"So, this is what happened..." Master Guerlon mused, stopping a step behind me. "I suppose we'll have to linger here. Apprentice, I need to precisely know where the safe zone is. Mark it with the paint."

I nodded and began to draw circles, casting glances at my discovery. The first temporal bubble contained the lower half of a human body. Everything above the chest had vanished, but the clothing, a spatial pouch, and several strange artifacts on the belt indicated that this had once been a mighty and great being on the path to immortality. Whether it was a human or demon was hard to tell at first glance. However, the contents of this bubble were not as intriguing as those of the second. There, seated in the lotus position and meditating, was a Taoist. His face was the picture of absolute tranquility, as if unfazed by the danger of the trap, with dozens of crossbow bolts suspended in the air before him. Someone had fiercely attempted to destroy the Taoist but failed: not a single bolt had reached its target. And the Taoist himself wasn't sitting on the ground — he was hovering, albeit at an odd angle. It was as if he had leaped back-first into the anomaly and managed to assume a meditative posture mid-flight.

"Apprentices, bow your heads and pay respects to a legend among Seekers," Master Guerlon intoned after I had finished marking the safe zone. "Before you stands the great Nurghal Lee, a Golden-ranked Overlord. A Seeker who had nearly become a nascent god."

Perhaps I should have done as the Taoist said, but instead, I picked up a couple of bones.

"Master, why don't we try to extract him?"

CHAPTER 11

"NO," GUERLON ANSWERED. "We won't be extracting anyone. We..." He halted so suddenly I felt a chill. As I turned, I saw Guerlon and Vyllea frozen in peculiar stances. A whirlwind of energy materialized before me, and without even fully grasping the situation, I leaped away just in the nick of time. A piece of light yellow slime started to detach from the closest enormous beast carcass right above me. This mass plummeted onto the rocks, but I had already been gone by then. Yet even though I managed to flee, Guerlon and Vyllea didn't, to my horror. They still stood there frozen, unaware of the time-stopping blob that had descended upon them. Guerlon's face showed complete disagreement with my proposal to rescue the Overlord, while Vyllea appeared shocked as she examined the bisected body. Both my companions were trapped in a timeless space, but it wasn't their immobilization that had shocked me. The fallen temporal anomaly gathered itself, transforming into a droplet, and then began to move. The thing was moving! As were the other droplets — those containing no living beings. They didn't need speed. A single touch was enough to ensnare a victim. The droplets were unpredictable in their movement, changing directions abruptly to ensure no one escaped this monstrous battlefield. The moving droplets skirted around those containing living entities as if they could see them — or were repelled by them. I backed away, eager to get as far away from the temporal anomaly aiming for me as I could. As soon as I distanced myself, the movement inside the droplet ceased. Whatever these temporal traps were, they reacted to living bodies — the bones scattered across the ground didn't interest them, apparently. One anomaly rolled over a pile, absorbed it greedily, and then promptly resumed its course. The bones remained undisturbed.

The decision to flee the battlefield and think on how to proceed safely outside its bounds was a hard one to take. I utterly loathed the idea of abandoning Guerlon and Vyllea. Yet I saw no way of rescuing them at that moment. Before I could do anything at all, I needed to get out of this accursed place alive and intact.

It seemed today was the first day my everyday vision had merged with my spirit vision. Any hint of delay could have cost me my life, which forced me to switch so swiftly that, at one point, I realized I was seeing two states simultaneously — the real world and the world of moving energy fields. This was very helpful, as I managed to evade the leaping anomalies as I darted about. It took several hours to cover the distance of about seven hundred feet, and when I finally left the stone plaza behind, I collapsed to the ground. My body shook as if after a week of training, albeit more from the rush of emotions. Now as I found myself out in the open, I felt completely overwhelmed. I wanted to scream, to curse myself for my folly — for getting distracted and allowing that damned anomaly to snatch my team. I was angry at Guerlon and his sudden desire to see the meeting point of two worlds, and angry at Vyllea, even though I had no real reason for that.

* * *

By the time I finished yelling and groaning, it was evening already. Looking back at the battlefield, I let out a string of colorful and intricate curses. My father would have smacked me for such words, while Guerlon would have just sighed heavily, remarking that such emotions did not suit a Taoist. The battlefield had stilled. As soon as it became devoid of living beings, the anomalies returned to a static state, as if inviting everyone inside. They acted just like they did in cases when stones got thrown at them — adapting first, and then eventually activating.

Only now did I notice I was still holding a bone I'd taken from the battlefield. I threw it at the nearest temporal droplet in irritation. The bone hung in the air for a moment before slowly descending to the rocks. The light yellow slime had found the object boring and "spat it out." My gaze shifted to the anomaly with the wolf that Guerlon had been pushing out. The stones still hung in the air. Just as those crossbow bolts that had struck Overlord Nurgal Lee did. This was so fascinating that my anger at everything and everyone in the world subsided. Temporal anomalies attacked living beings. Empty anomalies could move. Anomalies ignored ordinary objects, ejecting them almost instantly. They stopped moving chaotically when there were no living beings on the stone plaza. What did all of it mean?

The tremor in my body subsided, replaced by a wish to test a thought. The wolf served as my subject again, only this time I decided to push it in the opposite direction — towards the side where it was already practically dead. I had to run into the forest to break off a long stick; working with stones, as Guerlon did, didn't appeal to me. I entered the battlefield, ready to leap away at any moment, but the cunning trap didn't react, inviting me to move further into its territory. I was sure it wouldn't make the same mistake twice, and its timeless droplets would move much faster now. But since everything remained static for the moment, I circled the bubble with the wolf, aimed the stick at its mouth, and started pushing. The wood entered the anomaly reluctantly, as if I was pushing the stick into dense mud. At one point, I paused to adjust my grip, and in that moment, part of the stick crashed down. The temporal bubble had activated, placing the wood in two different dimensions. In the one where time existed, the weight of the stick worked against it, compromising its integrity. Yet I had managed to push the wolf out by almost two feet. Nearly all the stones that Guerlon had thrown were now outside the anomaly.

I had therefore been given new data: continuous movement was necessary for exiting an anomaly. As soon as there was an interruption, the object lost its structural integrity. But for as long as there was movement, the anomaly didn't activate.

So that much was clear. I needed another stick.

I had managed to gather a whole pile of sticks by sundown. I decided I would try out my conjectures tomorrow, with a fresh mind. Hunger reminded me that we had only eaten breakfast that day, but my mentor had taught me to go without food for a long time. I always wondered why he needed to do that, and now I saw how it could come in useful. Nightmares haunted me. A light yellow slime mold chased me, and I fended it off with sticks that shortened after each failed strike. I woke up in a cold sweat and barely restrained from cursing as I threw a glance at the battlefield. The positions of the empty droplets had changed overnight; they had moved again. Either a living being had entered the battlefield, or these things came alive at night and rearranged to confuse anyone who would venture into this dangerous territory.

In any case, my wolf had remained in place, which suited me just fine. I chose a stick that wasn't overly long, and as I started circling the temporal bubble, I immediately held my stick in such a way that I wouldn't need to adjust my grip at all. The stick entered the invisible viscous substance and, hitting the wolf, began to push it out. It almost worked perfectly: the stick entered the bubble almost entirely, never stopping. But the "almost" was crucial — the wolf's body fell apart into two pieces as it exited the anomaly. As soon as the creature felt pain, it began to twitch and, as a result, crushed itself with its own weight. Suddenly devoid of a living being inside it, the temporal droplet cleared swiftly, and all the stones and sticks fell to the ground. This pest had apparently sensed a living being nearby and moved towards me. I had to run around it, exit the battlefield, and think again. The wolf was no longer of interest to the temporal bubble. It was dead. By the way, the wolf emanated a strong force — it turned out to be a creature at the Apprentice stage. After making sure the droplet had frozen again, lying in wait for its next victim, I dragged the spilled remains off the stone platform and easily claimed the creature's essence. I would have liked to say I had expected it to come in handy someday, but that wasn't the case. I had to absorb this essence immediately.

Why was that? Because gradually, a plan on how to deal with this Heavens-forsaken battlefield was taking shape. I definitely wouldn't leave Guerlon and Vyllea here. There was much to do and much to test, but first, I needed to take care of myself. I was in an aggressive environment without a healer. The energy abrasions would kill me in a month at the latest. To ignore the ambient Qi energy, I had to open a node for myself and advance to the Golden rank, even though I didn't have Vyllea next to me. I also needed food and water. This problem also needed some solution, but here I would rely on the skills my father had given me. A hunter couldn't die of hunger or thirst in the forest. They could get killed by beasts, sure, but never hunger. Things were pretty straightforward in our village — if you were so poor a hunter and woodsman hunger or thirst could kill you in the woods, you deserved to die.

The first problem arose almost immediately. Knowing what to do was one thing; putting that knowledge into practice, quite another. Especially when I had a powerful mentor who'd been doing everything short of wiping my nose for me for the last two years. Now, reflecting on everything we'd been through, I realized that Guerlon had been shielding me from virtually everything. He'd never made me search for food, water, weapons, tools, or any items of necessity at all. It was quite hard to return to harsh reality for someone accustomed to having all their needs covered.

At any rate, water was my number one priority. Finding a puddle was no issue, and quite close to the battlefield, too. Fire was my second. This took some effort, selecting the right stones, dry grass, and twigs, but soon enough, I managed to start a proper fire. During my entire stay in the demon world, I hadn't encountered rain once, so I didn't bother building a shelter over the fire. However, I did gather lots of twigs to keep the fire going day and night. Third I needed a container for boiling. Drinking raw water in a foreign world was a sure path to death. I had to recall the basics of pottery and mold myself a small clay container to fire it in the flames subsequently. It wasn't the most reliable means of boiling, but it would have to do for now.

Finally, having quenched my thirst, I placed the wolf's essence before me, sat in the lotus position, and closed my eyes. My body's energy took a long time to understand why it was alone, where its red counterpart was, and for what inexplicable reason it was so severely restricted in mobility. It slowed down so much that I almost screamed from pain — my body rebelled against being left without Vyllea! Had this happened yesterday, I would have terminated the meditation and run to the girl to restore wholeness as quickly as possible. But now I was alone, angry, hungry, and wrestling with my own body's energy! Wasn't this utter madness? Sure was!

The warmth yielded reluctantly, as if

reestablishing circulation pathways anew, and as soon as the flows stabilized, I reached for the source. The power of the Apprentice-stage beast scratched my invisible hands, burning them, while I lacked a partner capable of taking and dissolving a part of the fire within them. I had to endure and keep working ceaselessly, recalling how I handled my first lower demons. What I had felt back then was pain. This was just temporary discomfort. At some point, I even managed to detach from the pain and begin to wind energy streams where nodes should form. Yes, it had a feeling of wrongness to it. The body should have produced these things of its own accord. It should have entered a state of readiness on its own. But I simply didn't have the time for that. It was either this way — or I'd die in a month. I'd deal with the body later. If there would indeed be a "later."

The moment the first pea-sized foundation for the nodes (which was how Guerlon had described these things) had appeared was something I'd never forget. I almost lost my concentration then. It felt as if a foreign hand was operating inside my chest, yet causing no discomfort. On the contrary, the more energy I wound up, the more pleasant these movements became. It reached a point where I started trembling; my body couldn't handle the sheer joy that had befallen it. I craved more and more, wishing the moment would never end, but I nonetheless managed to stop. The energy flows storming within me were so intense it seemed I could be blown away. The pleasure I was giving myself generated additional energy in my body, which began to tear my muscles apart. A bit more, and they would have simply ruptured, unable to withstand such pressure. I had to pull back, despite my intense desire for more. If not for our daily training with Vyllea and the subsequent craving for a new exchange that I had to learn to quench, I wouldn't have been able to deal with the current problem. The process of winding energy threads was too enticing, sweet, and pleasant.

Nonetheless, I did lay the foundation. My body continued to feel the abrasions, but significantly less than at the beginning of the meditation. Having managed to quench the raging energy flows, I directed the incoming external power into the formed node's foundation and opened my eyes. Now I understood what Vyllea had experienced and why she didn't want to tell me about her sensations. I wouldn't have told Guerlon about it, either.

Not a trace remained of the wolf's essence: I had absorbed it completely. The fire had died out so long ago that even the coals had cooled down. I was terribly hungry. Thirsty. Sleepy. I wanted to return to the world of humans, hide underneath a bed, and think that everything that had happened to me over the last three years was just a bad dream. But I liked this dream, and I didn't want to end it just yet. I had learned more over this relatively brief period than the inhabitants of our village would in several lifetimes! How could I give up in such a situation? How could I retreat when my group's life depended on me? Retreat absolutely wasn't an option! I swore to myself that I would see this through and that I would give it my all.

I found sustenance swiftly — the wolf meat, extricated from the temporal bubble, still lay scattered across the stone platform, of no interest to the battlefield. The fire blazed anew, and water boiled, but this time, the scent of searing meat filled the air — tough, fatty, and horrendously foul. I had to char it nearly to cinders to mitigate the stench somewhat. Taste-wise, the wolf was as repugnant as its smell, yet my choices were stark: eat or perish. My stomach protested long and hard against such fare, but body fortification kicked in on my behalf, quelling the spasms and the urge to expel the distasteful meal.

A series of simple experiments revealed that dust and small inanimate objects lingered on stationary temporal anomalies for thirty seconds, and on moving ones for ten. I trekked into the forest for bugs and spiders. Since the invisible mounds reacted only to living beings, it made sense to halt them all. But all I'd managed to do as a result was turn a part of the battlefield into an impenetrable barrier. The temporal anomalies consumed the bugs without a hitch, freezing in place. Yet after two hours of ceaseless toil on one side of the field — having supposedly drawn all the anomalies there — I returned to the opposite edge only to huff in frustration. The number of light-yellow mounds remained unchanged. It reminded me of what Guerlon said once about the number of anomalies always being static. If you sealed one, another would appear elsewhere instantly. He had referred to the world of humans, but what if the same principle applied here? Did every anomaly I blocked with a cockroach or some such creature give birth to a new one?

I had no desire to test this theory. My priority lay in rescuing my team, not delving into research of things that must have been researched well enough years ago. Since such anomalies were left only at the border of the demons' lands, the Taoists must have long figured out how to deal with them. Thus, it seemed there was no choice but to embark on my wild plan.

Once more, I ventured into the dense Forest of Dandoor, grateful for how thick it was for what must have been the first time. It was perfectly suited for my scheme. Even if I manage to extricate my team (a plan still in need of rigorous testing), fleeing with them from the battlefield wasn't an option. I could see the darting temporal anomalies; those I'd rescue would be blind to them. And the paint-soaked boots would clearly be no help. Thus, I needed to somehow eliminate the blindness issue, allowing Guerlon and Vyllea to sprint to freedom unaided. How so? Simply by constructing a platform above the battlefield, unreachable by the temporal bubbles! There were plenty of trees, and their webs could serve as bindings — were those massive spiders within some bubbles there for nothing? Where there were spiders, there was webbing. Strong and dense — precisely what I needed. All I required was time, more time, and just a tad more time...

Before anything else, I was itching to test my wild theory. Getting the wood was a breeze, but finding spider silk meant delving deeper into the woods. Surprisingly, Vyllea's voracious appetite had done me a service here — Guerlon had almost cleared out all the dangerous creatures for her. Sure, I encountered a few wolves, and even a tiger, but all the animals were just Candidates and thus no match for me. After gathering enough silk, I headed back to the battlefield, reminding myself to go hunting later. My plan required a live beast, and searching for one amidst anomalies wasn't the most prudent move.

I secured six vertical posts with a bunch of horizontal braces. The top platform sat some ten feet off the ground, and it struck me that height mattered. Assembling the platforms alone was tricky; sticks kept falling, snapping, or getting untied, but I was determined. It took me a whole week to construct five rickety-looking structures — spider silk was not that easy to come by. Finally, preparations were complete, and I hauled my creations onto the battlefield. The light yellow clusters didn't react — to them, my structures were just more debris on the stone plateau. But once I climbed onto a platform and sat there for about thirty minutes, the battlefield stirred to life. The temporal bubbles sensed prey, but couldn't pinpoint its location. Heart pounding, I watched several anomalies slam into the posts I was perched on, and then proceed onward swiftly. My crazy plan was working. I stood up and gazed toward where my group was stationed — five hundred feet away. In theory, five platforms would suffice if I kept moving the rear one forward. This method would allow me to reach my goal in a day, provided I had the strength. I also had to see whether hauling a platform up was indeed feasible.

Dealing with the platform presented no major hurdles, but, as fate would have it, challenges emerged from unexpected quarters. I hunkered down on my platforms for four hours. The empty anomalies began to move about thirty minutes after I had entered the battlefield, but failing to catch their prey, they gradually picked up speed. Three hours in, the light yellow clusters were zipping around twice as fast as they had been at the beginning. This odd escalation of speed made me stay put to observe. After another three hours, the temporal anomalies moved as fast as a running person, and by the day's end, they reached at the speed of a runaway horse. It was sheer madness: temporal bubbles raced, collided, and nearly engulfed the entire area without finding me. They couldn't jump, and having once hit my posts rooted in the battlefield's rocky base, they didn't crash into them again. The anomalies behaved as if they were alive, remembering the locations of the "unappetizing" bits and avoiding them on subsequent passes, flying so close to the posts it seemed they'd graze them — all at incredible speeds!

The option to lift the platform and reset it at the end for descent was gone; there was simply no room for my feet. I jumped, sacrificing one platform as I caused it to topple and splinter into bits almost instantly. Only the anomalies had the right to move across the battlefield. An hour after I'd left, the chaos ceased. The temporal bubbles dispersed and froze in place as if nothing had happened. Yet I was certain their initial speed next time would be substantial. I wouldn't be able to move platforms around to reach my group. A continuous, secure five-hundred-foot path was essential, and the platforms needed to be tied together thoroughly for stability. I saw no other way to tackle this insane battlefield.

I glanced at my jian with a heavy heart as I headed into the forest. I needed trees and spider silk. Lots and lots of both. The upcoming months promised to be a grueling challenge. Additionally, capturing another beast was on the agenda. Whether I liked it or not, advancing to the Candidate stage of the Golden rank was imperative, lest the energy of the demon world's Circle Zero should shred me to pieces within a few months.

CHAPTER 12

I FELT COMPLETELY EXHAUSTED as I pondered whether the Heavens had truly ordained this ordeal for me, or perhaps mistook me for some hero from the ancient legends.

Constructing a stable platform for my group took three grueling months. During that time, I cursed my "brilliant" plan countless times, yet persisted. The main challenge, as often happened, awaited me at the very end. A massive hovering mass of light yellow jelly harboring a deep-sea monster within its depths, which had also ensnared Vyllea and Guerlon, had set its sights on me. Foolishly placing a platform too close, I had a chunk of temporal anomaly crash onto it from above. The droplet lingered on the platform briefly — finding no living being, it slid off, forcing me to devise alternative routes away from high formations to avoid unexpected surprises.

Finally, the path was laid out, and I moved to the second phase — reducing the amount of light yellow jelly on Guerlon. I decided to extract him first, but wanted to perfect the rescue method beforehand. Thus, I needed to do some hunting — my plan required a sacrifice. A Bronze-ranked Candidate stage wolf had ventured too close to me at its peril — possibly sent by his kin to scout the area. It could have returned to his pack a trailblazer and a hero, but it didn't, falling prey to a Golden-ranked Candidate Taoist instead. I had indeed formed four nodes, shielding myself completely from the energy of Circle Zero. I had to empty several temporal traps to harvest beast essences, and then diligently absorb their energy, wrapping it around the forming nodes. Each time, it became harder to detach from this process, so I stopped at four nodes, fearing that starting a fifth would be my undoing, leaving me forever stranded in the world of energy, craving more pleasure. It was unpleasant to admit, but I really needed Vyllea.

I was therefore about to conduct my first experiment in extracting living bodies from an anomaly. The wolf whimpered fearfully, wrapped into a cocoon, and I genuinely pitied the beast. Yet I had no right to end its misery and fear by granting the wolf a swift death. Those accursed temporal anomalies disregarded the dead, craving only the living!

Thus, the wolf was out of luck. I hoisted it

over my shoulder as I made my way to my group. I avoided using the platform — the anomalies would remain calm for the first thirty minutes. Upon reaching my destination, I laid the twitching animal near a trap encasing half a human body. The light green jelly seized the opportunity, enveloping the wolf. The subject froze, and I grinned in satisfaction — the volume of the temporal bubble hiding the corpse had significantly reduced. With plenty of time left before the anomalies started moving, I dared another experiment. This time, I used my latest invention — a stick with an end resembling a splayed hand. Pushing an object out of a temporal anomaly at a single point was fraught: any bend would lead to destruction. The subject had to be pushed uniformly in all directions, preventing the body from bending. This approach worked perfectly with the wolf — it shot out of the temporal anomaly unscathed! The pesky anomaly pursued it immediately, but I had anticipated something like this, managing to circle around the bubble, grab the cocoon, and throw it onto the platform. The battlefield stirred, sensing something amiss and determined to reclaim its prey. But I had no intention of giving anything back. I leaped ten feet into the air effortlessly, grabbed the ensnared wolf, and ran off. Five hundred feet with a load were a trifle for a Taoist of my level. An hour later, when the anomalies ceased their frenzied motion, I repeated the experiment, this time bringing a new splayed stick. Unfortunately, the previous one was turned out to be single-use.

It took three "cleansings" to reduce the amount of light yellow jelly around the corpse to a thin shell. I refrained from reducing it further; exposing any part of the body could lead to its detachment. I needed to extract what remained of the body in one go. After placing the freed wolf away from the anomalies to prevent accidental consumption, I returned to my subject. A new stick, specifically created for extracting this body, came into play. Two branches for each leg, two for the waist. My contraption looked dreadful and threatened to fall apart during transport but was perfect for the task. Taking a deep breath, I aimed and struck the anomaly with the forked stick.

The result was flawless — the body emerged from the temporal trap unscathed. However, I'd overlooked one critical factor: only another Overlord, or, perhaps, even a Nascent God, could contend with an Overlord. Despite the body being long dead, the items that had emerged from the anomaly unleashed such a monstrous wave of energy that I nearly perished. The situation deteriorated to the point where even my four nodes couldn't cope. My internal organs began to feel abrasions, and the malicious anomaly, realizing the body it had released was no longer a living being, had no intention of reclaiming its catch. I was on the verge of fainting when I managed to leap after the wolf and hurled it towards the body ejected from the anomaly. I had lost my assistant, but saved my life — the light yellow jelly covered the wolf along with the body that was emitting that monstrous energy. The battlefield stirred to life again, forcing me to literally crawl onto the platform. My body suffered greatly. Moreover, a couple of platforms became unusable — the energy from the corpse had eroded their supports, and they began to crack under my weight.

I had to take a two-week break to recuperate. My body bore so many scars that I started to genuinely worry. Meditation no longer worked; the energy couldn't penetrate what my body had become. It was somewhat miraculous that I hadn't died. I coughed up blood for three days straight. It became clear why Instructor Guerlon had been reluctant to extract Overlord Nurgal Lee. The items worn by that Taoist would have annihilated both Vyllea and me. Master Guerlon didn't want to lose his apprentices, so he decided Overlord Nurgal Lee could stay in the anomaly a while longer. Funnily enough, despite his outward coldness, the instructor cared about us deeply.

However, as painful as it was, the task at hand awaited completion. I ventured back into the forest for another victim, and once again, a wolf was chosen. It seemed to be their fate. I had to craft a special extraction stick for mentor Guerlon. It was doubtful the Taoist would be pleased if his head had remained in the anomaly. Each branch had to be calibrated with perfect precision — they all needed to touch my mentor simultaneously.

It took three attempts to reduce the volume of the bubble encasing Instructor Guerlon, after which I had to pause to overcome the fear that surged within me. What if I made a mistake and the instructor was torn apart? What if a limb, or his head, was severed? What if my stick broke before the Taoist emerged from the anomaly? It took a day to conquer the overwhelming fear that had completely paralyzed my actions. I had never thought fear could be so potent as to entirely deprive one of any agency — until I faced it myself.

Finally, the moment arrived. Four months had passed since Master Guerlon and Vyllea were engulfed by a cluster of temporal anomaly. Today would be the day of liberation — for our mentor, at least. Taking aim, I stepped forward before my brain could spiral into panic again. The stick entered the anomaly and scooped up the Taoist's body in ten places simultaneously like a caring parent. I pressed on relentlessly, knowing all too well from the past four months that any hesitation or pause meant death. The moment felt eternal — the Taoist's body emerged from the temporal anomaly reluctantly, as if it resisted letting him go until the very end. I applied pressure once more, and the stick broke — it had reached the opposite end of the anomaly. Discarding the now useless stick, I circled the anomaly. There stood Instructor Guerlon, frowning, baffled by the sudden appearance of a massive wall of sticks next to him.

"Follow me!" I grabbed the Taoist by the hand and pulled him away. To his credit, he didn't argue or try to resist. As we reached the platforms, I let go of the instructor and leapt atop. The Taoist had already gotten there before me. He didn't ask what to do next. Suddenly, I was airborne: the instructor grabbed me and sped forward with astonishing velocity. The interconnected platforms shook and creaked under such treatment, but held up. Only when we landed did the Taoist set me down. After giving my makeshift construction, me, and my emaciated body a once-over, he placed his hand on my shoulder, sending a jolt through me. The spasm that gripped my body was so intense that I moaned. The scars left by the garb of the unknown Overlord (if an Overlord at all) reluctantly began to fade from my insides.

"How long has it been?"

"Nearly four months. Mentor, do you have any food? I..."

I couldn't finish. My body, overwhelmed by a hefty dose of healing, declared it needed rest, responding to such treatment. Dark circles formed before my eyes, and I slipped into oblivion. When I opened my eyes, there was no pain. None at all. After four months of constant discomfort, I'd initially thought I was still dreaming. But the appearance of the irascible Taoist dispelled that notion. It's unlikely a grumpy mentor would show up in a dream.

"You've reached the Golden rank," Master Guerlon observed.

"I had to. Otherwise, this world would have literally ground me to death."

"How did you manage the growth of the nodes without Vyllea? How did you extract me unharmed? What exactly have you been up to these four months? Food's right next to you."

Only then did I realize I was inside a vast tent, lying on a soft and comfortable bed, with a table laden with a variety of food beside me. It seemed I had drifted away from reality for a while. I devoured the food so quickly I barely had time to chew. Four months of surviving on subpar meat alone could bring anyone to their knees. Only after realizing not even a small bite could fit in me anymore did I push myself away from the table and smiled. Life burst into color again! Master Guerlon, who had patiently waited while I feasted, coughed politely, reminding me that he had asked a question. Gathering my wits and overcoming the urge to collapse onto the bed and sleep for several months, I recounted to the Taoist all my endeavors over the last four months. I didn't omit how I almost perished due to the attire of a bisected corpse and how I'd gotten out of that predicament.

"Understood. I need three days to prepare the platforms. Rest up."

Instructor Guerlon kept his word, dedicating himself to crafting the platforms. The Taoist ventured into the forest and engaged in a flurry of activity — chips flew in all directions, trees fell as if mowed down, and the hammer's pounding echoed constantly. Periodically, the instructor brought his creations to the clearing. All I could do was smile ruefully at what could be accomplished with strength, tools, and resources. Each platform crafted by the Taoist was a masterpiece of carpentry — they were stable structures standing on six perfectly straight legs, each around twelve feet tall. The top platform was five feet wide, and the constructions were interconnected by several blocks fitting into specially-made grooves. In three days, the instructor had erected a structure that would have taken me years. But I harbored no envy for the Taoist's skills. My much more primitive creation had enabled us to extract the instructor from the battlefield. Everything else was trivial.

Setting up the new platform road was a breeze. Mentor Guerlon carried his creations effortlessly, leaving me merely to point out where to place them. I didn't bother asking why the mentor felt the need to choose his own path. He wouldn't have answered anyway. Instead, I focused on reducing the volume of Vyllea's temporal trap. Her situation was more complex: not only did we need to extract her, but we also had to avoid getting too close to the massive pile of light yellow jelly that was also hiding part of a sea monster. A couple of times I had approached too closely, and a huge drop of jelly would attempt to fall on me, forcing me to activate the entire battlefield so the clear anomalies would disperse somewhere else. At one point, we even considered moving the carcass aside, but that endeavor failed. Mentor Guerlon couldn't budge it and narrowly escaped a "spit" from the anomaly.

Nonetheless, extracting Vyllea proved relatively easy. After significantly reducing her trap's volume and creating a pushing stick tailored to her body (how easy it was to work when you had access to unlimited resources and tools!), Mentor Guerlon and I synchronized our actions perfectly. I pushed the girl out and leaped away, dodging a drop falling from above. Mentor Guerlon caught the bewildered girl emerging from the anomaly and with a single jump, landed atop the new aerial road. A second drop fell onto an already empty space.

"Four months? I was trapped for four months? Is this some kind of joke? I just blinked!"

Vyllea struggled to accept the reality of her absence. For her, only a moment had passed. The drop had fallen so swiftly she hadn't had time to feel anything. She only realized something was amiss when she felt a poke with a stick, and for some reason, the mentor was scooping her up. The existence of two wooden roads made her believe in the unfolding events somewhat. And yes — my platform road began to collapse gradually. After all, spider silk wasn't the most reliable means of fastening heavy logs. Still, it had served its purpose.

"What do you mean you've reached the Golden rank?! How?!" The next piece of news seemed to shock her more than falling into a temporal anomaly. "Mentor, when are we leaving?"

"Leaving?" the Taoist marveled. "Didn't we come here to see the wormhole? The first attempt might have failed, but that doesn't mean we should give up so easily. Besides, we now have a safe way to reach the heart of the battlefield. Opportunities like this are rare, Apprentice Vyllea. The Heavens won't forgive us if we don't seize it. I need three days to prepare new platforms."

"That's great! I want to reach the Golden rank too, Mentor. Zander, lie down! We need to exchange energy!"

"Remember the sensations you experienced while forming the nodes?" I asked, taken aback by her insistence. "They'll be tenfold more intense during the node formation. Trust me — I know what I'm talking about. The method I used isn't the most appropriate one. You'd be better off achieving it through meditation."

"No!" Vyllea flushed deeply, but stood her ground. "I won't allow anyone to surpass me in rank! If it takes... Whatever it takes! I won't be outdone by you!"

"Having nodes isn't the sole criterion for advancing to the Golden rank," Mentor Guerlon interjected. "It requires an enhancement of the spirit. Your body is ready for the nodes. Your mind, however, lags behind. I forbid Apprentice Zander from forming any nodes in your body. He's right: if you so desire to ascend to the Golden rank, achieve it on your own. You will receive help from a fellow aspirant only after I deem your mind ready."

"Mentor!" Vyllea protested vehemently. "That's not fair! I shouldn't depend on Zander for this!"

"You need to control your emotions,

apprentice, unless you seek punishment. Cultivate your mind, train, and only once I find you worthy will I allow Apprentice Zander to work with your nodes. Not until then. You have three days. Meditate."

"Don't even think about it!" Vyllea grumbled angrily, deliberately avoiding my gaze. "I'll reach the Golden rank no matter what it takes!"

The stubborn demoness sat down in the lotus position not far from me, hands on knees, eyes closed. She remained like that for hours, flinching every time the mentor felled a tree. The manic determination of the Taoist to reach the wormhole was disconcerting, but I had no right to contest it. Perhaps he was indeed guided by the Heavens, and without witnessing the junction of the two worlds, the mentor would never break through to the Overlord stage. What did I know about ascending to such lofty ranks, anyway?

Lofty ranks... My head automatically turned towards the battlefield. There, sprawled on his back, lay a high-ranking Taoist. A legend among Seekers. Yet, the mentor hadn't even hinted at the idea of rescuing him. He deemed it either impossible, too dangerous for his apprentices, or perilous for himself. The latter couldn't be ruled out, either. Perhaps, Overlord Nurgal Lee had vowed to kill any Seeker he'd encounter. Still, the notion of extracting the Overlord as well wasn't half bad. If successful, there'd be a chance to obliterate this battlefield, severing the wormhole and disconnecting our worlds at this juncture.

B O O K   T W O

While everyone was busy or pretended to be, I dashed to the Overlord. His pose, of course, was extremely unfortunate. He was suspended in mid-air, collapsed onto his back. Using sticks to push him out would decapitate him. Extracting the mentor and Vyllea had been straightforward: they were in contact with the stone foundation, offering a point of leverage. But here, the Taoist was hanging suspended. As soon as any part of him became free, it would tip the balance and detach, much like what happened with my first wolf.

I circled the overlord several times, memorizing all the pertinent details, and then headed back. Vyllea had stopped feigning meditation and just sat there, sulking at the world. The mentor, lost in his own world, continued to fell trees without so much as a glance in our direction. He had a goal in mind and pursued it relentlessly. So, all that was left for me was to rest, but of course, I had no intention of doing so. The novelty of the challenge stirred my mind. How to extract a Taoist floating in mid-air, considering the peculiarities of temporal anomalies? Ideas came and went, all dismissed almost immediately. It reached the point where I grabbed a stick and started sketching various lift and platform schemes on the ground — ones that could catch a body emerging from an anomaly mid-air. But I came up with nothing viable. Extracting a floating person without injury seemed impossible. Achieving the necessary synchronization among a rescue team would require practice, but what could we practice on?

"Zander!" Vyllea finally broke and approached me. "I can't meditate alone! I need you!"

"Let's try later; I'm busy now."

"I don't have a later! I've started experiencing some weird withdrawal! When I look at you, my body shakes all over! There's this strange dryness in my mouth, my head's spinning, and I can't concentrate on anything. I'm drawn to you! And it's infuriating! I can't be this dependent on anything or anyone!"

"Your body has realized my rank is higher and wants to take some of my strength to ascend. What you're describing is a feeling I know very well. I lived like that for six months."

"It was your choice! What's happening to me now isn't my doing — it's yours! You're the one who has to fix it! I need a conjunction, or else I can't be held responsible! Lie down on your back!" Vyllea was so unlike herself that I had no right to object. Indeed, I had gone through what was now overcoming her, so I understood that without at least one conjunction a day, the body would start rebelling — and fiercely. Just recalling my first meditation without Vyllea still sends shivers down my spine. My own body wanted to kill me. My only salvation lay in that I was forming nodes at the time and quelled the pain with pleasure.

"Just lie down already!" Vyllea couldn't stand it anymore and pushed me, forcing me down. She immediately climbed on top of me and took a convulsive breath, pressing her forehead to mine.

She was clearly suffering. I didn't touch the nodes, following our mentor's orders. And I hardly had the time to — Vyllea was like a woman possessed. She generated so much bodily energy that I barely managed to control it. She couldn't do it herself. Only after twelve hours, when had I extinguished the last traces of warmth, did she collapse to the side and fell asleep instantly. It seems she had even fell asleep while falling. All that was left for me to do was to cover her with a blanket and approach the mentor with an interesting proposition. But I needed to ask him a question first. I really wanted to know why the Taoist had no desire to extract the legend of seekers from the anomaly? After exchanging energy with Vyllea, I was certain of how to accomplish it. And no platforms or braces were needed. Astonishingly, extracting the Overlord was even simpler than the mentor. I think I even knew why the ancient seeker was sitting in the lotus position. To ease the task for whoever came after him. Yet, for two hundred years, no one had bothered to do so. Could there have been a reason?

CHAPTER 13

"...SO EXTRACTING HIM wouldn't be difficult at all. But why are you opposed to the idea?"

Mentor Guerlon had heard out my proposal with his usual calm. He'd even stopped chopping trees. Instead of sending me to rest, the Taoist sat on a felled tree and silently stared at the axe in his hands for a while. I felt somewhat uneasy. Could it be that his disagreements with the Overlord were so severe he'd kill me and Vyllea just to ensure the information about the found Taoist wouldn't reach the wrong ears? Yet I felt no tingling between my shoulder blades — a sure sign of danger had it been real. My combat intuition may still have needed refinement, but it had never misled me. When real danger approached, it felt as if my spine was being pricked with needles. Finally, the mentor stopped examining his axe and looked at me.

"According to the surviving information in the records, Overlord Nurgal Lee was an exemplary Seeker. Great, powerful, and fair. He dedicated his life to destroying battlefields, closing wormholes, and annihilating demons, without getting involved in clan disputes. Even in his last hour, realizing he would remain in a temporal anomaly, he'd managed to release his pet, turning this region of the demon world into a desert."

"So you're saying he might kill Vyllea as soon as he sees her?" I asked, noticing the mentor's pause.

"There was no mention of madness in the archives, so I hope he won't do that. But we cannot completely rule out the possibility."

"Then why don't you... Mentor, that corpse that nearly killed me — that's not a demon, is it? It's a human, right? You recognized the clothing, or rather, what was left of it. One glance was enough for you to decide not to rescue the overlord. Who wanted him dead, mentor? Some clan from the Third Tier? The Fourth?"

"The belt worn by the corpse is an artifact of absolute protection. A unique item personally created by the Emperor and tailored for a specific person. This artifact can protect its owner from almost any attack for a few minutes. With such a belt, one can swim in the maw of an active volcano, fall from great heights, or travel through the deepest parts of the ocean. One could even enter the mouth of a Nascent God level beast. Briefly, but it would still be possible. This is how those who have encountered individuals entitled to wear such items describe the artifact. They are called imperial officials, Judges, or Executors of Fate. There are many names, but they all convey the same — these people are the Emperor's hands, acting on his behalf. What happened here has nothing to do with demons. It was a trap set for one particular person — Seeker Nurgal Lee. Such actions were sanctioned by the highest leadership of the Deforean Empire. And not only sanctioned, but also executed, although the Executors of Fate do not normally act independently."

"So, rescuing the overlord means going against the Emperor, may he reign eternally?"

"I doubt the Emperor even knows who Overlord Nurgal Lee is. To him, such a figure would be too insignificant. Merely dust underfoot that just so happens to move from place to place. This involves a power struggle within the Fourth Tier — or, possibly, even the Central Tier. The overlord had almost reached the Nascent God stage. Such Taoists must be admitted to the capital and given access to the Primordial Soul. Not everyone likes this. Competitors — especially Seekers — are most unwelcome. Rescuing the overlord could provoke a conflict within the Deforean Empire. Much has changed in the two hundred years since this Taoist's disappearance. Demons have made significant advances in the eastern part of the empire; battles are now being fought in the Third Tier. It's only a matter of time before the vanguard reaches the Fourth, allowing demon Overlords to enter our world in full force. If a vengeful Golden-ranked Overlord revealed himself to the world at such a point... I simply cannot predict the consequences."

"And yet you started making a new batch of platforms instead of leaving this place and forgetting about it forever. The Heavens won't accept retreat. We didn't just happen to come to the Forest of Dandoor by chance. Nor was it by chance that we have destroyed a huge tree and found the Overlord's turtle. The Heart of the Ocean, miraculously suitable for Overlord Nurgal Lee, isn't in your spatial pouch by mere coincidence, either. Even finding the place where the Overlord had fought his last battle did not happen by accident! The battlefield is vast; we could have gone elsewhere, and never encountered him. But the Heavens have led us here. Maybe we should take heed?"

"What do you want with the overlord?" The mentor grinned. "If you're hoping for his gratitude, I must disappoint you. A Taoist of his level will consider that you've merely fulfilled your duty. He might even punish you if he thinks you've dawdled."

"I don't know, mentor," I admitted honestly. "It's just that... There's a certain sense of wrongness that won't let me be at ease. We can't leave the Overlord here. I honestly don't know why. But I have this feeling we just can't."

"The Seekers do need him," the mentor

agreed unexpectedly. "But that's precisely the problem stopping me. A Judge had decided to eliminate the Overlord, making it seem as if demons were to blame for his death. Imperial officials rarely act alone, which means someone within the Empire had ordered the removal of Overlord Nurgal Lee. Two hundred years are but a moment for Taoists of high ascension. When the Seeker reappears in the world, a hunt will begin — not just for him, but also for those who've brought him back. That means me, you, and Vyllea. The Judges won't let such a thing slide. I'm a Diamond-rank Master. To kill me, they'd need to bring in someone serious. And they'd have to find me first. But you and Vyllea are different; you're still Candidates. Any Silver-ranked Apprentice could handle you effortlessly. A Warrior might kill you with their aura alone. The Judges are too vengeful to ignore this, and solving the issue of passage from the upper tiers to Tier Zero wouldn't be too hard for them."

"To seek vengeance, one must know whom to seek vengeance upon. Do you think Overlord Nurgal Lee will wander the empire proclaiming his liberators were Master Guerlon and his apprentices?"

"That's exactly what he'd do. If freed, the Overlord would start provoking conflicts, stirring up the morass that is the Deforean Empire. He'd use every means available, including the elevation of minor Taoists. Namely, us. To identify who's displeased by this and punish them."

"You consider yourself a minor Taoist?" I couldn't suppress a smile.

"Compared to the Overlord, I am."

"And yet, you're still here. The Heavens never send us any easy opponents, do they? So, why not meet it halfway and make enemies of our own?"

"Are you that tired of living?"

"No. I just know we can't leave the Overlord on the battlefield. He needs to be rescued, and I have a perfect plan for it. I just need your help for the final stage. I'm afraid the Taoist's attire might be the end of me. By the way, can the Imperial official's belt be sold? I understand wearing it is impossible, but surely it could serve as a power source for some Master."

"Whoever touches that artifact faces death. That's why even retrieving the body wasn't considered. It's useless."

"What if the belt is destroyed? Like the seeds of wormholes? Or a Seeker's plaque?"

"With a massive energy discharge?" The mentor pondered. "If we bring the body to the wormhole and activate the belt, the energy surge would tear the wormhole apart. But whoever does that will die."

"You mean the belt will explode upon contact with any living being?"

"I don't have that information. Planning to throw an animal at it?"

"Why not? As experience shows, they can be quite useful in operations on this battlefield."

"A good idea, definitely worth considering.

When will you be ready to free the Overlord?"

"Not me. You will have to do it. I'll prepare the body for extraction from the temporal anomaly, but I won't do the extraction myself. The energy will kill me, even with four nodes. The Overlord will be ready by the end of the day. But I'll need a few extra platforms. One needs to be placed directly above the Taoist."

"Let's go. I want to see how you intend to execute your plan with my own eyes."

The mentor lifted one of the platforms with such ease that I felt envious. I definitely couldn't handle such weight right now. Moreover, he acted without any techniques. Just raw strength. We reached the trap where the Overlord was located, and I indicated where to lower the platform. I needed to hover over the temporal anomaly's prisoner to set my plan into action. It was ridiculously simple — why extract the Overlord upside down, when you could lower him to the ground? It turned out to be quite easy. First, I leaned against the Taoist's chest and pressed him down to the stones. The first stick broke. Next, I needed the mentor's help: I pressed on the legs folded together, and the mentor pressed on the upper part of the back. This way, we managed to flip the Taoist vertically. The last step was to press down on the Overlord from above, increasing contact with the stone platform. All that was left after this was to use the services of a tied-up wolf to reduce the volume of the temporal anomaly. When the crossbow bolts fell out, I was again scorched by energy: the bolts turned out to be very powerful artifacts. However, I had a mentor who skillfully used a stick to toss them over into the temporal anomaly with the huge sea monster's carcass inside. The Taoist decided not to risk grabbing unknown artifacts with his hands. We left the battlefield three times, waiting for the agitation to end, and returned three times to reduce the volume of the light yellow jelly until, finally, only one step remained — to extract the Overlord.

"Here," I handed the mentor a stick, calibrated to the last fraction of an inch. Mental absolutes had their advantages, after all — you could create complete blueprints in your mind and work with them. The mentor couldn't do that. Heavens, but it felt good to be able to do something even a diamond-rank master couldn't! It was highly motivating to continue work.

"You have twenty minutes before the anomalies start running. I've marked where you need to stand. I've inserted a leaf into the points where you need to press. The main thing is not to stop. Maybe we should test this with an animal first? I'd spoiled several animals before getting to you."

"Leave," the mentor replied and jumped down from the platform. The Taoist approached the designated spot with such confidence, as if all his life he had done nothing but extract living beings from temporal anomalies. I wanted to stay and watch how it all worked out, but I remembered too well what the Judge's belt had done to me. Hastening, I found myself beyond the platform, and... even at a distance of five hundred feet, I felt a wave of released power. The Golden-ranked Overlord Nurgal Lee was freed.

However, something strange happened — the energy vanished as abruptly as if the Taoists had gotten covered by a temporal anomaly again. The invisible clumps began to move, but then two bolts of lightning flashed over the platform raised above the stone path, materializing into two Taoists. In comparison with Overlord Nurgal Lee, my mentor looked like a youth, yet the Overlord couldn't be called old. I would guess he looked about fifty, no more. Lean, majestic, and powerful. He reminded me of my father, only with way more severity. I thought it wasn't possible to surpass that. I was wrong.

"A demon?" a pleasant low voice inquired, and the force of the Taoist crashed down on me. Resisting it was futile — I was pressed into the ground. It seemed something broke.

"He is a human, Elder. My apprentice, whom I've mentioned to you."

The pressure vanished. I tried to inhale but couldn't — my body refused to function. My mentor's hand descended on my back, and I was pierced by sharp pain — bones snapping back into place. Overlord Nurgal Lee didn't just press me into the ground; he literally smeared me across it. The pain receded, and I felt myself jerked to my feet. Overlord Nurgal Lee was not gentle.

"Yellow eyes. The scent of death. Are you trying to mock me, junior?"

Judging by how my mentor paled, the Overlord had hit him hard with his power. Yet, the Taoist managed to maintain his composure.

"No, Elder. He truly is human. He temporarily became a demon after a complete conjunction with my other apprentice. Who happens to be a demon."

"Complete conjunction? Hmm..."

The Overlord waved his hand, and we found ourselves inside a large tent. The freed Taoist settled into a comfortable chair and propped his head with his hand.

"Judging by what I see, the very demon with whom this young human had achieved complete conjunction is nearby. Junior, take the trouble to bring her here."

"Apprentice, proceed." It seemed the overlord referred to Master Guerlon as the junior, not even recognizing me as a Taoist. Vyllea was still asleep. I wasn't given time to wake her, so I lifted her in my arms and brought her into Elder Nurgal Lee's tent. He paid no mind to us as he listened to Master Guerlon's account. From the conversation about closing the first wormhole, the Taoist decided to share the entire story of how he'd acquired such unusual apprentices. The mentor concealed nothing, recounting how he had delivered Vyllea to the Wang clan, but the leader of Tier Zero refused even to hear of the demon. Our journey to Zou-Lemawn, the exchange of prisoners, their interrogation, the destruction of wormhole coordinators, meeting Vyllea, and the realization that the Heavens themselves had presented him with this trial. The first conjunction, the trek into the Forest of Dandoor, their capture on the battlefield, my near-heroic actions, and, finally, the liberation of the Overlord.

"So, it's you I owe my life to." Elder Nurgal Lee looked my way again, making me exceedingly uncomfortable. "Come closer."

I approached the Overlord on stiff legs, and he placed his hand on me. Streams of energy surged into my body, but before I could grasp their purpose, they vanished.

"A Candidate of the Golden rank. A mental absolute. Acceptable spirit level, but the body is in an abysmal state. However, those four nodes concern me. When did you achieve the Golden rank?"

"Four months ago, Elder," I responded with a bow. How unusual it had become! "I had no choice; I had to act swiftly."

"You weren't asked..." the Overlord began, unleashing his wrath upon me once again, but it immediately dissipated. "What do you mean by 'having no choice'? Clarify."

"When I was left alone, I had to create nodes within myself to survive without healing. One node wasn't enough: there was too much energy near the battlefield. I stopped at four."

"Junior, wake her up," the Overlord commanded, nodding towards Vyllea, and then turned back to me. "Describe the process of creating nodes."

Having already discussed this with the mentor and answered all of his clarifying questions, I could now provide a full explanation of the process of forming nodes. By the time I finished, Vyllea had awakened and sat next to the mentor, too scared to even lift her head.

"Come here," the Overlord ordered her reluctantly. The mentor had to nudge the girl, as she didn't immediately realize she was being addressed. The Taoist hesitated for a long time before deciding to touch the demon, but eventually managed to force himself.

"Acceptable spirit, acceptable body, and a catastrophic mind. Two nascent nodes. Hmm... And yet, their conjunction... What an interesting compensation... Body for mind. But why then... I want to see you perform the union. Lad, work on her foundation and form a node."

"I beg your pardon, Elder, I don't have such a right." I bowed before the overlord. "My mentor..."

I couldn't finish — my world ceased to exist. It simply vanished. When I opened my eyes, I felt terrible pain. For some reason, I was lying on the floor, surrounded by a pool of blood. Next to me stood the mentor, still placing his hand on me. Noticing that I had regained consciousness, he stood up and said, without looking at me:

"Apprentice, when the Elder gives you an order, you must do everything within your power to fulfill that order. Any refusal or excuses will be perceived as an attempt to resist the elder and will be severely punished. You should learn this lesson."

"Thank you for the lesson, mentor." I managed to get to my feet. The overlord was still looking in my direction, so I turned to the mentor and bowed deeply: "Mentor, please lift the ban on working with Vyllea's nodes."

"So, my word is no longer sufficient for you, lad?" It seemed the Overlord freed from the anomaly's clutches even deigned to be surprised. I understood I was being foolish, but could not act otherwise. The Heavens would not forgive such weakness in a Seeker.

"Please forgive this junior, Elder, but you are not my mentor…"

Darkness enveloped me again. When I regained consciousness, Vyllea was lying next to me. From the looks of it, she had suffered greatly, too. One hand of our mentor was on me, and the other, on Vyllea.

"The complete technique for healing demons. You are an endless source of surprises, junior," came the voice of Elder Nurgal Lee. "I want to see the conjunction."

"Yes, elder. My apprentices will demonstrate it. Apprentice Zander, I grant you permission to work on one of apprentice Vyllea's nodes. What do you need?"

"A Bronze-rank Apprentice essence. There's not enough energy here for forming a node."

"Give him a Golden Apprentice," the overlord

demanded. "I understand what that entails. With a Copper Apprentice, he will take too long. And moreover, one node is not enough. A Golden warrior will suffice for three."

The Overlord's tone didn't imply refusal. The mentor handed me the scorching essence, after which I lay down on the floor. Vyllea positioned herself on top of me, and our foreheads touched.

"You'll owe me," I heard her whisper. "When the Overlord punished you the second time, and the mentor just looked away, I was the only one who stood up for you. I told that Taoist everything. That if it weren't for you, he would still be sitting in his anomaly for another two hundred years."

"I owe you," I agreed and closed my eyes. A warmth and pleasantness filled my soul. I knew Vyllea was reckless, but I couldn't even imagine she would defend me in front of the Overlord. I wanted to repay her kindness, and as soon as the warmth began to circulate between us, I reached for the essence's energy. Three nodes? No problem, I'd make it three nodes!

"I see a full bodily union. I see the formative stages of a soul union. But why have you set up a barrier to the mind, lad?" the voice of Elder Nurgal Lee pierced through my concentration. Or was it not concentration? It seemed that the words arose in my head, not interfering with my control of the whirlwinds.

"I get it. You don't know what to do. You don't even know how to talk to me. Astonishing. A self-taught opener. It's the first time I'm seeing something like this. You need to remove the barrier that prevents the circulation of mental energy between you. Concentrate on your head. Find the coldness in it. The body burns. The mind cools. Between you and the cold will be a barrier — you must break it. Proceed!"

To feel the cold? Vyllea even groaned in pain — judging by the Overlord's words, I momentarily lost my concentration. Struggling to regain control over the warm currents and the transfer of energy from the beast's essence into the girl's nodes, I allocated a part of my consciousness to my head. Cold. I needed cold. A cold mind. Act with a cool head. That's what the mentor always told me. Emotions are dangerous and harmful. A Taoist must be calm.

It felt like a huge weight was lifted off my shoulders when I uttered these, seemingly trivial and simple words. My body relaxed, despite the whirlwinds of energy. I had no idea about the cold the overlord spoke of. I didn't feel it anywhere. But, since he required coldness and it was produced by the head, I began to draw invisible streams of coldness, sending them through the circulation cycle. Perhaps I was deceiving myself, but after a while, my invisible hands indeed felt the coolness. To seek its source was as foolish as going against the Overlord, so I simply clung to this stream and pulled it towards me, sending it into Vyllea. The girl groaned — the cold caused pain. However, as soon as it formed a complete circle with my body, the groans ceased.

"Enough," the overlord's voice emerged again. "For a start, that's sufficient. Stabilize the currents. Finish with the nodes."

It seemed Elder Nurgal Lee understood what I was doing perfectly. I ceased to amplify the cold and mixed it with the warmth of body energy. Or, rather, I wove them together — they refused to mix. However, in their intertwined state, the whirlwinds calmed, turning into two energy cords. They stabilized completely on their own, allowing me to focus on Vyllea's nodes, managing three streams simultaneously. By the time the source vanished, three bright spots had lit up in the girl's body. I was about to stop the energy flows, but the overlord didn't allow it.

"Don't interfere — let them circulate. This way, she might become smarter, and you stronger. Now, lad, comes the hardest part. You must unify the conjugated nodes. Form meridians, but not in your body or hers, but between you. Start with one meridian. To your right is an energy source. Take it and act!"

The energy flow that flared up nearby almost blinded me. What the Overlord provided was clearly beyond my capabilities, but, surprisingly, the combined streams of mind and body energy protected us from getting harmed by Qi. Our bodies seemed to be shielded. If this was indeed the case... Huang Lung had detailed the process of forming meridians extensively. Now, with Vyllea and me as one, why not use the knowledge and form what the Overlord had demanded? I scooped up so much energy that I almost burnt my hands. I was screaming in agony, yet even such extreme external reactions of the body couldn't stop my work. I placed everything extracted from the source between Vyllea and me. Exactly between our two identical nodes. Vyllea screamed. I screamed. The world screamed. Yet the meridian wouldn't form. The energy was insufficient. My scream intensified when I dragged a second batch. This time, I enveloped her node with it, stretching the remainder towards mine. Again, it wasn't enough. I had to draw a third portion and wrap my own node with it. At that moment, I understood why Vyllea had quieted down: such monstrous pain had swept over me that my consciousness nearly slipped away. How I managed to stay conscious remained a mystery. Probably, the unwillingness to appear weak in front of the Overlord had something to do with it.

But even the third portion didn't make the meridian work. Energy enveloped both nodes, laying between them, but something was missing. This aimless force looked like fresh snow. Fluffy and useless. No — not snow! Wool gathered from sheep! A huge, shapeless mass, but once it was spun and given form, true wonders could be crafted from it. Just like here! All I needed was to spin the energy. Twirl it so it turned into a thin, saturated thread.

I needed a fourth infusion of borrowed power for the extraction, which I funneled between the nodes. Additionally, a slender stream of energy was used to entwine the fluffy mass of energy between our nodes. The pain gradually subsided until it vanished completely. When half of the structure was formed, the remaining energy coalesced into a fine thread, and both nodes shone with a bright golden light. A third circle of conjunction emerged, but I had no intention of halting there. It was necessary to envelop the inner energy with the external flow completely. Once I was done, a sensation of immense pleasure coursed through my body. Now, it was not only the nodes that glowed, but also the energy thread intertwining them.

"Enough," declared the overlord. "Cease the flows. Now your conjunction can truly be termed complete. Welcome to this amusing world, Candidate of the Diamond rank. Now the two of you have finally piqued my interest."

CHAPTER 14

"JUNIOR, HAD YOU MENTORED OTHERS before encountering this unusual duo?"

"These are my first, Elder. The Heavens had considered me unworthy previously."

"Your concepts of worthiness intrigue me. To what extent must one have vexed the Heavens for them to bestow upon a Seeker a mental absolute with a void in place of a body, along with a demon completely devoid of rational thought? I'm uncertain where to start. Full conjunction isn't unheard of. I am... I was aware of ten such pairings. Yet to achieve such conjunction, Taoists traditionally spent a century in mutual observation. Here, however, two adolescents, barely fifteen, exhibit such profound mutual trust that it facilitates a complete union! And such a match! The human embodies all the intellect, while the demon encompasses all the physicality. Heavens, to whom do I speak this? It's apparent from your expressions that my words are quite beyond your grasp. Are you completely oblivious to your capabilities?"

This inquiry, I surmised, was directed at Vyllea and me, prompting me to shake my head. Vyllea, remaining silent beside me, struggled with the realization of having ascended to the Diamond rank, bypassing Gold. The notion of skipping ranks was as foreign to us as it was to Guerlon.

"Had anyone told me yesterday that today I'd be lecturing a demon, I'd have turned the insolent fool to dust. The Heavens do love to conjure up amusing tricks, playing with our feelings and desires. Well, down to business. What are Candidates? They are individuals beginning to prepare their bodies for future achievements. Not yet Taoists — merely strong humans. Even their rank gradation is more formal than actual. In truth, there's only one rank — Golden, at which a couple of nodes are formed. All the others are superfluous, attributed merely for showcasing progress without bringing any substantial changes to the body. Occasionally, however, a miracle occurs, and geniuses emerge among ordinary people. Those who cannot follow the Taoist path, but who have crossed the boundary of the ordinary human. The Diamond rank. A rank at which a person continues to develop their body, which has hit its limits, becoming comparable to the lower ranks of the Taoists. How does this happen? The answer is clear — through the formation of nodes. A Taoist can form two hundred and fifty-six meridians. For them to function, two hundred and fifty-seven nodes must emerge in the body. These usually complete their formation at the Silver Warrior stage. But here we clearly have an exceptional case. A rarity — about once in ten years, a person is born who can form nodes without the need to tie them with meridians. And these nodes can interact with energy just as the Taoists' meridians do. They cannot store energy — only dispense it, but spirit stones and scrolls with techniques become accessible. In an ideal world, a Diamond-ranked candidate could unlock all their nodes and gain the ability to use Third-Tier techniques without harming their health. But we do not live in an ideal world. A human body cannot withstand the stress created by the nodes. It would disintegrate. Normally. But as I said, that doesn't concern us."

The Overlord paused. A table, a goblet, and a decanter filled with some green liquid appeared beside him. An exquisitely sweet, tart, and simultaneously enticing aroma wafted through the air. While for me, the liquid was merely a pleasantly fragrant one, Guerlon couldn't take his eyes off the decanter. The Overlord took a few sips, clearly pleased with the effect, and continued,

"On the average, a Taoist at the Apprentice stage, whether of Copper or even Bronze rank, needs several weeks to master energy flows and understand the nuances of the technique. The more complex the technique, the more time it takes. Hold hands." The order seemingly was for me and Vyllea. The girl squeezed my hand, and unexpectedly, I felt an unprecedented warmth — as if I touched a kindred soul.

"During your full conjunction, you managed to form a meridian between two nodes. Now you must utilize it and actualize the technique. Execute!" I wanted to protest that there was no meridian between us, but the elder's gaze spelled nothing good. It dawned on me — if I asked any questions about how to do what he demanded, the lesson would end instantly. And in the brief the time the Elder had been with us, I had learned more than in three years with my mentor! Missing out on such an opportunity was not an option!

Why did the Elder command us to hold hands? Why did I feel a strange sense of wholeness as soon as Vyllea's palm was in mine? Spirit vision showed nothing, and it seemed wrong to delve into energy exchange. That would be too obvious, and thus the wrong step. Furthermore, the elder stated it took several weeks to comprehend the intricacies of the technique. But we didn't have several weeks. Results were needed here and now. Nonetheless, it was indeed about technique. The semi-transparent figure of a Taoist, within which a meridian shimmered, reappeared before my eyes. But I was not yet a Taoist — I had no meridian. Nor did Vyllea. Yet it existed between our bodies, or so the Elder claimed. Meanwhile, the technique was designed for one Taoist. But there were two bodies. It seemed I'd found a crucial point. I recalled how our meridian was positioned perfectly. I didn't need to engage in conjunction for that. Two figures appeared next to the semi-transparent figure of the Taoist, lying atop each other. Focusing on the bodies, I first caused all the formed nodes to appear, and then the meridian between two of them. It was challenging — I even broke into a sweat while striving for the image to match exactly what I remembered. Once satisfied with the result, I moved the Taoist's semi-transparent projection next to the lying bodies. The pulsating meridian flared on its own for a while, but soon the one that arose between Vyllea and me began to burn alongside it. They synchronized. I released the girl's hand, and our bodies disappeared. Only the Taoist remained. I took Vyllea's hand again — the bodies reappeared, immediately in the right place and with the pulsating meridian. All that was left was to release the accumulated force, enveloping me and the girl in a thin protective film. It worked!

The Overlord spoke in an irritated voice, "It's taken you too long. You should have finished earlier. Have mental absolutes really degraded so much over the last two hundred years that it takes you this long to learn a simple technique? What is this world coming to... Well, that's your mentor's problem, not mine. My task was to demonstrate the purpose of conjunction. Energy exchange and mutual development are just side effects. The ability to use techniques without formed meridians is the key feature of conjunction. Now, Demon, it's your turn. As I see it, you're following the path of the Tiger? I despise the idea of teaching a demon to open their mind, so let your partner handle that. But it's crucial for you to learn to unlock the cold and let it circulate. It will help you accept your partner's mind and share your skills with them. Figure it out yourselves. I've never taught demons before... And one more thing. Young man, use the technique until the meridian empties."

Creating the spirit armor the second time was significantly easier and quicker. By the tenth attempt, I stopped visualizing the image before my eyes. By the fortieth, I activated the technique with a single act of will. All I needed was physical contact with Vyllea. The depletion of the meridian hit me like a mace — the girl's hand felt foreign, and not just to me — to her as well. We disconnected as quickly as if repulsed by holding each other. It was... an unpleasant experience. I wouldn't want to go through the complete nullification of our invisible meridian again.

"Fifty-three techniques. What do you say, Junior?"

"That's the level of a golden-ranked Apprentice, Elder," came the surprising response, but even more astonishing were the Overlord's words,

"Apprentice? Where have you seen such Apprentices? No, Junior, this is the level of a Copper-ranked Warrior! No issues with the meridian fading, its nullification, or degradation. And notably, they didn't even need a spirit stone for the process. Just physical contact. The energy absorbed during the conjunction had dissipated completely. Yet at the crucial moment, it manifested from what had seemed like complete nothingness. Isn't that a miracle? I studied the conjunction process thoroughly in my time, but I'm still thrilled by the possibilities of those who dare to take such a step. But let me warn you, young man. I see that glint in your eyes. Using a Warrior's techniques will kill you. Without an energy core, they're not just useless — they're mortally dangerous. Until you open all seven threads, you can't move on to the next three plaques. I won't even mention the Master and Overlord. The full technique description constantly tempts low-rank Taoists. It forces them to fight their thirst for knowledge. It's a useful training, especially for a Seeker. Are you planning to follow in your mentor's footsteps, junior?"

"Yes, Elder. Back when we were traveling through the lands of demons, I managed to find a plaque from a fallen Seeker. By returning it, I'll take his place."

"A commendable aspiration. I fully support it. And what are your plans for this life, demon?"

"In the world of humans, conjunction will make me human. Since Zander will become a Seeker, why shouldn't I also..." Vyllea couldn't finish — she collapsed to the floor. The Overlord gestured, and Guerlon, her mentor, bent over his apprentice, restoring her bodily integrity.

"You must respect your elders, demon," the Overlord's voice cracked like a whip.

"My respect must be earned!" Vyllea growled back. "You can't take it by force!"

"You'll owe me." These words flashed through my mind, and before I realized what I was doing, I grabbed Vyllea by the hand and pulled her to me, wrapping her in my arms. Circuit integrity was no longer there, but it wasn't needed: I scooped up half of my body's energy and activated the spirit armor, opting to take the hit myself. Blood trickled from my nose, a fire blazed in my chest, my legs began to buckle, and I leaned on Vyllea. But I achieved what mattered the most — we were covered by the spirit armor. Perhaps that was why the Overlord's strike didn't finish us off. The girl wheezed, we fell to the ground, bones crunched, and pain overwhelmed us, but despite this, we remained conscious.

Mentor Guerlon healed us again, following the Overlord's instructions. It took a bit longer for me — even a spirit stone had to be used. Burning body energy never ended well.

Vyllea and I took each other's hands as we stood up. She had made her choice long ago when she threw herself to protect me, and it was time for me to choose. The mentor had stayed aside. So let the Heavens judge him. We made our choice.

"So, this is how it is," the Overlord grinned unexpectedly. "This is odd. I don't sense any attachment in you. I sense no love. So why are you ready to die for each other?"

"One cannot demand respect, mighty Taoist," Vyllea replied and squeezed my hand as if expecting a blow. "I recognize your power and bow to it, but you are not my lord."

"A demon always remains a demon," the Overlord's voice contained no mockery. He was merely stating a fact. "So, you wish to become a Seeker?"

"I do. Mentor Guerlon has told me a lot about your world. I don't want to get involved in any clan disputes. None of that is of any interest to me. I want to become strong and independent, return home, and advance my tribe to the Third Circle."

"A worthy desire. Well then... You were among those who came to my aid. Though you did nothing yourself, it doesn't negate the fact that you've saved your partner. It was solely because of you that he survived and managed to overcome the temporal anomalies. You want to be a Seeker? So be it. If my memory serves, demons have never achieved this before. It will be interesting to see how you fare."

A Seeker's plaque appeared in the Overlord's hands.

"This is the emblem of one of the greatest Seekers of his time, Overlord Gurpal. Return it to the Phoenix Clan, and you will be exalted, as will the Silver Heron School. The Overlord had once counted among them. They will help you achieve great strength."

"Begging your pardon, Elder, but you'd be

sending my apprentice to her death with a plaque like that," Mentor Guerlon contradicted the Overlord for the first time. "The Silver Heron School no longer exists."

"What do you mean, no longer exists?" Overlord Nurgal Lee was taken aback. "I want details, Junior!"

"Fifty years ago, the Silver Heron School was destroyed by the School of Spirit Power. All students, mentors, and elders were killed. The school's founder was executed by the emperor himself, may his reign last forever."

"My mentor is dead?" For the first time, I saw the Overlord dumbfounded. "A Silver-ranked Nascent God Taoist had been destroyed? How did this happen?! And why are you still alive if the entire school has gotten annihilated?"

"I'm unaware of the details pertaining to the execution, Elder. Only the outcome is known. Now, even mentioning the Silver Heron School can cost a Taoist their head. As for me — I lost the right to bear the Lung name ten years before the attack on the school. My mentor, Overlord Lamik Lung, had personally relieved me from service in the school, sending me off to explore and conquer in the name of the Heavens."

Learning that the man before me had once been an apprentice of Huang Lung and that my mentor had once belonged to the Silver Heron School was quite a revelation. Had I known this right after the Overlord had taught me full conjugation, I would have immediately shared everything I knew about the last days of the great Taoist with him.

But now, the desire was gone. I understood that the younger must always respect the elder and that disobedience should be punished, yet I couldn't shake the feeling that there was a wrongness in all this. I was convinced that Seekers, who prided themselves on their freedom, should interact without all these formalities. Otherwise, it seemed that they were only all about freedom in front of outsiders — when it came to interactions within their group, they demanded strict obedience and adherence to ceremony. Wasn't this hypocrisy?

As for Mentor Guerlon... I certainly wouldn't be sharing the secret of Huang Lung's cache with him. It was Vyllea who'd stood up for me — not he. He'd yielded to the power of the ancient Seeker, allowing him to do whatever he wished with us. But it was up to the Heavens to judge him. The only living being worthy of the founder of the Silver Heron School's secret was the one holding my hand. Even though Vyllea had been utterly terrified, her pride wouldn't allow her to bend even to the Overlord.

Because, as the demons always said, once you became a servant or a slave, you could never return to the caste of lords.

"The School of Spirit Power, then," Nurgal Lee muttered slowly. "Chen Feng, a Silver-ranked Nascent God... A worthy enemy. And favored by the Heavens, it appears. Junior, this demon must become a Seeker."

"As the Elder commands," nodded Mentor Guerlon. "I'll make sure she grows into one."

"When are you returning to the Third Tier?"

"In a year, Elder. That's how much longer my voluntary exile in the lands of demons will last. Even though the goal of my training has already been reached, leaving them unmonitored is not an option. They're not ready for freedom yet."

"In a year, they'll only be sixteen. So, they'll spend at least another three years in Tier Zero. Not good. We need to act now. But they'll get killed... We need resources..."

The Overlord's habit of thinking out loud was confusing. The Taoist sank into thought for a while, and finally made a decision.

"Alright, you have a year. Your task, Junior, is to prepare your apprentices so they can stand against any First-Tier Apprentice. I don't think they'll send a Warrior after this pair. Even the Executors of Fate won't be able to solve such a problem right away. In a year, I will reveal myself to the world. By that time, your apprentices must have at least thirty nodes and the meridians between them opened. Do not let them open more than three nodes a week. It's dangerous. And don't you dare to form meridians in their bodies. That can only be done in the First Circle. Now, about the techniques."

The bound planks were brought into use again.

"The full techniques aren't necessary; we'll

limit ourselves to Apprentice-level material. I believe the classic set will suffice: Spirit Arrow, Steps, and Support. They already possess the Spirit Armor. For survival in Tier Zero or even the First Tier, this is more than enough. Figure out a way to pass on the spirit stones to them. Each of the conjugated meridians will require a golden rank Apprentice-stage stone. I will now destroy this battlefield, and in a year, when I reveal myself to the world, I will announce that the wormhole was closed by me, accompanied by Master Guerlon and his apprentices. I want to see who starts squirming. When you return to the Third Tier, find me. I will assign you a new task. That should be enough for you. Now gather your belongings and leave. I'm giving you two days to leave the impact zone. What is it, junior? Your face looks like you want to ask something. Go ahead. Your pair is so unusual that I won't even be angry with you."

"Is the Elder a mental absolute? Does he also see temporal traps?"

"A mental absolute?" the Overlord chuckled. "No, junior. This Elder is not a mental absolute. This Elder is a pure absolute. Now leave. I need to meditate. The fight with the Judge drained much of my energy. I hope I don't need to say that everything you learned today must stay within this tent? The world is not yet ready for the news that the Executors of Fate have played their hand too far and no longer deal in the fates of individuals. They are now interested in dictating the fates of entire clans, tiers, and even worlds. Junior, be cautious if you encounter an imperial official on your path. I suspect you're not the only one who traffics with demons."

CHAPTER 15

"ZANDER, HOW DID YOU SURVIVE while we were stuck in the anomaly? Need a hand, or can you get up on your own?"

"Shut up, Vyllea," I responded, attempting to rise from the ground. It was futile. The demoness had thrashed me so thoroughly that my arms, legs, and body felt like mincemeat. It was a bitter pill to swallow, but the damn girl had indeed become stronger than me — in everything. Handling the jian, endurance, speed, and hand-to-hand combat. Vyllea truly worked miracles in the latter, even managing to hold her ground against the mentor. Not for long, of course, just until he employed speeds beyond a normal human's capability, but still, her performance was impressive.

"Oh, what's this? Will the angry Taoist punish

the poor demon?" the demoness smirked.

"Stop it already," the mentor interjected, his voice carrying a note of fatigue. Six months in the company of two teenagers, one of whom did nothing but argue and act contrary could exhaust anyone. I got the impression that the mentor regretted taking the unruly girl on as an apprentice a hundred times over, but it was too late to back out now.

We settled near the bay that once was the fearsome and dangerous Forest of Dandoor. Overlord Nurgal Lee didn't hold back and destroyed everything within reach. That meant the battlefield, the forest, all the beasts, and even a vast portion of the land. So much energy lingered in the air after the great Taoist's work that letting such a gift from the Heavens go to waste would have been a sin. Meditation, training, sparring, and healing — and then start again from the top. Mentor Guerlon made us work sixteen hours a day. I grew to loathe my fifteenth birthday with every fiber of my being; that day — the "celebration" was so intense that I passed out about ten times.

In theory, such a regimen was supposed to turn me into the strongest Taoist of our time, but reality proved quite harsh. My physical condition still left a lot to be desired. The last time I managed to land a hit on that annoying girl was before pulling her out of the temporal anomaly. Conjunction undoubtedly made me stronger, but compared to Vyllea, I was less than a child — I was a mere embryo! Much as I regretted to admit it, she outclassed me in every aspect.

It seemed logical that if my body was weak, my mind and spirit should compensate, but here too I encountered a setback that Overlord Nurgal Lee hadn't warned me about. It turned out the limitation of opening three nodes per week was not for the person being operated on, but for the operator. After opening three nodes for myself and doing the same for Vyllea, I nearly died. It was the first time the demoness had to take control of the energies, stopping them, severing the connection, and running for the mentor. I remained out of circulation for two weeks, and then I couldn't enter into conjunction properly for about a month. So, in half a year, I'd only managed to open fifteen nodes, and could only wrap ten of them with meridians. However, there was a silver lining: even ten meridians were enough for Vyllea and me to start using techniques. And while Spirit Armor and Spirit Arrow were quite standard defensive and offensive techniques, Steps and Support were something incredible. Steps allowed us to accelerate and move to another location at high speed. Considering we could use the technique fifty-three times in a row, it was very powerful indeed. Now, even if a hypothetical Warrior from the Second Tier attacked me and Vyllea, they would have to work hard to catch us. Unless the Warrior in question knew the next place we'd hop to, of course... Come to think of it, it would be better if no Warrior ever attacked us. But we could definitely escape from any Apprentice, even a Diamond-ranked one.

Support enabled us to move along vertical walls, turning us into proficient climbers. Again, we could do fifty-three repetitions, and if used continuously, one could scale a rather high mountain in one go this way. However, each of the movement techniques, whether in horizontal or vertical direction, required Vyllea and me to work in sync. It was challenging initially — either I would surge ahead too quickly, or she would. Mastering the movements required practice, and often ended with the need for urgent healing.

Another significant development that happened over these six months was my acquaintance with the Tiger Style. Not the interpretation demonstrated by Mentor Guerlon, but the fundamentals Vyllea had learned from the beasts. She never managed to open her mind to me as Overlord Nurgal Lee had required, so I had to act independently. I couldn't even see or understand my own block, let alone how to fully remove it (I had to forcibly draw out the cold from my head every time during conjunction), so finding some semblance of mind in my partner was an even harder task. I had to remove the cold from her head by force, too, which was a singularly complex task — I'd never achieve success immediately. It was painful, too — when there was so little mind to begin with, sharing it with another wasn't the best idea. Vyllea gasped and suffered, but endured. However, surprisingly, such harsh treatment bore fruit — a month ago, the girl had managed to play a simple tune on the pipa without a single mistake for the first time. As for me... I didn't even know how to explain it... I began to understand better why I kept losing. I wouldn't twist my leg or arm right, or block the attack properly. I still analyzed every lost fight, but now I only saw my own mistakes. I had reached the limits of my body — it physically couldn't keep up with Vyllea. Not even the pills Mentor Guerlon fed me helped. They had no effect anymore — the simple ones didn't work on me, and the more serious ones required meridians.

Regardless, we were disastrously behind the schedule set by the Overlord. I couldn't possibly form another fifteen nodes and wrap them with meridians over the remaining six months, after which time Mentor Guerlon would leave us. No way. Especially since the mentor declared unexpectedly,

"I believe the world of demons has given us all it could. We're returning home."

"Not everyone here considers the world of humans home," Vyllea couldn't resist butting in, but Mentor Guerlon had stopped paying attention to his apprentice's snide remarks. Once, he had said, "Reeducating a demon is just spoiling it," and thereafter ignored any signs of disrespect. The Heavens themselves would decide when someone will come along to shorten Vyllea's sharp tongue.

"Mentor, shall we go through Zou-Lemawn?" I asked as the Taoist tucked the tents into his spatial wallet. "Won't they be waiting for us there?"

"They doubtlessly will be," the Taoist pulled out a self-moving carriage and climbed into the driver's seat. "It irritates me enormously that Master Nars-Go Li didn't keep his word. He had promised to destroy me, after all, and what was the result? Not a single demon showed up near the suddenly-vanished Forest of Dandoor. Six months have passed; someone should have taken an interest in what's happened here. But no! No one cares! And that includes Vyllea's former mentor. So, I sincerely hope he arranges a warm welcome for us in Zou-Lemawn. He might even hire mercenaries. Demons have mercenaries, too, don't they, apprentice?"

"Demons have adopted many vile practices from humans. Including that one," Vyllea replied.

"So it's a safe bet to say a well-prepared group led by an Overlord of Copper, or even Bronze rank, will be waiting for us in Zou-Lemawn,"

"You talk about it so lightly..." I was astonished.

"Avoiding danger is only commendable in one instance, apprentice, and that is when you set off to seek out even greater danger. Without formidable enemies, progress is impossible. The Heavens have no use for the weak. Besides, I gave my word to deliver Vyllea to Zou-Lemawn by a certain deadline. Remember, apprentices — a Seeker must never break their word. If a Seeker is not sure they can keep it, it's better not to give it at all. The Heavens deal harshly with oath breakers."

"But you couldn't have known Vyllea would achieve the Diamond rank..."

"I couldn't have. And yet, she did."

"Thanks to Overlord Nurgal Lee."

"That's irrelevant, apprentice. A promise has been made, and a promise has been kept. Vyllea became a Diamond-ranked Candidate. The path she took to get there by the deadline does not matter. Only the result does."

"But..." I wanted to object, but decided against it. One thing I'd definitely learned during three and a half years with my mentor was that he couldn't be swayed. If he decided that the Heavens willed it, he'd follow a specific course of action unswervingly. The fact that it took a miracle for Vyllea and me to achieve the Diamond rank had nothing to do with the Heavens. It was unlikely they'd compelled Overlord Nurgal Lee to train two demons.

"So, we head to Zou-Lemawn," the mentor concluded. "I'm sure we'll have some very interesting encounters there. Get in; we're wasting time."

"I often wonder — are all humans like this, or did we just get lucky?" Vyllea whispered, settling on my lap. I didn't intend to respond to rhetorical questions, so I just hugged her and closed my eyes. If I remembered the map correctly, it would take several weeks, if not a month, to reach Zou-Lemawn. Such a gift from the Heavens should be fully utilized. Throughout our time in the demon world, I learned one thing: I loved sleep, and sleep loved me. Ours was a mutual but, unfortunately, oft-separated love. We had to love each other from a distance, only reuniting briefly on rare occasions. I wasn't planning to waste even a minute of sweet communion with my beloved. And no amount of jolting could interfere with that.

It took four weeks for the walls of Zou-Lemawn to appear on the horizon. Although we had once lived in this city for four months, we had never seen it from the demon world's perspective. Therefore, the presence of a huge tent city near the walls was a surprise to me — and, apparently, not just to me.

"Have the tribes of the entire Circle Zero gathered here?" Vyllea frowned. "And it's not just them. Those two flags belong to the tribes of the First Circle. What are they doing here? They're supposed to be under our tribe's command. Did some war break out here while we were training?"

"War? No, Apprentice Vyllea, there hasn't been a war here yet. They're only preparing for one. Apprentice Zander, any thoughts on what's happening here?"

"Training is what's happening here, Elder. The tent city seemed unified at first glance, but a closer look reveals borders between separate areas. Each has a small plaza, and there are folks training almost everywhere. And it's not group against group, but one-on-one. There's a younger demon fighting an adult demon... This is... unbelievable! Are they preparing for a tournament?"

"One that's set to begin in five days," our mentor confirmed. "It has all turned out quite interestingly. What was initially planned as harmless entertainment has evolved into a full-scale clash between various tribes. Given the presence of First Circle representatives, the rules have been changed, allowing participants of lower ranks to compete. I assume there are just as many tents around Zou-Lemawn in the human world. Demons will be demons..."

"You knew?! You knew what was happening here! That was why you hurried us, right?" Vyllea exclaimed.

"Let's say I suspected," our mentor nodded, and the carriage moved forward again. "Well, let's see who's gathered here. Zander, I need a complete report. Mention everyone who remains opaque to you. We need to understand how many Masters and Overlords have come to Zou-Lemawn."

My spirit vision was confidently nearing a mile. The mentor deliberately moved slowly, allowing those gathered to take a good look at us. Judging by the shocked glances, we were quite the sight. Not only were two teenage demons riding calmly next to a formidable human, but the boy was constantly whispering something to the Taoist; besides, the teenagers sat provocatively close, as only a couple deeply in love, with relationships formalized by all the rules of the demon world, could sit.

There were few Master demons in the tent

city. I only managed to find four black figures, and they were near the flags Vyllea identified as belonging to the First Circle tribes. However, demons weren't strong because of their Masters alone. In every camp, there was at least one Warrior, sometimes two. In total, I counted thirty-seven Warrior stage demons on just one side of the city wall! As we approached Zou-Lemawn, the number of Warriors inside the walls made me tense. It seemed every tenth demon in the city was a Warrior! To even mention the ten Masters I could spot within Zou-Lemawn's walls was unnecessary. Mentor Guerlon was right — we were in for some extremely interesting encounters.

Our mentor's spirit armor had long since covered both Vyllea and me. He couldn't trust ours. No one touched us as we approached the city gates. They glanced over, whispered, and even followed us, but didn't engage. The four Masters I had detected outside Zou-Lemawn's walls were now standing nearby. The tents obscured them, but there was no doubt: if any trouble started, they would rush to defend the city. After all, they were Masters, and there were four of them. They could easily deal with any trespasser daring to enter the demon city.

"The purpose of your visit to Zou-Lemawn, human?" A squad of guards blocking the gate confronted us.

"Participation in the tournament," the mentor replied calmly.

"Humans are forbidden from..." the guard

began but stopped short, noticing us. Vyllea and I certainly didn't appear human at that moment.

"Has Overlord Shang Li arrived already?" The mentor asked as if in passing. "Inform him that Seeker Guerlon has arrived."

"Seeker Guerlon?" It seemed the guard almost choked upon hearing the name. "May I see the plaque?"

"Will you mind if I don't hand it over?" The mentor smiled and showed the demon the plaque. The guard's face paled as he leaned in to read the name on it.

"Welcome to Zou-Lemawn, Founder," the guard stepped back and bowed.

"Founder?" The mentor's face expressed surprise. "Now, I'd like to hear more about this."

"The Zou-Lemawn tournament has grown into a major event drawing demon Candidates from across Circle Zero, as well as the First and even Second Circles. Every month, the tournament determines the top ten, who then compete annually for the title of the best demon. Zou-Lemawn has become one of the most popular places in Circle Zero, growing and developing, but none of it would have been possible without the Founder. The one who laid the foundation for the tournaments. Seeker Guerlon. You are granted the right of unimpeded entry and exit from the city at any time you choose. A decree to this effect has been signed by three Overlords. Moreover, the tournament rules include a clause allowing your students to participate in the final stage. That's what you're here for, aren't you?"

"Of course."

"I must warn you, Founder. The winners determined eleven months ago were at the Candidate stage, but they have continued their ascension since. Many have reached the Apprentice rank, yet they still have the right to participate in the final tournament, as they won it as Candidates. Such are the rules."

"Thank you. Do I need some kind of identification to show I'm in Zou-Lemawn officially? I wouldn't want to cause any conflicts."

"No, founder, no signs are needed. Fools who attack a guest of the city will be responsible for their own deaths. Zou-Lemawn will have no complaints. This, too, is stated in the tournament rules."

"Such well-thought-out rules," the mentor smiled. "One last question. In which world does the tournament take place?"

"Where you founded it. The tournament will be held on the other side."

Not "in the human world," but "on the other side." Were demons already considering our world theirs? Wasn't it a bit early for that? The guards stepped aside, letting us into the city. The prickling sensation between my shoulder blades sharpened — someone very powerful was displeased by what had happened. Yet, no one attacked. Apparently, the guards here held a high status, and whoever attacked them got punished.

The problems started almost immediately: the

city was overcrowded with demons, and it was impossible to move forward with the carriage. Sure, we could have run everyone over, disregarding their status, as if to deliver the message that it was the victims' fault for being too slow to clear the way for their betters, but the mentor decided to proceed on foot. In the four months we had spent in Zou-Lemawn, we never got to visit its demon world side. We were now filling in that gap in our experience.

"Wow!" Vyllea suddenly exclaimed, stopping near one of the shop windows. Judging by the sign and the merchandise, it was a women's clothing store. "That thing's beautiful!"

I approached to get a better look. Vyllea couldn't take her eyes off a training dress. Or not exactly a dress. It resembled a classic kimono, but even a cursory glance made it clear: this was attire for girls. No boy I knew would be seen dead wearing something like this.

"Mentor! I want it!"

"If you want it, buy it," the Taoist replied calmly, without even turning towards the display.

"I need thirty spirit coins!"

"So? What does that have to do with me, apprentice? My job is to provide you with the essentials — to wit, weapons, food, and clothing. You have all these. If you want something new as a personal possession, nobody's stopping you from buying it. Just make sure it's practical for you."

"I don't have any coins! You know that!"

"I do. But I fail to see why you think I should

be the one to fix this oversight."

"My mother will reimburse the expenses!"

"Do you have the right to manage your tribe's finances?" The mentor even looked at Vyllea. She frowned. "I thought not. No, apprentice. I won't buy you this useless item. It's impractical. The fabric is too cheap, the design too elaborate, and there are way too many extraneous details that could hinder in a fight. If you want this dress that much, you can buy it yourself."

"I hate you!" Vyllea grumbled at the back of the Taoist, who had ended the conversation decisively and moved on. "When I become an Overlord, I'll destroy that show-off! No, I'll devour his cores! I definitely will devour them! This is my word as a scion of the Urbangos tribe!"

Vyllea remained silent for the rest of the way. She didn't even glance at the displays, though there were plenty of interesting things to see. Zou-Lemawn had changed drastically. It had evolved from a backwater borderland town to one of Circle Zero's major trade centers. I had never seen so many high-stage ascension demons in one place before. Here and there, skirmishes broke out — the temperamental demons got into fights over any trifle. Someone looked the wrong way, someone breathed incorrectly, someone just didn't like someone else's look. We were left untouched. A human calmly wandering through the city was intimidating because of their unknown status. Or perhaps we were left alone because of the squad of guards that had been following us from the gates.

Either way, we reached the palace without incident.

"Thirteen black silhouettes," I reported as we approached the city center. My back was not just prickling — it was burning. It was dangerously unsafe here, and I disliked how calmly the Taoist was walking into what seemed like a trap. The mentor nodded, acknowledging he had heard the information, and then approached the main gates. They opened immediately — we were expected. A demon in a fine black suit came out to meet us.

"Seeker Guerlon, on behalf of the city mayor, I welcome you to Zou-Lemawn. We were expecting you in two days, so your quarters have not yet been prepared. Elder, the city mayor bows before you and humbly asks you to stay in the guest room. Your quarters will be ready for habitation within five hours at most."

"I accept the junior's apologies and agree to the proposal of temporary accommodation," the mentor replied, with such pomposity that Vyllea and I exchanged looks. Such behavior was never previously observed from the Taoist. We were led to a huge room — a two-bedroom suite with two bathrooms.

"Elder, you may rest from the journey and freshen up. Dinner with Overlord Shang Li is scheduled in three hours. I humbly ask for your forgiveness, but you are not permitted to eat until then, as per Overlord Shang Li's directive."

"Apprentices, this bathroom is mine," the mentor turned away from the demon, without bothering to respond to his words. "I plan to spend the next three hours in there. Manage your time in the second bathroom yourselves. Junior, why are you still here? Be gone."

Vyllea locked herself in the bathroom for two hours, declaring she needed it because she was a girl. When I went in after her, I growled in annoyance: the demons only had regular bathtubs. There wasn't a hint of an artifact in sight. The bathroom smelled of dirty water. I had to refill the tub anew, thankfully having learned to use the plumbing. All of this took time, so when they came for us, my hair hadn't dried yet. Gathering it into a bundle and feeling relieved that my kimono, albeit worn, remained clean, I followed the mentor.

We were led to a vast hall where all thirteen black figures were present. Along with the masters and overlords, several warriors were there, including Almyrda, Vyllea's mother. Upon our entrance, the demons stopped their chatter. Their gazes turned towards us, and I nearly ran away — their desire to kill us was that apparent. Overlord Shang Li was at the head of the table.

"Welcome, junior. I'm glad you didn't rush and try to break through to your world elsewhere. Please, have a seat. Your apprentices may stand by the wall."

Ah, so they weren't inviting us to sit at the table. Fine, we'd survive if we skipped a meal — it wouldn't be for the first time.

"Thank you, Elder," Mentor Guerlon bowed

and took the only vacant seat. As he looked at the demons continuing to glare at him, the Taoist said, "Which one of them, Elder? And what are the terms?"

"Is it all so obvious?" A chagrined grimace appeared on the Overlord's face. "I thought this would be a surprise for you."

"Besides you, elder, I see two more Overlords here. I also see ten Masters, who are their apprentices. Five each. I didn't come here to exchange pleasantries with the weak, elder. I came here to kill them. I hope the rules of your tournament don't forbid this?"

"No, junior. They do not. There is just one small clarification. It applies to your apprentices as well. There will be two fights. Ten Golden-ranked Master demons against you and one hundred and ten Candidate and Apprentice stage demons against your apprentices. The only way for you to leave Zou-Lemawn is as victors. That is my word."

"I have a counter-clarification, Overlord. Ten Golden-ranked Masters are dust under my feet. I would like something more challenging. Such as, for example, fighting these two nameless Overlords sitting on either side of you, neither of whom merits an iota of my respect. Let them step up with their apprentices and show the world of demons what they and the tribes that sent them here really are: weak and useless. As for my own apprentices, I feel somewhat offended on their behalf. One hundred and ten Candidate and Apprentice stage trash? Against my duo? You might as well have brought in ordinary demons to make the crowd bigger. Elder, I request you to find ten Silver-ranked Apprentices you no longer care for and add them to the one hundred and ten future corpses you've mentioned earlier. The weak have no place in this world, Overlord Shang Li. My apprentices and I are ready to prove it."

"So be it, Seeker Guerlon. Win, and I will call you equal, despite the difference in ascension levels. Bring chairs for the Seeker's apprentices! The condition set by their mentor allows them to take their place among us. Or does anyone have objections?"

There were no objections. When the food was served, I was astonished at how the realization that I might die in five days affected the taste. The food was magnificent! Yet, for some reason, only four of those present ate — namely, Overlord Shang Li, Seeker Guerlon, and his two apprentices. For some reason, none of the rest had any appetite. Well, it was their problem. That simply left more of those assorted delicacies for us.

CHAPTER 16

"SEEKER GUERLON, I SEE you have enjoyed my dinner. I'd like something of equal value in return. How about an interesting story? They say human Seekers are masters of the spoken word, and the chance to converse with a still-living human, not strapped to a torture table, is exceedingly rare in our parts."

Overlord Shang Li leaned back in his chair, signaling the end of the meal. A pity! There was a plate with a few pieces of royal pudding left in front of me. I had never tasted anything even a tenth as delicious and satisfying as this dessert in my entire life, so I attacked it with unabashed fervor. Vyllea didn't lag behind, and we engaged in a competition — who could eat more. Naive girl! No one could compete with me in consuming sweets! At least in this I managed to defeat the brat! But our feast was cut short: servants rushed in, and the table was quickly cleared.

"As the Elder wishes. What story would you like to hear? About how Overlord Lurth Mink had his rear end presented to him on a plate after a duel? How we conquered the Forest of Dandoor? How the battlefield with temporal anomalies was destroyed? Or about how the Forest of Dandoor was subsequently erased from the face of the planet completely?"

"What nonsense is this?" unexpectedly spoke one of the unnamed overlords. "Three days ago, I met with Overlord Lurth Mink personally! He was alive and well! Elder, why do you make us listen to the ramblings of this man?"

Overlord Shang Li frowned.

"As far as I know, Seekers consider lying unacceptable. I myself saw Overlord Lurth Mink a month ago. I would like to hear the details, Seeker Guerlon."

"There are rumors of a special bond among demons who are blood relatives that allows them to discern whether one is telling the truth or lying. Is that so?"

"Yes, it's true. But I don't see the relevance of this question," Overlord Shang Li was losing patience.

"Among those gathered here, I see Almyrda, chief of the Urbangos tribe. Apprentice Vyllea, tell your mother about the battle between me and Overlord Lurth Mink."

"Yes, mentor." Vyllea blushed. "But there's

not much for me to tell, really. It happened about a year ago. Zander and I were about to head to the training grounds to level up..."

"The Zou-Karteen Training Ground?" Almyrda clarified. Vyllea nodded, and her mother frowned. "Why together? That training ground is for Silver-ranked Candidates."

"That's irrelevant to the discussion," Overlord Shang Li interjected. "Continue, junior."

"So there we are about to leave, but unexpectedly, Overlord Lurth Mink shows up at this very moment. My future mentor had just destroyed some city, so he came for revenge. I didn't see the fight itself; they were moving too fast for me to see anything. I can say it lasted only a minute. When they stopped flashing around like lightning, my future mentor was standing over the fallen overlord, contemplating what to do. He had severed the Overlord's leg, but then reattached it. Overlord Lurth Mink was lucky my Taoist mentor had the complete technique for healing demons. For some reason, the Taoist decided not to finish off the opponent, but let him go. He even healed him enough so he could leave on foot. And off he went. Walking."

"She's not lying," Almyrda said, astonished, as the demons' gazes concentrated on the Urbangos tribe leader.

"Regrettably, elder, my apprentice has made an unforgivable mistake and will be punished for it. The fight didn't last a minute. It lasted twenty-seven seconds."

B O O K   T W O

"Oh! I completely forgot! Before letting the Overlord go, the mentor took his weapon, rings, amulets, and spatial pouch!" Vyllea exclaimed. Ignoring the ascension stages of those present so casually could play a cruel joke on her sooner or later, but at that moment, no one paid attention.

The room fell into silence. Overlord Shang Li clearly didn't know about the incident. But how could that be, especially since Vyllea's former mentor was supposed to report everything to him? It seemed I wasn't the only one thinking this.

"Elder, forgive me, but didn't my former mentor report this to you? The Golden-ranked Master Nars-Go Li had left me in the care of this human and headed straight to you to report the attack of Overlord Lurth Mink on him and the demons of the Urbangos tribe."

"The Golden-ranked Master Nars-Go has been a personal apprentice of Overlord Lurth Mink for a year now," one of the unnamed Overlords informed us. Even Vyllea had the sense to keep quiet and not voice the obvious fact — one of Overlord Shang Li's inner-circle disciples had betrayed him and switched his allegiance to Overlord Lurth Mink.

"Do you still have Lurth Mink's possessions? Have you looked into his spatial pouch?" Judging by his tone, Overlord Shang Li was barely holding back his anger. The mere fact he referred to another Overlord by name, without mentioning his ascension stage, and in the presence of witnesses, was tantamount to an open declaration of war.

"I'm not well-versed in the art of artificing, Elder," Master Guerlon stood up and walked around the table to Overlord Shang Li. "Besides, I had no intention of delving into the possessions of someone as unworthy as that character. He showed no remarkable qualities during the fight, so I doubt there's anything of interest in his spatial pouch. Please accept this as a token of my gratitude for such a refined dinner. It was truly splendid."

The spoils taken from Overlord Lurth Mink appeared in Mentor Guerlon's hands all of a sudden. Overlord Shang Li grabbed the spatial pouch and closed his eyes. An unpleasant smell of burnt flesh followed, and then a snap. The demon broke the artifact's binding, apparently. He placed a set of brightly-red garments on the table.

"The ceremonial outfit of an Overlord," came the astonished voice of the demon who claimed my mentor was spouting nonsense. "A month ago, Overlord Lurth Mink was seen without it..."

"You said it took you twenty-seven seconds, Seeker?" Overlord Shang Li looked at the Taoist.

"Unfortunately, yes, Elder. Lurth Mink was running away too fast. Besides, that was a year ago. I've grown significantly stronger since then."

"Take your seat, Seeker. The spoils are rightfully yours. I've removed the binding."

Overlord Shang Li returned the spatial pouch to the Taoist, but kept the rings and amulets for himself, presumably along with a pile of other interesting items that were in Lurth Mink's storage. However, Mentor Guerlon paid no attention to this and calmly took his seat.

"I liked your story. But I want more. The Forest of Dandoor. What about it?"

"It no longer exists, Elder. It had to be destroyed. Ditto the battlefield with temporal anomalies. Though I must admit — in that affair, my apprentices deserve more credit than I. It was their training assignment, and they handled it. I acted mostly as a supervisor."

"Two Candidates destroyed the Forest of Dandoor?" The unnamed Overlord exclaimed in shock again but was silenced by Overlord Shang Li's gaze.

"Well, if the destruction of the forest is the juniors' merit, I'd like to hear their story again. If you will, junior."

Overlord Shan Li was addressing Vyllea, not me. Apparently, to have Almyrda confirm or refute her daughter's words.

"After the Taoist let Overlord Lurth Mink go, we headed to the forest. That was where the mentor showed us a map, pointed somewhere, and said he'd wait for us at that point. Zander said he understood how to get there, and off we went. On the way, we encountered a Silver-ranked tiger, and I accidentally consumed its essence. This caused me to lose control of my consciousness for a while. When I came to, we were in a tree. Spiders had dragged us there. We'd killed a couple, but staying inside the tree was impossible. The energy there was burning us from the inside. We had to leave the spiders alive and get down from the tree. Then, the mentor found us and punished us. Apparently, he didn't like the fact that we'd killed too few spiders. The Taoist was greatly upset and took his anger out on the tree. He later told us the tree was fed by an item called the Heart of the Ocean. But I never saw it myself, so I cannot confirm it."

"The Heart of the Ocean is a fairy tale!" Exclaimed the impulsive overlord. Where did he even come from?

"My daughter has told the truth! I swear on the honor of the tribe!" Pride for her daughter resonated in Almyrda's voice so much she seemed ready to burst. Overlord Shang Li stared at our mentor for a long time, as if deciding how to proceed. Finally, he asked,

"Tell me, Seeker, does the Heart of the Ocean truly exist? Is it in your possession?"

"Yes, Elder. It does. And it is."

"And you can demonstrate a Nascent God level item here and now?"

"Of course. But before I do, I request that my apprentices be sent away. I've grown accustomed to this pair, and I wouldn't want them to burn up. I don't care about any of the others here, but I'm confident that Overlord Shang Li can subdue the power of such a source."

"Your words have been heeded, Seeker. What happened next, junior?" The overlord asked after a brief pause.

"Next, I found myself in a temporal anomaly, elder. The mentor pulled me out, and then the

Forest of Dandoor became transformed into a beautiful bay, along with the battlefield. I don't know how this was achieved — Zander and I were meditating at that moment."

"Pray pardon me, but how could two Diamond-ranked Candidates defeat a Silver-ranked tiger?" The second Overlord frowned. That was the one trying to keep himself in check. Apparently, it didn't work that well.

"The tiger was defeated by techniques!" Vyllea declared. "And I finished it off when I ripped the essence from its still-living body! And when I did that, I was at the Bronze rank!"

"My... my daughter speaks the truth." Almyrda's eyes were like two large saucers, while I was amazed at how Vyllea had manipulated the facts. The tiger was indeed killed by techniques. Spider techniques. And she did indeed finish it off by ripping out the essence from a still-living body. It seems I began to understand what the mentor had in mind. Vyllea belonged to that breed of demons who would claim any victory for themselves. She wouldn't mention the freed Seeker in her story because it would tamper with her narrative. So she chose her words in such a way as to seem much stronger than she actually was. As for our mentor... He wanted to defeat the opponent before the fighting would even begin. To destroy them not just physically, but psychologically as well.

"This is impossible! I sense a lie!" The more tempestuous Overlord was clearly out of sorts.

"Even assuming the Seeker has told us the truth about defeating Overlord Lurth Mink and managed to prove it, the notion that a Bronze Candidate has used techniques to defeat a Silver-ranked tiger is a blatant lie!"

"The Elder accuses me of lying?!" Vyllea flared up and jumped to her feet. "I can prove my words right here and right now!"

"How will you do that, junior?" Overlord Shang Li's voice was so cloyingly sweet it made my skin crawl with foreboding.

"You see through me and Zander completely. You see we only have nodes. No meridians. No spirit stones. Elder, I request permission to attack the one who didn't believe my words with a Spirit Arrow!"

"You want to attack a demon of the Overlord stage?" It seemed everyone was taken aback by such audacity.

"Would that be dangerous for him?" Vyllea wondered. "Can't he block a Diamond-ranked Candidate's attacks without breaking a sweat?"

Silence fell in the room again. Even to me, who was far from the higher echelons of power in the demon world, it was clear that Vyllea had earned herself several death sentences. She wasn't struck down only because she needed to survive until the tournament to provide amusement for the crowd. But even I did not expect such audacity, accustomed as I was to my partner being somewhat unhinged. She didn't care who was in front of her — they could be a Warrior, a Master,

BOOK TWO

or an Overlord. She acted as her mind suggested. Which, as I knew better than anyone in the world, was hardly her strongest feature. *"Why are you so fearless, Vyllea?"* — *"Because I don't have the brains to be scared..."*

"Using spirit stones is prohibited. Healing you if you burn out your body's energy is prohibited. If you want to die now, that's your choice. I give you permission to attack me," declared Overlord Shang Li.

"I didn't say that I would be the one to attack, Elder. I said it would be a Diamond Candidate. Zander, give me your hand!"

With the tacit consent of those gathered, I stood up, and our fingers intertwined.

"The Elder knows what complete conjugation is, I presume?"

The Overlord nodded, and his eyes narrowed. It seemed it was only then that he realized why I looked like a demon, not a human.

"Zander, we've been given permission to attack. Shall we try to kill Overlord Shang Lee? When else will such a chance arise?"

"Let's," I smiled and extended my hand towards the Overlord. The first Spirit Arrow flew off and vanished, not reaching the target by more than three feet. But I wasn't going to stop: perhaps the Heavens would make the Overlord slip up, and one of my strikes would land? But the demon made no mistake, and all the spirit arrows evaporated in the air. When I used the technique for the fiftieth time, Vyllea said,

255

"Okay, Zander, that's enough. I think that's more than enough to show how we survived in the Forest of Dandoor. You can't breach the defense. Enough!"

I managed to launch three more arrows while she spoke. The meridian zeroed out, but from the outside, it looked as though I could keep firing endlessly.

"Fifty-three techniques in a row without stopping, and none of us know how much longer they could keep going for," Almyrda's voice broke the silence. "This is at least the level of a Bronze-ranked Warrior. Overlord Shang Li, as the chief of the Urbangos tribe, I must withdraw my participants from the upcoming fight. My warriors are strong and brave, and more than ready to prove their strength in battle against an equal or higher-ranked opponent. They are prepared to lay down their lives to prove the strength of demons, but against those who operate with techniques at the level of a Bronze-ranked Warrior, they would be useless. And the same goes for any other demon who'd have won the tournament. As for you, Taoist... I've always thought Seekers were people of honor, striving to please their Heavens. Ten Silver-ranked Apprentices? Seriously? These two would make mincemeat out of them! Would such a beating please your Heavens?"

"Full conjunction," Overlord Shang Li mused, not taking his eyes off us. "It's been a long time since I've last encountered it. Just the Spirit Arrow? Or have you learned anything else?"

Instead of answering, I took Vyllea's hand, and we were covered in Spirit Armor. Since we were still standing, I indicated the direction with a familiar hand gesture, and we moved to the other end of the room, where we easily climbed up to the very ceiling. A few more jumps, and we were back in place.

"Spirit Armor, Steps, and Support. The classic set for an ascendant Apprentice. Considering the way they synchronize their movements, they've worked long and hard at it. There are minor flaws, but those are trivial. Not bad at all."

"The chief of the Urbangos tribe is right: even considering the addition of ten silver apprentices, the participation of this pair in the tournament is unreasonable. There's no point in setting the tribes against the tournament by staging a blatant slaughter here. I am cancelling the juniors' combat and allowing them to leave Zou-Lemawn at any moment. Moreover, as long as this pair is in the city, they are my personal guests. This is my decision. Who dares to challenge it?"

No one did. The demonstration of our capabilities was too vivid and too baffling. Using techniques without meridians, spirit stones, or scrolls was something normally considered impossible.

"Elders, send one apprentice each to the Forest of Dandoor. I need precise information about what is happening there currently. There are five days until the tournament. They should manage to return by the time it begins."

This decision by Overlord Shang Li had not only spared us from an unfair fight, but also placed us under his protection, shielding us from any potential retribution. The implication of full conjunction and our ability to utilize advanced techniques without the typical prerequisites intrigued and perhaps even alarmed the assembled demons, demonstrating a level of power and synergy uncommon even among the most seasoned warriors.

"Aye aye, Elder." The overlords seemed to have gone pale, but they dared not defy the elder's will. What was the difference in their ascension levels, I wondered?

"I wish to see the Heart of the Ocean with my own eyes. Water is my native element; it won't harm me. Follow me; I know the perfect place for this demonstration."

"As you wish, Elder." The mentor rose but hesitated. "Elder, forgive my audacity, but I must ask — is my battle still on? My students might be somewhat unusual, and they'd easily handle the group you've assigned to them. But I swear by the Heavens, I'm merely a Master without any conjunction to anyone. I wouldn't want to miss the opportunity to enrich my collection with two more spatial pouches. The two Overlords for whom I have already expressed having zero respect will bring their artifacts with them, am I correct?"

The Overlords seated beside Shang Li turned pale. Not out of anger or fury — it was fear that enveloped them, and it was visible not just to me.

"Your fight will proceed as planned, Seeker. That is certainly an event no one will want to miss. Everyone is dismissed. In five days, I expect a report on what's happening with the Forest of Dandoor and the battlefield with temporal anomalies."

The mentor and Overlord Shang Li departed. The demons hesitated to leave their seats for a long time. The first to recover were the two Overlords. They exchanged glances, as if reaching a silent agreement, and then rose and exited swiftly, followed by the Golden-ranked Masters. Soon, only three remained at the table: myself, Vyllea, and Almyrda.

"Full conjunction? And which one of you is the leader?" Almyrda asked.

"Zander. He controls all the flows."

"Do you trust him that much, my girl?"

"Don't call me that!" Vyllea snapped. "Yes, I trust him! Because only he could make me what I am!"

"You both are now demons. What do you seek in the world of humans? Stay with me. I can aid in your ascension."

"Listen to yourself, mom! You're asking me to stay in a world ready to pit one hundred and twenty demons against two Candidates, yet the moment we showed this world our true strength, it cowered! Where's our fight? We could do with some training, you know! Duh, had someone told me two years ago that demons were so weak, I would've torn out their throat, no matter who it was. It's better to die a lord than live forever as a slave. The mentor has showed me the true strength of humans. He, while still a Master, has defeated a demon Overlord with incredible ease. He plans to kill two more Overlords, and I know he can! Which demon Master is capable of something like that? None! No, mom. I won't gain any strength in this world. So I won't stay here! I'll go with Zander, become human, and find out why humans are so strong. By myself!"

Almyrda smiled, hearing exactly what she wanted from Vyllea. But the smile faded when her daughter, who had just vehemently asserted her independence, suddenly said,

"Mom, can I have some spirit coins? I saw such a pretty dress in a store, and the mentor's too mean to pay for it!"

* * *

"Will this place suit your needs, seeker?" Overlord Shang Li brought Master Guerlon onto the arena. Not only had all personnel been sent away, but the demon had also established a protective formation to minimize the influence of the immensely powerful source on bystanders.

"Yes, Elder," the mentor nodded, breathing heavily as a sparkling object appeared in his palm. It resembled a fist-sized frozen droplet, emitting such a force that the sand beneath their feet started to turn into black dust.

"This is indeed it. The Heart of the Ocean," the demon said reverently, reaching for the source. It instantly reacted to the shared element, striking the demon with a thick blue beam. The moment was brief before the overlord ceased the flow.

"Ah! Refreshing," the demon remarked. Master Guerlon stored the source back into his spatial pouch and placed his hand on his hip, using healing. Being close to such a powerful source was dangerous even for him.

"Why are there protective shields on the Heart of the Ocean?"

"Without them, I'd turn into this." Master Guerlon gestured towards the dark dust scattered underneath their feet. "I prefer being alive, Elder."

"You do realize I cannot let you leave with such a source, Seeker? It belongs to the world of demons. It must return to its rightful owners."

"My element is fire, and I believe a fair exchange is always beneficial."

"Are all the fire-aligned places of power in your world taken?" the demon smirked. "In five days, you'll receive a source that could help you break through to the overlord stage. My word! But I need the Heart of the Ocean here and now."

"Yes, Elder. I have no reason to doubt your words." Master Guerlon materialized the source once more and calmly handed it to the demon.

"That's it? No demands, assurances, or promises? Just like that?"

"The Heavens have no use for foolish words, Elder. They care only for actions and results."

"And you'll face off those two Overlords, even after giving me the source?"

"I don't need this source to defeat those two worthless Overlords, Elder. One of them is even weaker than Lurth Mink, whom I wouldn't even consider a proper Overlord. However, I suspect the fight won't happen. I've seen the eyes of those overlords, Elder. I've seen the fear that has taken root in their souls. They've already lost, and they know it. Elder, are you a betting sort of person?"

"You're too confident, Seeker." Overlord Shang Li was unsure how to respond to the proposition. Coming from a human, especially one of a lower ascension stage, it seemed like a challenge. But so was the essence of his words, anyway.

"Your terms?" After a pause, the overlord decided to indulge. The Seeker amused him, as did his apprentices.

"Here are a hundred spirit coins." Master Guerlon showcased a hefty pouch. "I wager ten of these that by our return, the Overlords I was supposed to fight will no longer be in Zou-Lemawn."

"The very notion is absurd! They wouldn't risk such damage to their reputation."

"Between life and reputation, many would choose the former. They're not Seekers, Elder. They're merely demons, and far from the strongest or bravest ones, their lofty ascension stage notwithstanding."

"Accepted! A thousand coins against a

thousand coins. But why do you need such an amount? I've heard Seekers shunned money."

"Not exactly. Coins are merely a means to an end, not the end itself. Education in my world's Tier Zero is quite expensive, and I have two apprentices. I have to resort to such measures to give them everything I can."

"Well... In that case, I'll take pleasure in giving you extra trouble finding those spirit coins. I believe in the Overlords. They will come for you in five days."

Half an hour later, the demon and the Taoist returned to the palace. The steward, still dressed in the same impeccable suit, greeted them at the entrance. He bowed, offering the demon two pieces of paper.

"Overlord Shang Li, there's a message for you."

The demon snatched the papers from the steward's hands, scanned them, crumpled, and tossed them away. Not a muscle moved on Master Guerlon's face, but the Overlord could feel that the human was laughing. At him, at the Overlords, at the demons, and at this entire world. And he had every right to do so.

"The fight is off. Quite suddenly, both Overlords remembered they had vital tribal affairs to attend to that they cannot postpone. How long their issues will take to resolve remains to be seen, but they promise not to delay unduly. They'll return and fight the Seeker at first opportunity. Disgrace. This is just a disgrace..."

The steward turned pale and sweaty but dared not leave. No one had dismissed him.

"Alright, Guerlon. The fight didn't happen, but it's none of your fault. From now on, you have the right to call me simply Shang Li. Without titles. My word is bond. You'll get your thousand spirit coins and leave Zou-Lemawn alive and hale. However, it wouldn't be right to leave those on the path to immortality without a spectacular duel, would it? How about a little friendly sparring? I can't promise anything, but I'll try not to kill you. I'm too curious to see what you can do with that pig-headed apprentice of yours. You do realize that with her temper, she won't survive in the world of humans for too long?"

"Either that, or she'll make the entire world of the humans bend to her will," Master Guerlon shrugged. "It's all the will of the Heavens. Our part is merely to follow its decrees. Yes, Shang Li, I'd gladly engage in a friendly sparring with you. And I, too, will try not to kill you. But I won't promise anything, either..."

CHAPTER 17

"WELCOME THE VICTOR of the final contest! Loukree from the Prantir tribe! Let's remember the path our hero took to claim her title!" The announcer began listing Loukree's opponents, while I glanced at Vyllea, sitting beside me with a gloomy expression. Her good mood had vanished five days ago, right after the conversation with her mother — which, frankly, suited me just fine. A sullen Vyllea didn't create any chaos, get into any trouble, or argue with anyone. Almyrda refused to sponsor her daughter. Since Vyllea was heading to the human world, it was up to the humans — or herself — to indulge her in life's luxuries. So the beautiful dress for thirty spirit coins went unpurchased, transforming the unbearable demoness into a sullen demoness.

While the winner bowed to the vast crowd, a

number of demons entered the arena. Initially, as city's honored guests, Vylea and I had been allocated a box by Overlord Shang Li, but so much had changed in these five days it was a wonder we were allowed in the arena at all. Our seats weren't the most comfortable, but I managed to observe the masters' movements and the energy they generated. The seals formed by the demons were extraordinarily complex yet fascinating. They definitely merited a closer examination in a more tranquil setting. Following the seal masters, artifactors began setting up protective formations. While such preparations might surprise some, as I've mentioned, too much had changed in five days.

And I couldn't say I liked these transformations. Why? Because the sharp pain between my shoulder blades hadn't eased one bit during these days. Directly opposite us, in the central box, sat Overlord Lurth Mink, who was watching the preparations on the arena with what looked like complete indifference. Beside him were the two Overlords who had suddenly remembered urgent tribal matters and fled, unwilling to confront the seeker. Yet the most conspicuous figure in the central arena wasn't them. Three Overlords, big deal. The central figure was, of course, a gray-haired demon of the Nascent God ascension stage. He watched the preparations with interest and occasionally glanced our way. Those rare moments felt like being whipped, so tangible was the demon's gaze. Greakon Mink, the grandfather or great-grandfather of the Overlord my instructor had defeated — the accounts varied — had personally come to watch the battle between Overlord Shang Li of the Silver rank and Master Guerlon of the Diamond rank. Demon against human. The promise of such a spectacular show had turned Zou-Lemawn, already packed, into a teeming hive in just five days. The city's portal operated non-stop. Demons arrived by the dozen. All minor candidates had long been evicted — there was no place for them among the spectators. And everyone was expelled from the city to avoid interference. Warriors, Masters, Overlords — there were all sorts. Even a Nascent God, as it turned out.

However, it became clear why no one dared to touch Overlord Lurth Mink, and even Overlord Shang Li turned a blind eye to one of his students defecting. Greakon Mink cherished his young relative dearly. He personally took charge of his ward's elevation, supported him with resources, and shielded him from any calamities. Anyone who so much as glanced sideways at his favorite heir was annihilated by Greakon without a shred of mercy. This very attitude caused Overlord Lurth Mink to lose touch with reality and commit acts that would have long warranted execution for other demons. Seeker Guerlon turned out to be the first being in decades to openly fought against Overlord Lurth Mink and, precisely because the Overlord had remained alive, the Seeker himself continued to live. Overlord Shang Li relayed as much to us four days ago. The demon had even offered to cancel the fight to allow the Seeker to escape from Zou-Lemawn — an idea my instructor merely scoffed at. The day the Seeker ran from a fight would be his last. The Heavens would not forgive such cowardice.

Finally, all preparations were complete — a dome capable of protecting spectators from the combatants' stray attacks was formed over the arena. Vyllea mentioned that the demons were so engrossed in the upcoming battle that serious bets were placed on who would win. This event hardly seemed like a friendly sparring match anymore.

An amplified voice announced,

"A warm welcome to the participants of the final contest! The one we've all been eagerly awaiting! Demon versus human! Overlord Shang Li against Seeker Guerlon!"

The arena buzzed with excitement as the seeker appeared. The demons that had arrived in Zou-Lemawn thirsted for human blood, hence they jeered, showing their contempt. When Overlord Shang Li emerged into the arena, the jeers turned into cheers of approval. The crowd supported their hero.

"Overlord Greakon Mink knows about the Heart of the Ocean," Overlord Shang Li stated and bowed to his opponent.

"Has he already demanded its delivery?" The Seeker mirrored the greeting.

"Of course. Once I destroy you, I'll take it from your corpse and hand it to the Elder. You understand I have no right to hold back? This is no longer a friendly spar, Guerlon. This is war."

"War it is," the Seeker confirmed. "The Heavens see all, Shang Li. I might surprise you yet, if they sanction it."

"Get to it already!" A disgruntled voice from the stands called out. The Nascent God was displeased with the delay. As if waiting for just that command, the Taoist leaped a few dozen feet away from the demon. Six circling green blades appeared around the Seeker. The Taoist made a few circular hand movements, and the blades followed like obedient dogs. Finally, the Seeker extended both hands towards the demon, and the blades shot forward, leaving only a green trail behind. It was impossible for a being of low ascension levels to see them.

Overlord Shang Li stood his ground until the last moment and only vanished to the side an instant before the first blade reached him. He simply disappeared and reappeared next to the Seeker. Two streams of water erupted from the demon's hands, and their power was palpable even through the protective formations. These streams were supposed to sweep the Taoist away, but they didn't reach him in time: the Seeker was capable of moving with the same speed as the demon. Where the human had just stood, only a bright fiery orb remained, exploding with incredible force. Despite the elevation difference, the water streams were deflected aside, and then six green blades that seemed to move on their own raced towards the demon.

I didn't notice where the dark blade in the demon's hands came from. I only heard a clang and saw bright flashes of artifacts being destroyed. Overlord Shang Li decided to eliminate one of his opponent's weapons. But this only granted the seeker a few additional moments — more knives appeared in the air, though they were no longer knives but two sets of paired blades. The mentor created another artifact as he charged at the demon, and, for a while, two blurred shadows raced around the arena, periodically shooting fire and water at each other. The Seeker demonstrated astonishing control over the artifacts. He could never defeat a Silver-ranked Overlord in a one-on-one fight, but attacking simultaneously from four directions gave him a chance for success. The Overlord had to twist and turn as if on a frying pan. Judging by how he was defending against the daggers, the blades, and the mentor's sword, they were all quite powerful artifacts.

It may have seemed Seeker Guerlon had the demon cornered, but the demon swatted away another blade and launched a counterattack. Suddenly, everything underneath the protective formations became engulfed by dark waters. Judging by the demons scurrying around the seals and formations, the defense was unprepared for such an assault. The force unleashed by Overlord Shang Li exceeded its limit. Even the Nascent God Greakon Mink rose from his seat. A large flag flew from his hands, splitting into a dozen smaller ones mid-air. These flags plunged into the arena's sand, a lightning bolt ran between them, and a dome began to form. The demons responsible for the arena's protection found themselves trapped between two formations: their own and the one created by the Nascent God. Judging by the panicked looks of the captives, things had gone completely awry. The dark water inside the formation wasn't going anywhere. Moreover, it pressed with incredible force, and at one point, a crunch was heard: the seals and formation broke. From my vantage point, it was clear to see the demons flattened by the unleashed water. Overlord Shang Li didn't hold back and immediately applied monstrous pressure to the water mass.

This lasted for a long time — about five minutes. Inside the element, nothing was visible, but gradually the color of the water began to change. From dark blue, the element reached blue, then light blue, and then became completely transparent. The arena gasped. On one edge of the arena stood Overlord Shang Li in an air bubble, alive and unharmed. On the opposite side was a fiery orb, within which, in the lotus position, sat Seeker Guerlon. The pressure that had managed to destroy protective seals and formations was powerless against the Taoist's fiery element.

The water vanished instantly, as if it had never existed. Only the wet stone, into which the compacted sand had transformed, remained as a reminder of the clash between two elements.

"Is this all a Silver-ranked Overlord is capable of?" The Taoist's surprised voice rang out. "How odd. I always thought that merging with an element meant this!"

The stone dried instantly — the dome became filled again, but with fire this time. Remarkably, a mere Master forced the Nascent God to rise to his feet again. Another flag flew from the demon's hand to form another protective formation. The silence that fell over the arena was deafening. No one could have imagined that a human possessed so much power. The fire raged for about five minutes before its intensity began to wane. I didn't even attempt to perceive what was happening with spirit vision, fearing blindness. The energy employed by the adversaries was beyond my comprehension.

The flame subsided, and the arena was filled with a triumphant roar. Overlord Shang Li stood, arms crossed, slightly tilting his head as if waiting for the Taoist to tire of his silly games. Finally, the last sparks died down, and the demon said,

"Interesting artifacts you have, Guerlon. But they won't help you. I suggest you surrender, so as not to spoil my future loot. It will be interesting to rummage through your spatial pouch. I promise to kill you quickly."

"All is as the Heavens will. You try to defeat me first, then think about my belongings," the instructor replied, and I felt uneasy. Tension was evident in the Taoist's voice. While the Overlord looked as if he had just gone out for a stroll, the

Taoist looked as someone who'd undergone a six-month intensive training program compressed into one minute.

"As you wish. Let's see what else you're capable of."

What followed could only be described as a thrashing. Overlord Shang Li got serious. Massive streams of energy erupted from his hands, thick snakes of compressed water flew out, and water walls formed around the Taoist from all sides. The demon demonstrated a remarkable unity with the element, making it obey his every wish. Seeker Guerlon no longer thought about attacking. All he could do was position his fiery shield against dangerous blows, absorbing simpler ones with his spirit armor. Within a minute of this frenzy, blood appeared on the Taoist's face. It came from his nose — the Master's body couldn't withstand the strain. Yet, somehow, inexplicably, my mentor managed to hold on. His fire couldn't completely evaporate the demon's streams, but weakened them enough for him to survive.

The Overlord ceased his attack so abruptly that the Seeker continued moving and attacking the void for a few moments, not realizing it was over. Overlord Shang Li's face was devoid of sweat, whereas Instructor Guerlon looked the way I did back when I had still been the outlet for Vyllea's numerous frustrations.

"This is the end, Guerlon. I must admit, you're the first to have lasted so long against me. The fact that you're merely a Master only emphasizes my respect for you. However, everything comes to an end eventually. It is now time to end your life. I hope your Heavens will be kind to you."

A dark sphere began to form in Overlord Shang Li's hands. Judging by how the Nascent God rose and leaned forward, he did not expect such an ability from the demon. All I could do was bite my lip, watching the final moments of Seeker Guerlon's life. All artifacts he had used were destroyed by the Overlord effortlessly. The difference in elevation between an Overlord and a Master was clearly demonstrated today.

However...

"The Heavens are always kind to those who act according to its will. Farewell, Shang Li. You were a worthy opponent."

What happened next silenced the entire arena. A huge bell formed around Overlord Shang Li, and another artifact, resembling a hammer, tore from the instructor's hands. It struck the bell, and a shockwave of sound blasted over the audience. Despite the protective formations set by the Nascent God, the front rows turned to mush. Demons nearby hastily set up their defenses, but they were all swept away along with the demons themselves. The wave reached myself and Vyllea, passing through. The spirit armor set by Overlord Shang Li before the fight, along with two protective amulets given to us by the Taoist, had withstood the blast. We were severely shaken, blood ran from our noses, and stars danced before our eyes, but we remained alive. The same couldn't be said for our neighbors. The Masters were pulverized as if they were mere Candidates! I struggled to gather my strength, barely managing to rise — the spectator stands were a horrific sight. Most demons were motionless. Only a few showed signs of life, but it was clear they wouldn't last long without immediate help. With just one strike, Instructor Guerlon had managed to annihilate an enormous number of demons of the Warrior and Master stages. Only four demons remained standing: three Overlords and a Nascent God. The latter was found on the arena, freeing himself from the protective formation. I couldn't see the demon's face, but his movements were noticeably furious — too abrupt. Finally, the last flag flew into the hands of the nascent god, who instantly appeared next to the bell. I had no idea what the demon had done then, but the artifact vanished. Simply evaporated. Overlord Shang Li was still standing, but he swayed as if only his incredible willpower kept him from falling.

"Weakling," The nascent god flung the demon aside. He flew off and splattered on the ground. The ancestor of Lurth Mink turned towards my mentor. Astonishingly, the sonic wave seemed to have bypassed him. In an instant, the Nascent God was standing next to the Seeker. Grabbing the Taoist by the neck, the demon lifted him off the ground as if he were a feather.

"You, a Seeker? Since when did the Emperor's lapdogs become Seekers? I will consume your essence, human. Make you pay for everything you've done here. Your death will be long. I'll extract every core, every meridian, everything that makes you a Taoist, but you will still live. You will feel on your own skin what it means to anger..."

"Everything is Heaven's will," came a wheeze, followed by something unimaginable. The Nascent God froze in place. The mentor grabbed the fingers clutching his throat and, not even trying to hide his cry of pain, broke free from the grasp. Judging by the immediate need for self-healing, the Taoist had to break his own neck in the process. But the demon didn't react — he remained motionless.

"Heal him, Guerlon!" Overlord Shang Li commanded, appearing in front of the nascent god. "Remove the plaques. I need the chest."

Only then did I realize that there were Seeker plaques on the chest and the shoulders of the Nascent God! There were three — no, four of them! Simultaneously! Artifacts created by the head of the Phoenix Clan, a Nascent God of the Golden rank, a true immortal, who had managed to deal with another Nascent God. They couldn't destroy him — Greakon Mink's rank allowed him to survive, but he had to exert all his strength to withstand four seeker artifacts simultaneously.

The instructor complied with the demon's demand and placed his hand on his captive. A red glow appeared — the Taoist began healing. Simultaneously, Overlord Shang Li delivered his strike. His fist pierced the Nascent God's chest and pulled out a core. Judging by the meridians trailing behind it, it was an energy core. Without missing a beat, Shang Li stuffed the core into his mouth and began to shove the meridians down, trying to absorb them before the energy disappeared. Judging by the Overlord's dexterity, he had extensive practice. After the first core came the second — the elemental core. Then, the spirit core. All the while, the Nascent God remained alive — Seeker Guerlon didn't allow him to pass away.

When the body hit the compressed sand, there was no life left in it. However, Overlord Shang Li didn't stay in place to relish his victory. He vanished, only to materialize in the main box with the three mortally terrified Overlords. The frenzied demon didn't bother with grandiose phrases. He appeared beside Lurth Mink and lifted him into the air by the neck, just as the Nascent God had done seconds earlier with my mentor.

"Not even worth speaking to!" The Overlord eventually declared and squeezed his fingers. Lurth Mink's body hit the floor, but his head remained in the demon's grasp. Tossing it aside as if it were some distasteful object, the overlord materialized next to the remaining two demons. Shang Li didn't bother inventing anything new — two more decapitated bodies hit the floor simultaneously.

The whole city seemed to freeze when Overlord Shang Li's voice echoed through the air.

"This is Overlord Shang Li speaking. Master Guerlon of the Diamond rank has defeated me in a fair training duel. Nascent God Greakon Mink of the Copper rank decided he was dissatisfied with the result of the training sparring and entered the arena, ignoring all the laws of friendly duels. I don't know how it happened, but somehow, the Master has managed to destroy Nascent God Greakon Mink and the three Overlords who were accompanying him. Thus, a curfew is declared in Zou-Lemawn. The portal is locked until further notice. I need to figure out how a training duel between myself and the tournament's founder could have become part of a revenge plot by a high-ranking demon. Everyone go home. Anyone seen on the streets in the next twenty-four hours will be considered an enemy of my family. My Golden-ranked Master apprentices have been sent out on patrol. The curfew will begin in an hour!"

My attention was drawn to movement in the arena, pulling my focus from Overlord Shang Li. His personal apprentices were walking through the rows, finishing off the survivors. Some tried to defend themselves, but to no avail: the Masters didn't even notice any resistance. My heart stopped as I waited for the Overlord's apprentices to reach us, but they passed by as if Vyllea and I didn't exist. They didn't even glance our way. Five minutes later, there were no survivors left in the arena.

Overlord Shang Li jumped down to the arena and approached the body of the Nascent God. After tossing three spatial pouches to the Seeker, the demon began to strip the consumed opponent of artifacts.

BOOK TWO

"Your twenty-four hours start now. I can't give you more. Good luck, Guerlon. I hope the hunt for you will be glorious. Do not return to the demon lands. You won't be welcome. Goodbye."

"Goodbye, Shang Li. I'll gladly kill you in a real battle if Heaven brings us together again. Apprentices, to the exit! We're returning to Vorend!"

* * *

(Four days before the tournament)

"...which is why this family has almost subjugated the entire South. The Prince turns a blind eye to what's happening here — his focus is on expansion in the East. The Mink family takes full advantage of this. Lurth has gotten used to absolute immunity, and Greakon just looks for a reason to attack.

"Can't the Overlords put a single Nascent God in his place?"

"They've tried twice. Other Nascent Gods didn't even deign to listen to their juniors. They do in their lands exactly what Greakon does in his. We had to resign to it and swallow the disgrace the Mink family drags us through. A Nascent God has expressed a desire to kill you. I've been ordered to detain you."

"How about a third attempt?"

"By whom? The three most vehement opponents had been killed, and their families annihilated. As for the rest… You've seen who has gained power now. Twenty years ago, I wouldn't have let such sycophantic nobodies through my door, and now I'm forced to share a table with them because they serve the Mink family."

"We don't need others. We can do it all by ourselves."

Guerlon placed four Seeker plaques in front of him, making the demon flinch involuntarily. His premonition clearly indicated they were deadly.

"So, this is how you were planning to destroy the Overlords?"

"This is how I was planning to destroy you. As for the couple that had fled — I would have killed them with elemental techniques. They're weak."

"But you're not planning to kill me anymore?"

"No. A far more interesting target has drawn itself before me."

"You cannot breach through a Nascent God's defenses. Your artifact requires bodily contact, I presume?"

"I'll make Greakon Mink come close to me. He'll want to consume me. At the end of the battle, when you're nearly victorious, I'll enclose you in the Bell of Negation."

Overlord Shang Li couldn't help but let out a string of foul curses.

"The Seeker is the Emperor's lapdog? How much lower can a Taoist fall?"

"The emperor isn't even aware of my existence. This artifact has been taken from a Judge. I had to leave the belt, but I took the Bell of

Negation with me. My mentor's mentor was the creator of these artifacts, so I knew how to remove their personal binding. To absorb an Executor of Fates, the Nascent God will have to approach him closely. Then I can use the tablets. They won't kill him, but they'll disable him. The grand finale will be up to you."

"Our fight must look genuine. Will you be able to withstand my attacks?"

"Here's all the high-level stuff I have with me. You can build your strategy around them."

Master Guerlon materialized several dozen items on the table.

"This one, this one, and this one here," Overlord Shang Li started to point at the items. "Yes, with their help, you'll manage to resist for some time. If you use the Bell of Negation... Say, I have an idea. It would please your Heavens for the number of high-ranking demons to be lowered, wouldn't it?"

"You want to lure everyone you have a feud with into the amphitheater?"

"If any of the tribes naively think I've forgotten the offenses committed hundreds of years ago, they are mistaken. Yes, I want to turn our fight into a spectacle. Send away everyone loyal to me, bring in all my enemies, and destroy them all in one fell swoop."

"My apprentices must be in the amphitheater, too. Otherwise, the Nascent God might suspect something."

"We'll cover them with amulets from head to

toe, and I'll use my Spirit Armor on them to boot. They'll survive. Tell me, Guerlon, if the Seeker Plates are so powerful, why doesn't every Taoist have them?"

"They're single-use, and each one carries a significant part of the clan head's power. If they start to mass-produce plaques, they'll simply die. Or be overthrown. There are plenty of contenders. No one wants a weak head, and each plaque weakens him significantly. One or two every half a year — that's the limit various groups can expect. After all, it isn't only Seekers who receive such items. There are too few plaques, so their return grants the right for a person to take the place of the deceased. Only the name changes, without the need to invest any power. Let's work out the fight sequence. Improvisation is dangerous in such matters."

CHAPTER 18

"THE SENSATIONS ARE STRANGE," Vyllea said, opening her eyes after the conjunction. The girl was lying on me and, as always, was in no hurry to get up. My partner's face was too close to notice details, but I saw something odd. I freed my hands, grabbed Vyllea by the head unabashedly and lifted her up a little.

"Wow! Your eyes are such an interesting color! I've never seen anything like it."

"What is it?" Vyllea worried and even jumped to her feet. "Teacher, I need a mirror!"

The Taoist materialized a small bundle with Vyllea's personal possessions without saying a word. The girl took out a mirror and inspected herself from various angles for some time. The bright green eyes looked so unusual that they immediately attracted attention. And, it must be admitted, they really suited Vyllea in her human guise.

"Beautiful! Wait, what do you mean 'never seen anything like it'? Don't humans have green-eyed individuals? Will everyone immediately recognize me for a demon?"

"Green eyes are rare in the South of the Empire," Master Guerlon explained. "They're common in the West, though — the lands of the Tiger Clan."

"That's where we need to go! There are bound to be tigers in the lands of the Tiger Clan!" The girl exclaimed. "Mentor, let's go to the West!"

"Getting to the West is even harder than returning from the demon world. The Tiger Clan only accepts outstanding Warriors or higher-level Taoists into their ranks."

"Why should we care who they accept? I'm not planning to join the Tiger Clan. I'm going to become a Seeker. Or are Seekers only free on paper? Can't they travel wherever they want?" Vyllea challenged the mentor.

"Seekers are free to travel across the entire Empire, regardless where they received their tablet. But you're not a Seeker yet," Master Guerlon responded.

"So what are we waiting for? I've become human, Zander has also returned to his annoying form. I liked him much better before. You stayed human throughout. Mentor, what's with the tent, anyway?"

"We need to ensure your disguise doesn't fail,

be it during training, from lack of energy, or over time. Start warming up — we're here for a month at least."

The news wasn't the most pleasant — there wasn't even a water source nearby to gather water for washing. A month in such conditions wasn't critical — we could always wipe down with a damp towel — but living without a warm bath was somewhat sad.

Vyllea turned into a demon precisely four weeks after the conjunction. During this time, the Teacher had us running around the area, building our endurance. Running, working with the jian, hand-to-hand combat, more running, strength exercises, breakfast... Each day lasted an eternity. If we mostly focused on meditation near the destroyed Forest of Dandoor, now the emphasis was on physical training. And the Teacher had no intention of healing us, believing that the body should adapt on its own. And adapt it did: everything that could hurt, did hurt. It got to the point where Vyllea and I started fighting on equal terms. Not because I had become so strong, but because it was easy to fight as equals when both parties were at zero strength. The Teacher put us on a week-long fast, not even allowing water. The Taoist wanted to see if such restrictions would affect the conjunction's disguise. Nothing did, except for time. As long as we engaged in energy exchange at least once a week, no one would ever realize a demon was running among humans. Which really invited the question: how many demons were living among the people undiscovered? I had no doubt they existed. Too many Taoists and demons knew about conjunction. Thus, both sides were using it actively. What if demons kidnapped a child, instilled a hatred for humans into them, and then bonded them with a demon and sent them to our world? This way, even a demon of a high ascension stage could remain hidden indefinitely. All you needed was a correctly-indoctrinated human. How would one go about revealing such individuals? Heavens, why was I even thinking of something that complex? I wasn't even a Seeker yet...

We arrived in Vorend several weeks before the mentor's amulet's effect was due to wear off. After Zou-Lemawn, the capital of the human Tier Zero appeared inferior in every aspect — both spiritually and visually. The Demons' architecture was compact, strict, and clear — akin to a vastly-enlarged castle within high walls. Humans, however, emphasized comfort with wide roads, vast parks, and low-rise buildings, each occupying an exorbitant amount of space. My first visit to Vorend had left me in awe of its grandeur — hardly surprising, given I had seen nothing but my village and our provincial capital until I was twelve. Now, I had to admit — compared to Zou-Lemawn, Vorend looked as my village did compared to Vorend, losing enormously in comparison. It was hard to accept that demons could be more organized than humans. Yet, I seemed to be the only one who thought that way.

"It's so beautiful here!" Vyllea whispered. She didn't get the chance to see the Southern Imperial capital's sights the previous time. "Wow! Zander, look! A park! People are just walking around in a leisurely manner! Everything is so well-arranged. No need to push, hurry, or cram. So much space! Wow! Mentor, what's that?"

We stood on a hill offering a beautiful view of the city, and Vyllea's gaze settled on a massive structure towering over the city. I had to admit — this particular building far surpassed anything I'd seen in Zou-Lemawn in terms of thought-through design and beauty. Even the mayor's palace, temporarily housing Overlord Shang Li, was no match for this creation of the human world's Tier Zero.

"That's the palace of House Dun from the Tiger Clan. A clear demonstration of who really wields power in Tier Zero — and, indeed, across the Empire."

"Is the Phoenix Clan weaker than the Tiger Clan?" Vyllea immediately inquired.

"Yes. Constant clashes with demons require considerable resources. The Westerners don't have this problem, allowing them to afford such gaudy structures."

"Why call it gaudy off the bat? I personally like the palace! So much so that I'd love to visit it. Does the Tiger Clan welcome guests?"

"Any Taoist has the right to choose which clan to serve. You and Zander became Diamond-ranked Candidates by sixteen. That's more than enough to interest the Tiger Clan's recruiters. I'm sure if you entered that palace, they'd immediately welcome you with open arms."

"So what are we waiting for?" Vyllea's eyes lit up. "This is our chance to become stronger! Why bother with the weaker clans? You can't gain everything you need from them!"

"The Tiger Clan doesn't have Seekers, apprentice. They allow them to travel through their lands, but they don't issue the plaques themselves. The Clan Head believes it's a waste of personal power. If you enter that palace and express your wish to join the Tiger Clan, you can forget about freedom. You'll be doing as your elders command," the mentor explained.

"No way! I've had enough of that crap at home!" Vyllea nearly shouted, turning away from the palace sharply. "Actually, there's nothing special about that building. Mentor, why have we stopped? I should have become a Seeker, like, ten minutes ago!"

"Do you wish to present yourself before the Phoenix Clan Head's Advisor looking like this?" the mentor asked, giving the girl a look that made her blush. "No, apprentice, we won't paying our visit to House Wang right now. First, you need to take care of yourself."

Words could hardly convey the sensation of a hot bath. Bliss multiplied by relaxation. Surprisingly, we didn't stop at the Seekers' tavern, but headed for what the Taoist considered the best hotel in Vorend. Initially, they wanted to refuse us

— our clothes, albeit clean, had turned into rags after years of constant wear. We urgently needed a replacement. However, as soon as the mentor pressed the hotel owner and half the guests with his aura, everything resolved at once. Rooms were found, and no further objections were made about us. I soaked for hours, but all pleasures ended eventually. There was a knock on the door. According to my spirit vision, it was Vyllea attempting to barge in.

"What's taking you forever?" The girl burst in as soon as I opened the door. "Get dressed quickly! The mentor said we're going shopping!"

"In five hours. It's only been three!"

"Zander, don't get on my nerves! Here!"

With those words, Vyllea pointed at an open book she brought with her. It was a textbook on basic artifact crafting, familiar to me — I knew it by heart, so I immediately understood what she was pointing at. The Reinforcement section.

"I can't do combining. The clothes can either be durable or clean. Not both at the same time."

"Zander, don't give me that! Look!" Vyllea flipped to a new page. She surely came prepared! It described the process of combining multiple properties. "Clean and durable. Ideally, also heat-resistant."

"You won't manage three conditions," I was flabbergasted and overwhelmed by her enthusiasm.

"Why?" Vyllea's surprise was genuine.

"Because you didn't read the textbook

carefully."

To prove my point, I took the book and flipped back a few pages. "Look. One condition can be applied to any base without problems. For an item to withstand two conditions and turn into an artifact, its base must be at least of the Apprentice stage, Tier One. For three conditions, it has to correspond to the lowest ranks of the Second Tier. Do you know what will happen to you if you start wearing Second-Tier items? You'll turn into a walking corpse. I've seen craftsmen in Vorend working with First-Tier items. They're not a pretty sight. We already have nodes, so First-Tier items shouldn't affect us. Two enhancements, Vyllea. No more. Choose what's more important to you."

"Cleanness and durability. I'm sick of patching holes. I'm not a freaking seamstress!"

"What's wrong with seamstresses?" I didn't get her point.

"They serve!" the girl snorted and jabbed her finger into my chest. "I refuse to serve anyone! You need to think about how you'll work on the clothes! What bases do you have? I need a full list so I don't buy anything unnecessary."

"I doubt the mentor will let you buy anything unnecessary," I couldn't resist the sarcasm but nonetheless began listing. Vyllea was right: the first thing was to turn clothes into artifacts immediately, considering it was embarrassing to show our noses anywhere in the garb we were wearing.

But what happened next... I anticipated a lot,

but certainly not that we would end up in Vorend's finest and most expensive store, where the Taoist, having first placed himself comfortably the guest chair, began issuing orders as if it was his personal shop. Sellers and tailors started scurrying around us, and the Taoist declared he needed to have traveling robes and a Seeker's attire made. I was measured from head to toe, which was quite uncomfortable. When they started showing me underwear and asking what color I preferred, I nearly ran out of there. What did it even matter what color my underwear was? Who cared about stuff like that?! Unlike me, Vyllea enjoyed every moment. This was exactly what she had missed in her two years of close interaction with the Taoist. All these frills, bows, ribbons. An utter and absolute nightmare that showed no signs of ending. It got to the point where I was handed a temporary set of clothes and sent to change. When I came out, the mentor was in the middle of a conversation with the store's owner. "Everything will be ready in two days, Elder. Two sets for each apprentice. You need to deposit three hundred and twenty spirit coins as a down payment."

"A down payment?" The mentor looked at the store owner with interest. "Has the junior decided to test the limits of my patience? I can burn half of this store right now. Would that down payment suffice for you?"

"The store is under the protection of House Dun!" The owner didn't even think to back down.

It seemed that Tier Zero lacked the skill of communicating those with those ascending towards immortality at high stages of elevation. Instead of further threats, the mentor extended his hand, and a fireball flew from it. Having traveled through several rows of clothes and turned them to ash, the ball hit the wall. Smoke billowed, cries for help sounded — someone got hurt. Only now did the store owner realize whom he was speaking to.

"If House Dun has any complaints, they can express them in any form they find convenient," the Taoist said, and the store owner was flattened to the floor. "I'll come to collect the clothes for my apprentices in two days. If they're not ready by then, Vorend will have a vacant spot for a fine clothing store. Have I made myself clear, junior?"

"Yes, Elder!" gasped the owner, pinned to the floor. He, like all his employees, was merely a Candidate — not even of the Golden rank. They had no right to oppose the will of a Diamond Master, but the habit of operating under the protection of House Dun had done the owner a disservice. He forgot how to behave with his betters.

"Apprentices, follow me," the mentor ordered. Vyllea had changed and was looking... pleasant, if not exactly stunning. The girl was attractive, especially with those bright green eyes, but I could not say my heart started to skip beats whenever she lay on top of me. It seems I had become so accustomed to her constant presence that I perceived her not as a sixteen-year-old peer, but merely as a partner in ascension. No romance. And there was none from her part, either. We simply did not perceive each other as romantic partners.

They were already waiting for us outside — a carriage with House Wang's crest on it stood near the store.

"Elder, the head of House Wang humbly requests a meeting with you," the coachman bowed and didn't even think of rising as he awaited his answer.

"At least someone knows how to speak properly to elders," the seeker grunted as he climbed into the carriage. Vyllea and I followed him, and as the carriage moved, I managed to see that the fire in the store had been extinguished after all. And the profit from making our clothes would hardly cover all the losses. The hole in the wall alone would be costly enough for sure!

Hurikki Wang was sitting in his office. The head of House Wang looked absolutely wretched. Dark circles under his eyes indicated he hadn't slept for weeks, if not months. Sunken and emaciated, he resembled a craftsman working with inner-tier artifacts and not the respected head of a major house.

"Seeker Guerlon, what an unexpected encounter," Hurikki Wang, as I had anticipated, was a Candidate of the Golden rank. Before arriving to the Wang family's palace, I had met only a few Taoists of the Apprentice stage in Vorend. Here, surprisingly, there were many.

There were even two Warriors. There were also plenty of power sources. Practically every door had artifacts installed, and every Taoist in the palace had a couple of energy-emitting amulets. For Tier Zero, this was quite strange: energy here tended to escape from dwellings, and artifacts had to be recharged with spirit stones each time. And that was an expense, and a significant one at that. It was surprising that House Wang would indulge in such expenditure — two years ago, when we were here last, this certainly wasn't the case.

"Junior," the Taoist nodded and sat down in a chair. Vyllea and I remained standing; no one offered us a seat. "You wanted to see me. Speak."

"The Elder has a new apprentice?" The head glanced at Vyllea. He hardly remembered her. The bound demon we had brought to his office a few years ago and Vyllea, looking and smelling human, bore no resemblance to each other.

"You called me to talk about my apprentice? Junior, I can find more interesting things to do. Who attacked you and what can you offer in return?"

"The Elder is already aware?" Hurikki Wang even seemed to deflate a bit.

"I have eyes. I have ears. I have a sense of dissatisfaction when juniors forget who stands before them. I give you five minutes to tell me everything clearly and thoroughly. After that, we shall either leave, or we shall stay and help, depending on whether what you have to offer interests us. Your time starts now."

BOOK TWO

"House Dun, Elder. The Tiger Clan has attacked us. They intend to take over Tier Zero."

Hurikki Wang's narrative was replete with woeful details. After certain events that had transpired two years ago, House Wang's position became rather shaky. A First Tier inspector from House Soth discovered a catastrophic shortage of spirit stones. Though they were useless for the First Tier, the very fact of exceeding official powers spoke volumes. House Dun sprang into action shortly afterwards. The Tiger Clan sponsored its representatives, spoiling them with abundant resources — spirit stones, artifacts, you name it. Many stores came under the management of House Dun — working with the strongest was profitable. But the most unpleasant part was that unknown attackers began targeting House Wang's businesses and lands. It had reached the point where one of Hurikki Wang's closest friends, the head of the School of Spirit Power, had gotten killed. It was the very old man who had conducted my inspection. It was a short-sighted move for House Dun: quarreling with an ascension school was never wise. A new head came from the First Tier, seeking vengeance, but somehow House Dun managed to quell the conflict and even prove their innocence. However, Hurikki Wang had no doubt that the murder of his closest ally was the work of the Tiger Clan. After all, there was no force in Vorend capable of such a deed. And now, the palace of House Wang had been under attack by unknown raiders for two weeks. They came at night, killed one or two defenders, stole artifacts, and left. Hurikki Wang hired two groups of mercenaries from the First Tier to deal with the madmen who'd decided to attack House Wang, but both groups were destroyed. And those groups consisted of Bronze-ranked Apprentice Taoists!

"I still don't get two things, Junior — what do you want from me, and what's in it for me?"

"The details about your apprentice are with me, Elder. My departed friend had intended to pass them on, but I convinced him to delay. There's a time for everything, after all, including revelations about a mental absolute, especially one who is a Seeker. I'd wager, throughout all of Tier Zero, only those of us gathered here know about Zander's true identity and his significance. If you, esteemed Elder, could eliminate the threat haunting House Wang, the entire Tier Zero will forget it had ever birthed a mental absolute. Your apprentices could then enroll into the School of Spirit Power under normal conditions, and when they turn eighteen, they'll head to the first tier as fully-fledged Taoists who had been given a basic education. Not as outcasts or fugitives — as Taoists. A fair exchange for a minor favor, don't you think?"

"Fair enough," conceded the mentor, "except for one small caveat: as soon as my apprentices join the School of Spirit Power, they'll be subjected to a mandatory examination."

"Your apprentice is another absolute?" Hurikki Wang's face fell.

"No. But does that change anything? Zander alone is sufficient."

"It changes everything, Elder!" The head of House Wang perked up visibly. "The fact that a Seeker's apprentice had undergone examination has been documented in all reports. Just providing the current head with the proper document would suffice…"

Hurikki Wang approached a steel strongbox, removed a key from his neck, and unlocked the heavy door. My spirit vision revealed a trove of fascinating items within, highlighting its worthlessness to me — for I saw the strongbox as nothing more than a hunk of metal. That it contained so many valuable items remained my little secret. Nevertheless, I memorized the safe's specific traits, knowing that should I encounter such an artifact (and it was indeed a high-level artifact), I'd know there was something valuable to plunder inside.

Hurikki Wang sifted through the strongbox for quite some time before finally extracting several documents. He read them and grinned.

"Yes, this is it. This report was sent by the head of the School of Spirit Power, treacherously murdered by House Dun. Should this document enter circulation, the information regarding the Seeker's apprentice shall become public knowledge."

House Wang's leader fearlessly handed over the sheet to the Seeker. He simply grunted in acknowledgment upon reading it and, as I had anticipated, handed the document back. The Heavens would disapprove if the mentor were to destroy such a paper and condemn it as a criminal act.

"But here's a document I prepared nearly four years ago, knowing it would eventually prove useful. It's an official document, Elder Guerlon, bearing the valid signature of the late head of the School of Spirit Power. This document will withstand scrutiny at any level, right up to the clan head."

A new sheet appeared in the Seeker's hands, and this time his grunt was a lot more eloquent.

"You've prepared well, Junior."

"I won't even mention what it cost me to convince my untimely departed comrade to sign here. It was expensive, Elder. Very expensive. But I knew it would come in handy sooner or later. It seems the Heavens itself has incited your return at this very moment. If your apprentice is merely on her path to immortality, she'll easily pass any scrutiny and fail to catch the new head's interest. Help me, and your apprentice will have the chance to become a fully-fledged Taoist."

"Consider the payment accepted. You can sleep easy tonight, junior. I'll find who's causing you trouble. Here, apprentice, this is your ticket to a normal life. Four years ago, I made a mistake, but thanks to the head of House Wang, it's been rectified. Fulfilling his request is worth it."

Evaluation results for Zander, Apprentice of Seeker Guerlon. Age: 12 years. Spirit: Zero stage.

Body: Initial stage. Mind: Initial stage. Conclusion: The youth is of no interest. Progression likelihood is minimal. Recommended for enrollment into the School of Spirit Power on standard terms. Fee: 400 spirit coins for 2 years.

Not a word about anyone being a mental absolute anywhere. I looked at the jubilant Hurikki Wang. The mentor made a mistake by sparing his life. People like Hurikki might be useful, fitting perfectly in their designated places, and convenient for everyone, but in my opinion, they didn't deserve to exist. My Heavens — apparently, a version that differed from the mentor's substantially — wouldn't forgive me if the head of House Wang remained alive. We needed to rid this world of such vermin. Otherwise, we were no better than demons. I had two years to keep the promise I'd made to myself. Hurikki Wang would die. I swore it to myself.

CHAPTER 19

THE NEXT MORNING STARTED OFF rather unusually. The mentor came into my room and gave me a minute to pack. A very sleepy Vyllea stood behind him, clueless about what was happening. A calm exterior masked the mentor's seething rage — he hadn't even been like this among demons!

"Follow me!" ordered the mentor. We entered his room, where a man's body lay on the floor. Fitting black clothing concealed his form, leaving only the eyes exposed.

"Thoughts?" the mentor asked, nodding towards the corpse.

"Silver, maybe Bronze-ranked Candidate. No nodes. A few small, nearly invisible power spots near the right sleeve. If I hadn't seen the safe of House Wang's head, I'd have easily missed them."

BOOK TWO

The mentor leaned over the body and slit the sleeve. Six long needles spilled onto the floor, emanating power from their tips. The needles looked odd, as if dipped in green paint, but the color gradually evaporated in the air. I fearlessly picked up a needle by the end devoid of power. There was no reaction, and the mentor didn't object. I examined the edge emitting power. It wasn't paint — this part of the needle was an artifact. The entire needle must have been an artifact originally, but it had lost its power. I twisted it around until I found where a seal was applied. Whoever did this was a true master.

"I can't make it out. It's too small," I lamented. The mentor silently handed me a glass — a magnifying artifact. Looking through it at the needle, I couldn't suppress a satisfied grunt — the magnifying properties of the artifact were impressive. Now, having adjusted the needle, I was able to fully decipher the symbol, or rather, its components.

"It's a First-Tier artifact. It has two conditions, but I have no idea what they signify. I've never encountered such before. Although... Vyllea, touch me."

As soon as her hand had touched my neck (physical contact was required for conjunction), I activated Spirit Armor and brought the needle close to my palm. It pierced the skin as if the armor wasn't there at all.

"One of the conditions is ignoring Spiritual Armor at the Apprentice stage. I have no idea why it works, but it does. Mentor, how do you defend against such needles?"

"Speed," Vyllea answered instead of the Taoist. "That's what training is for. It's an assassin's needle. Those are vile creatures who know no honor. Fiends who strike from the shadows. They're not even slaves. They're lower. The Urbangos tribe would never work with them!"

"Never say 'never,' apprentice. Sometimes, even Seekers must resort to their services."

"But what about the Heavens?" Vyllea immediately flared up. "Aren't Seekers supposed to solve their problems themselves? What's the point of hiring assassins?"

"To give one's enemy a chance," the mentor replied, as if it were obvious. "If I had decided to kill the head of House Wang, merely activating my aura would suffice. Everyone in this palace would die. But the Heavens wouldn't accept such a victory. There is no glory in it. However, if I hire an assassin of equal or even lower rank than the head of House Wang, it gives him a chance. There are many types of hiring, apprentice. Most set a specific goal — to eliminate the target. The Mercenary Guild must do everything it possibly can to fulfill the assignment. Even if it means spending all their resources to hire a higher-tier assassin. But there's the type of hiring that gives the target a chance. One attack. No follow-ups. The assassin either completes their contract or dies. There's no other way. In such a case, the Heavens decide if the enemy deserves to live.

There's no dishonor in this, apprentice."

"So, you've used their services too?" The girl looked at the Taoist as if seeing him for the first time.

"Apprentice, is that all you could deduce from this artifact?" The mentor ignored Vyllea's question, but it was clear he had indeed used assassins at least once. I twirled the needle, examining it until I reached its tip. There, I found several grooves filled with a liquid that gave off that green color. For some strange reason, the liquid didn't spill from the slots, as if held in by an invisible film.

"Penetrating spiritual armor is the first condition. The second keeps poison in the grooves."

Hooking a barely visible thread of energy on the needle, I drew it into myself, completely draining the artifact. The film vanished, and several green drops fell to the floor, emitting an unpleasant smell of decay. The mentor extended his hand, and a jet of fire shot out. The smell disappeared. As did a large section of the floor.

"Orimmal frog poison is dangerous even as a vapor. Apprentice, can you replicate the seal?"

"Yes," I was taken aback by such a question. "But there's no point without the recipe. The seal itself is useless."

"To clarify: could you apply the seal to a needle?"

"Yes," I responded less confidently. "I'd need a magnifying glass, a vise, a special pen with a fine tip, and a sealed container for the poison to dip the needle in. Not to mention the precision required to apply the ingredients, which have to be ground into dust to fit on such a small surface. And if there's a specific sequence to them... It would take a lot, but nothing's impossible. If I set my mind to it, yes, I could replicate it. But why would you want one?"

"Not for me. For you. For both of you. But more on that later. Let's go. I want to talk to a rather unpleasant person who thinks he's the cleverest Taoist in this world."

The mentor grabbed the corpse by the leg and headed to Hurikki Wang's office. The head of House Wang was already in his office, seemingly having had a rather pleasant night; the dark circles under his eyes had noticeably diminished. However, his reaction to the Seeker's arrival was odd: he went pale as if he had committed some cardinal sin. He paid no attention to the corpse that my mentor threw on the floor, his frightened gaze fixed on the Taoist.

"Elder Guerlon, you've agreed to the task!" Hurikki Wang said as the mentor sat down in the guest chair. "The paperwork will go to the school as soon as I have assurances of my safety."

"You're planning to solve all your problems with my help?" The Seeker's voice boded ill.

"You have accepted the assignment. You should have asked more questions!" Hurikki Wang repeated, looking like a rat cornered. Tense, frightened, but ready to lash out if necessary.

"Two years, junior. Exactly the time my apprentices will spend in Tier Zero. That's all I can offer you."

"That's not enough, Elder! Give me five years!"

"Two, junior. Who did you send to kill my apprentice?"

Given Hurikki Wang's further paling, he had indeed sent someone.

"I didn't use the Assassins' Guild! I sent about twenty groups I didn't want to pay for previous jobs. I promised them such a reward they couldn't refuse. I knew they'd be no match against you. It killed several birds with one stone. Got rid of the scoundrels and gave your apprentice a bit of training."

"I don't care about the small fry. They'd sent an assassin after us. I had to spend two years in the demon world, junior. Someone has to pay for that."

"It wasn't me! Why would I send an assassin after you when I was preparing for your future help? It was all my former partner! It's no wonder he got taken out! Despite signing the paper, he hired a guild to eliminate the mental absolute. Not me! I swear by the Heavens, Elder!"

"I need to arrange a meeting with the local leader. Make it happen."

"That'll be difficult, Elder. He doesn't meet with high-stage Taoists."

"Tell him a Seeker wishes to meet. If he's truly the head of the assassin's guild and not some madman who has just stumbled into power, he'll meet me. Tonight at eight, at the Old Hat tavern. It's in your best interest to ensure our meeting happens, junior. Deal with the body yourself. Apprentices, follow me."

The mentor was furious. He stayed in his room until the evening, giving us no tasks — an unprecedented occurrence. No matter what problems we would face, the mentor had always remembered our training. We had to train ourselves. Jumping and running didn't appeal to us much, so we resorted to conjunction practice, cycling energy aimlessly. Surprisingly, the Taoist didn't head to the meeting alone. He took us with him. We arrived at the tavern and sat on the open veranda. Vyllea instantly forgot everything else; the view was breathtaking.

"A Golden-ranked Apprentice," I said when an unusual Taoist entered my spiritual vision. What was commonplace in Zou-Lemawn seemed utterly bizarre in Tier Zero. The Taoist I detected was heading towards the tavern, and soon we saw a self-moving carriage with the crest of House Wang upon it. A short man stepped out, and I frowned. The needles in his sleeves felt familiar, but there was significantly more energy in them than in those I had held today. Besides the needles, this man could surprise you with a plethora of baffling artifacts. Outwardly, he seemed like a genial uncle — short, with somewhat puffy cheeks, strangely sparse hair, and even sporting whiskers and a beard, usually allowed to Taoists in their venerable age. Yet he didn't resemble an old man. He moved through the tavern as if he owned it, even managing to exchange greetings and a few words with someone on his way. Without the multitude of hidden artifacts and his unusually high stage of ascension for Tier Zero, no one would sense any danger in this peculiar man. But the danger was there, and it was substantial. The man finally reached our table and sat down uninvited. Vyllea, who had been looking at the city all this while, suddenly sniffed the air and almost purred with pleasure,

"Mmm, what a delicious smell. Blood. Lots of blood." The girl turned, and I saw something strange in her eyes — something that had never been there before. Vyllea looked at the uninvited guest with... interest? No, that wasn't the right word. Desire, that was it! Astonishingly, this was the first time I saw Vyllea regard someone not as food, but as a potential partner.

"I was told a Seeker who was highly respectful of his Heaven wished to see me." The man signaled, and a waiter rushed to our table, pouring a glass of water. "I usually don't meet clients personally, but I understand this is a special case. It might be unnecessary, but I must adhere to protocol: my death won't affect my people's work. You can call me Dee. What does our humble guild have to offer a Master Seeker?"

"I'm aware of your humble guild's rules. Here are five hundred spirit coins." The mentor gestured, and five hefty pouches appeared on the table.

"A very solid start," Dee nodded, not bothering to touch the pouches. "I'd like some details."

"First, I want to know the conditions regarding Zander and Hurikki Wang. It's not some horrible secret, is it? The details depend on what I learn."

"It's a standard contract. Irrevocable; must be completed. Means and resources are irrelevant. Business as usual."

"Postponement?" the Seeker clarified.

"Postponement is possible," Dee nodded. "But only for Hurikki Wang. The client was quite vague in his terms for him. As for Zander, his client was very precise in the contract's wording. Quite the quibbler, that one; had to meet him personally. So, Zander's contract cannot be postponed."

"Even if you receive a new contract on Zander? For a higher amount?"

"In that case, we'd have to consult with the previous client," Dee answered after a pause.

"However, the client is dead, and you can't consult him on new terms," the Seeker concluded.

"But we can't just refuse either. Reputation is too valuable an asset to jeopardize. You understand, we can't take a guarding job, so Zander will die. Sooner or later, even if the Seeker wipes out the entire Tier Zero. Those are the rules, and we'll follow them to the end."

"One last clarification: what does the humble guild do if Zander enters territory it doesn't control? As far as I know, transferring tasks to another humble guild requires the client's consent. Or will the humble guild of Tier Zero start operating in the First Tier?"

"If the client cannot arrange the transfer, the humble guild will wait for Zander's return to Tier Zero to fulfill the contract."

"I've heard everything I wanted to. As I said, here are five hundred spirit coins. The humble guild will receive the same if it postpones executing the order on Hurikki Wang for two years and also fulfills the Seeker's order. I need four apprentices. Bronze or Silver ranks. They work separately and independently. Candidates cannot be involved. The targets are Seeker Zander and Seeker Vyllea. The term is two years. Three months of guaranteed safety between each attack."

At that moment, I had completely lost the plot. Instead of taking out the scoundrel who had come to us, the mentor was issuing an order for our assassination? What on earth was happening? Was he in his right mind? Judging by the way Vyllea was looking at the Taoist, she was equally baffled.

"Candidates?" Dee looked first at me, then at Vyllea. "Against a quartet of Apprentice Taoists? Is the Seeker so confident in his apprentices? I'm fine with these terms. They don't break any rules. Anything else?"

"Zander is an artificer."

"And?" Dee didn't understand. "Am I supposed to react to this information somehow?"

"He can replicate this." The mentor placed on the table a needle nearly depleted of energy. A little more, and the poison would drip onto the table. Di understood this better than anyone. Judging by how energy flowed from him into the needle, restoring its original integrity, he had a direct connection to this artifact.

"Many can replicate that," Dee responded. "I still don't get you, Seeker."

"I was imprecise in my wording. Zander can replicate this with a hundred percent success rate. All he needs is the recipe, a base, and the ingredients. I won't even ask what the failure rate is for making such things; I'm not interested. Just confident that it's one successful needle out of ten, if that. In Zander's case, it would be ten out of ten. That's it."

"And when could Zander prove his skills in practice?" The man's gaze settled on me. No aggression, no curiosity. Just a look. Yet, for some reason, that look made me feel uneasy between my shoulder blades. The one who called himself by the strange name Dee was mortally dangerous.

"You've been asked a question, apprentice," Mentor Guerlon said. "When can you demonstrate your artificer's mastery?"

"As soon as I get everything I need," I grumbled. "A recipe, ingredients, and preferably a workshop. It's hard to do this on just any tabletop."

"Hey! I'm not Zander, so I won't stay silent!" Vyllea burst out. "Mentor, what the hell is happening here?"

"If the result of the inspection satisfies you, you'll pay him the standard rate for a First Tier artificer, plus a separate fee for silence," the Seeker ignored his apprentice's outburst.

"First Tier? He's just a Candidate."

"The needle carries two conditions. Its base was brought to our tier from the First. The creator of this artifact sits before me. I'm not asking how much time you spend on these needles. Nor am I asking what you even need them for in a tier where spirit armor is rare. Over the two years Zander is forced to stay in Tier Zero, he could save you a lot of time."

"Assuming that's true. But it doesn't exempt him from attack."

"Four apprentices. Bronze or Silver. The deal stands. If my apprentices are so weak they can't fend off some Tier Zero assassins, they have no business in the First Tier."

"You're missing five more pouches on the table, Seeker," Dee responded after a pause. "The standard rate for a First Tier artificer is thirty spirit coins per month for crafting thirty artifacts. The silence fee is an additional twenty."

"That works for me. I'll need a workshop in two days. Zander will demonstrate his skill. How do we contact you?"

"We'll find you," Dee nodded and scooped up ten pouches of spirit stones. Without saying goodbye, the man left the tavern. Outside, a self-propelled cart awaited him, and soon the head of the assassin's guild disappeared from my spirit vision.

"Apprentice, sit down. Don't make me use force."

Vyllea was breathing so heavily her breath could be heard all across Vorend. Still, she complied. Her experience of dealing with the Taoist had made her very aware that angering him was unwise.

"Firstly, the artifacts. Zander needs experience, but finding somewhere for an artificer to practice in Tier Zero is extremely difficult. We must humiliate ourselves before House Wang and ask them for employment — ask very humbly and politely. There are no Seeker artificers in Tier Zero. It's impossible to open a workshop here. I don't have enough spirit stones to leave you both set for life. What little I have left must be spent on your education. Working with the Assassins' Guild is the only way to earn a living without bending the knee to House Wang. Fifty gold pieces a month is more than fair compensation. Not to mention that in the First Tier Zander will also be of interest as an artificer, possessing specific and extremely rare recipes. All he needs to do is prove his mastery now. I know Zander can handle it. Zander knows he can handle it. I've connected you with clients willing to pay. The rest is up to you."

Vyllea and I remained silent. The mentor had laid everything out clearly, leaving no room for argument. Once he was sure we wouldn't protest, he continued.

"Secondly — the assassins. I've worked a lot with this guild. They have a particular understanding of honor. Even if every assassin in the belt dies, others from the inner belts will come. The order must be completed as long as the target is accessible. The former head of the School of Spirit Power had known I'd turn to assassins, hence he had prepared the contract very meticulously. House Dun didn't even consider this, for example. Their mistake. The only way to save your lives is to postpone the execution of the former head's order until you leave Tier Zero. That had cost a lot. As for the four Apprentices... You were prepared to face off against a hundred and thirty demons. What has changed since then? Besides, I've done everything to make your survival as easy as possible."

"There are few Apprentices in Vorend, especially of Bronze and Silver ranks," I mused. "Plus, there's a condition that Candidates cannot be involved. No Apprentice can approach us unnoticed. But by the Heavens, mentor, this is still wrong! Why do Seekers allow assassins to exist? Or why do people like Hurikki Wang still live?"

"Do you want to kill him?" the mentor smirked.

"It's not that I want to. I will. It's a fact, not a wish."

"Don't do it with your own hands," the Taoist suggested unexpectedly. "The death of a clan head will trigger an investigation. Assassins won't be punished — they are just tools. The order to eliminate Hurikki Wang has currently been issued by House Dun from the Tiger Clan. When investigators from the First Tier arrive, they will turn a blind eye. No one wants to have the Tiger Clan as an enemy. Did I make my position clear, apprentice? Or do I need to spell it out further?"

"You could have told us sooner," Vyllea grumbled angrily. "It's infuriating when a supposedly wise mentor doesn't think it necessary to explain his actions."

"If that's all, we should be going. I assume the head of House Wang is already nervously awaiting the outcome of our meeting. Tomorrow, you'll become Seekers, apprentices of the School of Spirit Power, and our paths will diverge."

"So we'll no longer be considered your apprentices?" Vyllea was surprised.

"Until you reach the Third Tier, you'll be on your own. You're Seekers, not blind kittens bumping around in search of their mother's teat. I've given you everything I could. Taught you how to learn. Taught you to defend your interests. Tell me, apprentice, what else do you expect from a mentor? Should I run after you wiping your noses? I can't help you with that in either the First or the Second Tier. Not in any way. Only in the Third. Or the Fourth, if by the time you reach the Third, I become an Overlord. If you want someone to wipe your nose, grow up to reach me. I swear by the Heavens, I'll do it if you really need me to. Any more questions?"

"No," Vyllea responded gloomily. "If there's no

mentor, there are no questions."

Vyllea couldn't accept the Taoist's stance. And from her expression, it seemed she never would. The Heavens be her judge. As for me, I was relieved the Seeker would soon leave us. I was eager to delve into the archives of Huang Lung and explore all the books stored there. Better to share this secret with Vyllea than with Guerlon. He had said his piece; now it was our turn.

The Wang palace was abuzz with activity. Too many self-moving carts, too many people rushing about, too much hustle. My spiritual vision revealed something odd amid all this commotion: a black figure stood out.

"There's a Master or an Overlord here," I said. "He's..."

I couldn't finish, for a sight has opened to me. Standing next to a dignified man was someone quite incredible, and my heart skipped a beat. It was She with a capital S. A girl of roughly my age, dressed in a beautiful traveling dress that couldn't hide the perfect figure of someone constantly practicing to ascend to immortality. A Diamond-ranked Candidate. Fifty-two open nodes. Several times more than either Vyllea or I had. Red hair styled in a complex fashion, yet the wind dared not touch it. The girl was talking to an older-looking Elda, smiling in a way that made my heart stop. The stranger was stunning. Dazzling.

"It seems the Heavens have decided to test us once again," came mentor Guerlon's thoughtful voice through the ringing in my ears. "It only remains to see why the advisor to the head of the Phoenix clan's daughter is here and why she's still just a Candidate."

CHAPTER 20

"ZANDER?! LOOK HOW you've grown!"

The exclamation of surprise pulled me away from admiring the beauty. A tall young man approached us. He towered over me, his long cold silver hair perfectly complementing his kimono and the crest on his chest. Carmin of House Bao, Third Tier. A potential absolute of the body, but as someone from a remote village in Tier Zero, I naturally wouldn't know something like that. The four years since our last meeting had changed the young man significantly. He looked stronger and more mature, and, for some reason, his hair was dyed. Though, as my mentor had told me once, hair growth ointments came in various types, and when you burned your own hair, you can grow it back in any color. Apparently, Carmin liked steel. Like Elda, he had no nodes yet. Just a Silver-ranked Candidate.

"Carmin. I see you've reached the Silver rank," I nodded in greeting, unsure how to act properly. Here was the scion of a powerful clan from one of the inner tiers, openly flaunting his grandeur. His kimono alone probably cost as much as all my personal belongings combined.

"Will you introduce me to your charming companion?" Carmin's smile was handsome, I had to admit. But it faded when Vyllea looked him up and down, and then asked disdainfully,

"Do I understand correctly that he's not even a Golden-ranked Candidate? Just a junior flaunting the wealth of his house, but really amounting to nothing? Though he moves interestingly. It feels like he knows how to hold a jian."

"Junior?" Carmin's brown eyes flared with anger. "And who might you be?"

"That's none of your concern, junior," Vyllea emphasized the last word again. "We won't keep you any longer. You can go back to the important business of your important House."

"To speak such words, one must be prepared to back them up, beauty," Carmin's voice had a steel edge to it. "Or did you decide to hide behind the Seeker and yap from behind his back like a little dog?"

"Here and now!" Vyllea made decisions quickly, though not always wisely. Drawing her jian, she pointed it towards Carmin. "Draw your blade, silverhead! I'll make you respect your betters!"

Carmin smirked, drew his jian, and stepped back, ready to attack. His winner's grin hadn't changed in four years. The young man knew his capabilities, confident that he was superior in swordplay. A clearing formed around us, and I realized then that everyone's attention was on us. Yet no one intervened; a dispute between two candidates was their personal affair. Mentor Guerlon calmly moved to the wall, indicating he had no part in what was happening. I followed him. Vyllea was within her rights. After all, she did rank higher than Carmin. The fact that the boy couldn't discern who stood before him was his problem.

"We got off on the wrong foot, beauty," Carmin made a few swings with his jian. "I'll give you another chance to acknowledge..."

He didn't finish. Vyllea charged forward. The sound of clashing metal, a few dull thuds, and Carmin was on the ground, Vyllea's jian piercing his shoulder, the girl herself sitting atop him, her knife at his throat. The blade had already penetrated his skin.

"Weak, slow, and useless. Exactly as expected of juniors who bask in their clan's greatness but are themselves worthless," Vyllea's voice dripped with venom. She vented all her frustration from the day's earlier meeting with the head of the assassin's guild, having found the perfect target. "I expect an apology, junior. Or shall I stop holding back and finish what I started?"

"Enough!" commanded the dignified Taoist perceived as a black shadow by my spiritual vision. He appeared next to Vyllea, even reaching out to push her away from Carmin, but he stopped abruptly. Mentor Guerlon's jian hovered near his neck.

"Just try to touch her, junior! She's within her rights! The weak must know their place and recognize the strong. If this junior hasn't been taught such a basic concept, he has no place in this world."

"Do you know who I am?" the man demanded, as if that alone should have made the Seeker fall to his knees and beg for mercy. But mentor Guerlon was not purely a Taoist. He was a Seeker.

"You're a dead man if you touch my apprentice. That's all I need to know about you."

"Should I finish this?" Vyllea didn't even turn around. All her attention was focused on Carmin. She pressed further, and blood spurted onto the ground.

"I apologize, Elder," Carmin wheezed. "You are stronger. I acted rashly."

Vyllea stood up and pulled her jian out of the wound. The dignified Taoist immediately leaned over the young man to heal his wounds, but the way he looked at the girl made it clear that we were in big trouble. Big trouble indeed.

"Apprentices, follow me. Don't engage in conversation, ignore those gathered around you," the mentor ordered and walked inside. Everyone parted way as if the Seeker emitted an aura of death. Hurikki Wang was found near the entrance. By the looks of it, the head of House Wang wanted to disappear into the wall but couldn't. Mentor Guerlon didn't even glance at the junior, merely pausing momentarily to say,

"I've secured two more years of your life. The paperwork for my apprentice must be at the school by tomorrow morning."

We headed to the palace. We had rooms there, and the mentor intended to take advantage of House Wang's hospitality to the end. But it was a strange kind of hospitality. We weren't invited for dinner or breakfast, and no one saw us off in the morning. It was as if we were guests, yet profoundly unwelcome ones, from whom they couldn't wait to be rid.

They were waiting for us at the shop. I could discern ten Apprentices of initial ascension stages, nothing special. Vyllea and I held hands just in case, but it wasn't necessary. As soon as the mentor entered the shop, all ten suddenly remembered urgent business in another part of the city. House Dun's fighters knew perfectly well how to assess their opponent and their own chances.

The shop owner approached us. Judging by his reddened face, he was struck by panic. The mentor waited for a while, expecting them to start bringing out the clothes, but no one hurried to us. The sellers hid, only the blushing owner stood, not daring to raise his head or look at the Seeker. It didn't take a genius to realize they hadn't even started on our order. The shop owner had complained to House Dun and thought he had solved all the problems.

"Tier Zero has forgotten what the right of the strong means. Well, it's time for a reminder. You and your employees have one minute to leave this place. Your time starts now."

The Taoist's voice left no room for objections. People rushed out of the shop, and exactly one minute later, a huge bonfire blazed where it had stood. Judging by the screams of pain, not everyone made it out. But the Seeker wasn't concerned. The Heavens disapproved of the weak surviving. Turning to us, he said,

"House Dun has insulted your mentor. Whether to swallow that insult or demand an apology is entirely up to you. Sit down."

The mentor conjured a self-moving cart and climbed inside. The raging fire and the screaming people were no longer his concern. Judging by Vyllea's satisfied expression, she preferred this version of the mentor much more than his previous demeanor. We returned to the Wang family palace. Numerous carts were still there. The guests hadn't dispersed to their estates. As I had come to understand, every great clan possessed its protected estate in Tier Zero. House Wang served merely as a transit point.

The mentor headed to a part of the palace previously off-limits to us. In one of the rooms, we found an inactive portal arch, almost a replica of the one shown to us in Zou-Lemawn. Hurikki

Wang was already there, his face strangely radiant.

"House Dun will raise objections about the shop, Elder," Hurikki Wang said, indicating that we had been followed and his servants had relayed information to him before we returned.

"Their problem. Disrespect towards elders was, is, and shall continue to be punished. If House Dun is too foolish to understand that, my apprentices will convey it to them in more accessible terms. Is everything ready?"

"Yes, Elder. We only need energy."

Hurikki Wang stepped aside and pointed to a container. Seeker Guerlon extracted several stones from his spatial pouch, placed them in the container, and sealed it. The portal trembled, and a shimmering veil appeared within the arch. Moments later, a Taoist in a white robe with the Phoenix clan's crest on his chest emerged. He resembled mentor Guerlon in some ways: equally young, majestic, and regarding the world as if it owed him.

"Greetings, Elder." The mentor bowed, indicating we were in the presence of at least an Overlord. "Seeker Guerlon requests a meeting with the advisor to the head of the clan to bring two more Seekers into this world. I have the plaques."

"Wait," the Taoist said as he vanished back into the portal. Only then did I realize I had been holding my breath. The individual who had entered through the portal wielded such an aura that my body had ceased to live for a moment.

Vyllea inhaled sharply beside me.

"Elder, may I leave?" Hurikki Wang clearly didn't wish to meet the advisor to the head of the clan. The Taoist didn't reply but nodded, allowing the head of House Wang to depart. There were no chairs or seats near the portal, so we had to stand. An hour passed. Then a second. A third. We stood as if our lives depended on it. Finally, at the end of the fourth hour, when even the enhancement began to fade, the shimmering veil rippled, and three Taoists materialized in the room.

Mentor Guerlon gave a deep and silent bow. Vyllea and I mimicked his gesture — before us stood a Nascent God of no minor rank. I dared not use my spirit vision, for fear of being blinded. The Taoist who had come to Tier Zero had to leave behind all artifacts and significantly dim his power. Yet, he still radiated such force that I struggled to remain standing. Judging by Vyllea's heavy breathing, she was also finding it difficult, prompting me to commit a monstrous breach of all norms of etiquette in the presence of elders. I stopped holding my hands in front of me and, without raising my head, extended my palm to her. She clutched at it like a lifeline, interlocking fingers. The energy from the advisor intensified, but now I found a way to control it. Capturing all the flows, I directed them into our virtual meridians, restoring their integrity. The pressure of the energy grew, but it no longer affected us as before. All the flowing meridians had filled, so I began to form a new one. Now, turning us to dust would require some effort!

"Indeed, a full conjunction," a voice sounded, and the energy abruptly vanished. "You may rise, juniors."

I straightened up and, before I realized what I was doing, pulled Vyllea closer to me, increasing our physical contact. She didn't resist; on the contrary, she pressed closer, as if seeking protection from the formidable advisor. One of the leading figures of the Phoenix clan appeared to be of significant age. If the beard of the head of the School of Spirit Power, who had conducted my examination, had looked artificial, here everything seemed exceedingly harmonious. The advisor appeared to be in his seventies or eighties, but by the way he carried himself, he seemed no more than thirty. There was nothing remarkable about his pristine white kimono, yet I couldn't shake the feeling it was the most powerful artifact I had ever seen in my life. His face and palms were dry. Likely, his entire body was the same — no excess fat, and no signs of aging whatsoever.

"Elder, during my travels, I have managed to find these plaques. My fellow Seekers perished, but their mission did not. I have brought two whom I deem worthy of the right to be Seekers."

"You haven't changed a bit, Seeker Guerlon. Still a mischief-maker, as ever. Did you really think full conjunction could hide the presence of a demon from my sight?"

The advisor's gaze fixed on Vyllea, and she squeezed my hand tighter. Judging by her trembling, she was either scared, in pain, or both.

"Elder, I've never concealed who my apprentice is. Information about her was sent to the Phoenix clan two years ago. I received neither approval nor denial. Vyllea's current form is due to the specifics of our conjunction, not an attempt to hide anything from the Elder, who surely already knows. The law of Seekers doesn't state that a demon cannot be one of us."

"The wording does indeed permit it," the advisor agreed. "Had you come with such a proposition two years ago, when you first took the demon as your apprentice, I would have personally rid the world of a pest like you. However, Seeker Guerlon has become too notable to ignore. Freeing the legend of Seekers, destroying the battlefield, killing a Nascent God... Many have become anxious, junior. They're wondering how to deal with you. After all, who knows what you might be capable of once you become an Overlord? The clan enjoys such disturbances. They force the juniors to crawl out of their mire. To return to the path of ascension. My only question is: did you consider what would happen to the demon, even in human form, when she takes the Seeker's plaque? There are many spies using conjunction. What you hold is the perfect means of finding them. We can make your demon a Seeker, and she will even become one, but only for a moment, until the tablet destroys her. Is this what you wanted by summoning me?"

"No, Elder. I request that the tablet be

adjusted so that the demon Vyllea of the Urbangos tribe does not suffer any ill effects when the status of a Seeker is conferred to her."

The mentor seemed to suggest the impossible, as both assistants twitched, but a gesture from the advisor stopped them. Seeker Guerlon continued,

"I am aware, elder, that it's impossible to adjust a tablet for a demon. It would have to be formed from scratch, requiring the life force of the clan head. I know how valuable a resource this is, therefore I offer my own energy in compensation. All of it, if the Heavens will it."

"Seeker Guerlon is prepared to sacrifice himself for a demon?"

"For an apprentice, elder. Not a demon. Not a human. Not a Taoist. One cannot undertake commitments without being prepared to fulfill them to the end. The Heavens would not approve. My apprentice possesses the spirit of a Seeker, far greater than mine or any other Seeker I know. She deserves what I am about to do."

"I accept your price, Seeker Guerlon. Demon, come forward."

Vyllea released my hand and took a few steps. Her legs buckled, and she began to collapse to the floor. The presence of a Nascent God of such rank was unbearable for her. I caught her in the nick of time, preventing her from falling. Our hands interlocked again, and disregarding the rules, we approached the advisor together. He showed no reaction to our audacity. Placing his hand on the girl's head, the advisor closed his eyes. Such powerful streams of energy flowed into Vyllea that I was affected as well. Without a word, the elder placed his other hand on my head. I was struck as if by lightning. It was both painful and pleasurable.

"Your auras have been registered," the advisor's voice cut through as the energy storms within us finally subsided. Vyllea, although standing, had slipped into unconsciousness, her form upright only because she leaned heavily against me. The advisor glanced over at Seeker Guerlon, then back to us, and gave a slight nod, indicating the gravity of the moment at hand.

"You have a minute to impart any final words you may have."

Seeker Guerlon's response was measured, his tone carrying the weight of his decision. "There's nothing more to say, Advisor. I've shared all that needed to be said, and given all I could. The last step remains mine alone to take — not theirs to bear."

"Put this on," the advisor directed, offering an amulet to the Seeker. "It will shield you from incineration. We're off to the central belt. The would-be Seekers are to remain here, undisturbed."

This command was clearly aimed at the two assistants, who received the instructions without a flicker of emotion. As the portal began to ripple, signaling departure, the room was left with four beings — among them, Vyllea, adrift in unconsciousness. The assistants showed no concern for her state; they simply stood up, their attention fixed on the door, awaiting further orders.

Compelled by necessity, I remained standing, Vyllea's weight against me the only assurance of her presence. She gave no indication of returning to the waking world anytime soon.

As I pondered our situation, bewildered by the turn of events, the weight of what had just transpired hung heavily in the air. The Seeker, a Master Taoist of the Diamond rank, was prepared to sacrifice his very essence for his apprentice — a Candidate demon of the diamond rank. Despite his teachings, urging us to think for ourselves, to fight, to stand up for our beliefs, and to always heed the Heavens, he was now ready to lay down his life. Such an act was beyond comprehension — a testament to his unwavering commitment to his apprentice in defiance of all expectations and norms.

After what felt like an eternity, marked only by the slow passage of time and the steady rhythm of my own heartbeat, Vyllea stirred. Three hours had lapsed into silence before she finally regained consciousness. Upon seeing the advisor's assistants, she immediately tensed, her grip tightening around my hand — a silent testament to the storm of emotions raging within her.

As we stood there, the fabric of the portal began to undulate once more, heralding the advisor's return. He emerged alone, his demeanor changed, as if he had witnessed the unimaginable and was still grappling with the reality of it. For a long moment, he remained silent beside us, lost in thought. Finally, he spoke, his voice breaking the silence that had enveloped us:

"To be a Seeker of the Deforean Empire is a great honor and responsibility. Seekers cannot afford to be ordinary; they must be better than the rest — significantly better. Like Master Guerlon of the Diamond rank. I hope he did not misjudge you, paying such a price. From now on, and until the end of your days, you are a Seeker, Taoist Zander. From now on, and until the end of your days, you are a Seeker, demon Vyllea. Even when you return home, consume the prince, and set off to destroy our world, you will still remain a Seeker. Such is the decision of the head of the Phoenix clan. Such is the decision of the Emperor. Accept your plaques, Seekers."

The advisor extended small plaques to us. As soon as I grasped mine, a strange wave of energy passed through me. It altered something within my body, though I couldn't catch precisely what before it dispersed, leaving me invigorated.

"The plaque will not kill you, even in demon form. The Emperor, may his days be eternally prolonged, personally imbued it with strength."

"The Emperor? Does that mean the mentor is alive?" Vyllea's eyes widened. "You said he was gone!"

"Elder never said that, Vyllea," I interjected before the advisor could react to such an indiscretion. "He mentioned we should strive to be better than Master Guerlon of the Diamond rank. That doesn't necessarily mean the mentor is deceased."

"But..." Vyllea started but then fell silent.

"Continue, junior," the advisor said, looking at me intently.

"Indeed, the Diamond-ranked master has vanished from this planet, having surrendered his life force to the clan head. The mentor would never go back on his word. The Heavens wouldn't allow it. Yet, I suspect that this very act was the final push he had needed to overcome the ascension barrier. The Diamond Master left, giving away all his life force, but a Bronze Overlord arose in his place. Not Copper, but Bronze. That's why you, esteemed Elder, seem so perturbed. I assume that jumping ranks at this stage of ascension was considered not just rare, but impossible until today."

"The Phoenix clan will monitor your progress, Seekers," the advisor declared, then smiled. "You are mistaken on two counts, young Seeker. Firstly, rank jumps to Bronze instead of Copper at the Overlord stage are not that uncommon. Masters often become so unified with their element that as soon as they acquire a spirit core, they immediately jump to the second rank. Secondly, your mentor did not achieve the Bronze rank. That would have been too simple, and as it turns out, nothing is simple with Guerlon. This is for you. Think thrice before you sign here."

The advisor handed Vyllea and me a golden sheet each. I took mine and read the following:

I, Silver-ranked Overlord, Seeker Guerlon, extend an offer to Seeker Zander to become my apprentice. The term of apprenticeship is until the death of either party. Challenges and troubles guaranteed.

"Do demons only sign like this?" I chuckled at Vyllea, pulled out a knife, and sliced across my palm. "I like this method. No need to fuss over an intricate signature."

"When I become an Overlord, I'll devour that bastard," Vyllea nodded, mirroring my action. "Given what he's orchestrated, there can be no other outcome."

The golden sheets vanished, and a moment later, the advisor and his assistants disappeared as well. As if sensing their departure, the Wang palace stirred. I looked at Vyllea and extended my bloodied hand toward her.

"So, Seeker Vyllea, shall we cause a ruckus here?"

"Let's do it, Seeker Zander!" She clasped my cut palm with hers. "We'll uphold Overlord Guerlon's reputation. As that guy who smelled of blood so deliciously said, reputation is too valuable an asset to jeopardize."

END OF BOOK TWO

Want to be the first to know about our latest LitRPG, sci fi and fantasy titles from your favorite authors?

Subscribe to our **New Releases** newsletter:
http://eepurl.com/b7niIL

Thank you for reading *Law of the Jungle!*
If you like what you've read, check out other sci-fi,
fantasy and A LitRPG series published by Magic
Dome Books:

NEW RELEASES!

Crossroads of Oblivion
a portal progression fantasy adventure series
by Dem Mikhailov

Gakko Academy
a portal progression fantasy adventure series
by Evgeny Alexeev

War Eternal
a military space adventure LitRPG series
by Yuri Vinokuroff

The Hunter's Code
a LitRPG series by Yuri Vinokuroff & Oleg Sapphire

The Order of Architects
a portal progression series
by Yuri Vinokuroff & Oleg Sapphire

I Will Be Emperor
a space adventure progression fantasy series
by Yuri Vinokuroff & Oleg Sapphire

An Ideal World for a Sociopath
a LitRPG series by Oleg Sapphire

The Healer's Way
a LitRPG series by Oleg Sapphire & Alexey Kovtunov

A Shelter in Spacetime
a LitRPG series by Dmitry Dornichev

The Village
a LitRPG progression fantasy series
by Dmitry Dornichev & Alexey Kovtunov

The Last Portal Jumper
a LitRPG series by Konstantin Zubov

Kill or Die
a LitRPG series by Alex Toxic

Living Ice
a portal progression alternative history series
by Dmitry Sheleg

Law of the Jungle
a Wuxia Progression Fantasy Adventure Series
By Vasily Mahanenko

Reality Benders
a LitRPG series by Michael Atamanov

The Dark Herbalist
a LitRPG series by Michael Atamanov

Perimeter Defense
a LitRPG series by Michael Atamanov

League of Losers
a LitRPG series by Michael Atamanov

Chaos' Game
a LitRPG series by Alexey Svadkovsky

The Way of the Shaman
a LitRPG series by Vasily Mahanenko

The Alchemist
a LitRPG series by Vasily Mahanenko

Dark Paladin
a LitRPG series by Vasily Mahanenko

Galactogon
a LitRPG series by Vasily Mahanenko

Invasion
a LitRPG series by Vasily Mahanenko

World of the Changed
a LitRPG series by Vasily Mahanenko

The Bear Clan
a LitRPG series by Vasily Mahanenko

Starting Point
a LitRPG series by Vasily Mahanenko

The Bard from Barliona
a LitRPG series
by Eugenia Dmitrieva and Vasily Mahanenko

**Condemned
(Lord Valevsky: Last of The Line)**
a Progression Fantasy series
by Vasily Mahanenko

Loner
a LitRPG series by Alex Kosh

A Buccaneer's Due
a LitRPG series by Igor Knox

A Student Wants to Live
a LitRPG series by Boris Romanovsky

The Goldenblood Heir
a LitRPG series by Boris Romanovsky

Level Up
a LitRPG series by Dan Sugralinov

Level Up: The Knockout
a LitRPG series by Dan Sugralinov and Max Lagno

Adam Online
a LitRPG Series by Max Lagno

World 99
a LitRPG series by Dan Sugralinov

Disgardium
a LitRPG series by Dan Sugralinov

Nullform
a RealRPG Series by Dem Mikhailov

Clan Dominance: The Sleepless Ones
a LitRPG series by Dem Mikhailov

Heroes of the Final Frontier
a LitRPG series by Dem Mikhailov

The Crow Cycle
a LitRPG series by Dem Mikhailov

Interworld Network
a LitRPG series by Dmitry Bilik

Rogue Merchant
a LitRPG series by Roman Prokofiev

Project Stellar
a LitRPG series by Roman Prokofiev

In the System
a LitRPG series by Petr Zhgulyov

The Crow Cycle
a LitRPG series by Dem Mikhailov

Unfrozen
a LitRPG series by Anton Tekshin

The Neuro
a LitRPG series by Andrei Livadny

Phantom Server
a LitRPG series by Andrei Livadny

Respawn Trials
a LitRPG series by Andrei Livadny

The Expansion (The History of the Galaxy)
a Space Exploration Saga by A. Livadny

The Range
a LitRPG series by Yuri Ulengov

Point Apocalypse
a near-future action thriller by Alex Bobl

Moskau
a dystopian thriller by G. Zotov

El Diablo
a supernatural thriller by G.Zotov

Mirror World
a LitRPG series by Alexey Osadchuk

Underdog
a LitRPG series by Alexey Osadchuk

Last Life
a Progression Fantasy series by Alexey Osadchuk

Alpha Rome
a LitRPG series by Ros Per

An NPC's Path
a LitRPG series by Pavel Kornev

Fantasia
a LitRPG series by Simon Vale

The Sublime Electricity
a steampunk series by Pavel Kornev

Small Unit Tactics
a LitRPG series by Alexander Romanov

Black Centurion
a LitRPG standalone by Alexander Romanov

Rorkh
A LitRPG Series by Vova Bo

Thunder Rumbles Twice
A Wuxia Series by V. Kriptonov & M. Bachurova

Citadel World
a sci fi series by Kir Lukovkin

You're in Game!
LitRPG Stories from Our Bestselling Authors

You're in Game-2!
More LitRPG stories set in your favorite worlds

The Fairy Code
a Romantic Fantasy series by Kaitlyn Weiss

***The Charmed* Fjords**
a Romantic Fantasy series by Marina Surzhevskaya

More books and series are coming out soon!

In order to have new books of the series translated faster, we need your help and support! Please consider leaving a review or spread the word by recommending *Law of the Jungle* to your friends and posting the link on social media. The more people buy the book, the sooner we'll be able to make new translations available.

Thank you!

Till next time!

Printed in Great Britain
by Amazon